THE LEGEND OF GREG

ALSO BY CHRIS RYLANDER

The Fourth Stall Series

The Codename Conspiracy Series

House of Secrets: Clash of the Worlds
(created by Chris Columbus and Ned Vizzini)

THE LEGEND OF GREG

— *Book One of* —
AN EPIC SERIES OF FAILURES

CHRIS RYLANDER

G. P. Putnam's Sons

G. P. Putnam's Sons
an imprint of Penguin Random House LLC
375 Hudson Street
New York, NY 10014

Library of Congress Cataloging-in-Publication Data
Names: Rylander, Chris, author.
Title: The legend of Greg / Chris Rylander.
Description: First edition. I New York, NY : G. P. Putnam's Sons, [2018] I
Series: An epic series of failures ; book 1
Summary: "Greg Belmont learns he's anything but ordinary when he discovers he's a real,
live, fantastical dwarf and sets off on the adventure of a lifetime"—Provided by publisher.
Identifiers: LCCN 2017053083 I ISBN 9781524739720 (hardcover) I
ISBN 9781524739737 (ebook)
Subjects: I CYAC: Identity—Fiction. I Dwarfs (Folklore)—Fiction. I Magic—Fiction. I
Kidnapping—Fiction. I Elves—Fiction. I Adventure and adventurers—Fiction. I Fantasy. I
BISAC: JUVENILE FICTION / Fantasy & Magic. I JUVENILE FICTION /
Action & Adventure / General. I JUVENILE FICTION / Monsters.
Classification: LCC PZ7.R98147 Leg 2018 I DDC [Fic]—dc23
LC record available at https://lccn.loc.gov/2017053083

Printed in the United States of America.
ISBN 9781524739720
3   5   7   9   10   8   6   4   2

Design by Eileen Savage. Text set in Apolline Std.

For everyone who has ever been made to feel small

STOP!

Before you start reading this book, what day is it?

If it's a Thursday, close this book immediately and start it tomorrow instead.

Only bad things can happen reading this on a Thursday.

Trust me.

THE LEGEND OF GREG

CHAPTER 1

—◆—◈—◆—

Flaming Lady Beards, Man-Eating Monsters, and Head-Exploding Rock Allergies

I t should come as no surprise that the day I almost got my face clawed off by a vicious monster was a Thursday.

Since pretty much the beginning of time (according to my dad and his dad and his dad's dad and his dad's dad's dad, etc.), bad things have happened to my family on Thursdays. A few examples:

- Great-Aunt Millie's legendary beard caught fire on a Thursday. Once the flawless envy of every Belmont (man or woman), it sadly never quite grew back the same again.
- Second Midwestern Bank repossessed the old Belmont family farm on a Thursday way back in 1929, dooming the family henceforth to dreary city life. Ever since, all my aunts and uncles call it a slimy *Pointer* bank. Nobody will tell me what that means, but it's almost certainly a curse word

since it's precisely what Aunt Millie screamed the moment she realized her beard was on fire.

- My cousin Phin lost his brand-new car on a Thursday. To this day we have no idea where it went. He parked it on a street in the city, but then simply forgot where. After looking for over an hour, he gave up and took the bus home. If you say it's impossible to just lose a midsize sedan, I'll show you a Belmont on a Thursday.

There are so many more, but the point is: I shouldn't have been surprised to nearly get torn limb from limb on a Thursday. I certainly expected *something* bad to happen, since it nearly always did. Just not something so drastic. I thought maybe I'd get gum stuck in my hair. Or perhaps Perry would try to stuff me into the toilet in the fourth stall of the boys' locker room again—which was actually *almost* as bad as getting attacked by a monster since this particular toilet was so notorious it even had its own name: the Souper Bowl. The Souper Bowl hadn't been flushed since 1954 due to some superstitious school tradition that ran so deep even the city's top health inspector (a former student) overlooked it. I can't even describe to you the horrible sights I've seen inside that stall—and the smell shall never be mentioned again.

But I'm certainly not complaining about Thursdays. They're just part of being a Belmont. Some kids are born rich, some are born poor; some are born with eight toes, some are born with blond hair; and others just happen to have been born with a Thursday curse.

Luckily, my whole family was pretty good at coping with it. We even had a saying: *Thursdays are why every other day seems so great!* Okay, so maybe it's not very catchy, but it worked. The other days of the week truly felt like a holiday compared to Thursdays.

That particular Thursday started out simply enough: with a supposedly harmless school field trip to the Lincoln Park Zoo.

The Isaacson Preparatory Empowerment Establishment (I dare you to try saying you go to a school called I-PEE with a straight face) is one of the fanciest and most prestigious private schools in the country. They had enough money to *buy* their own zoo if they wanted. But instead they sent us on "cultural enrichment" trips once a month to places like the Shedd Aquarium, or a local apple orchard, or another, much poorer school on the west side so my classmates could see firsthand just how much better their lives were than other kids'.

That Thursday, a convoy of luxury charter buses drove the entire school up Lake Shore Drive toward the zoo. Lake Michigan flanked us on the right, looking like an ocean with a sparkling blue surface that stretched on forever.

My first goal, after stepping off the bus at the entrance to the Lincoln Park Zoo, was to find Edwin. That was the good part about Field Trip Thursdays: getting to hang out with my best friend all day.

Edwin was easily the most popular kid at the PEE, and perhaps also the richest. And maybe that's not a coincidence?

Not that being wealthy was rare for the PEE's students (I was one of the few exceptions). Of the school's 440 students, only 45 of us paid reduced tuition. The rest came from families wealthy enough to afford $43,000 a year for something they could have gotten for free.

But Edwin's family was like a whole other level (or two, or forty) of being completely loaded. I spent my summers working at my dad's organic health goods store, whereas Edwin spent his summers jetting all across the world on his parents' fleet of private luxury planes. Yeah, that's planes—as in they owned more than one private jet. I didn't even know what exactly Edwin's parents did for a living. They worked downtown doing something vague and financey—like CEO of a Money Management Investment Firm, or Executive Commodities Director, or Market Analyst Portfolio Broker Financial President Administrator.

But the point is: despite us coming from two different worlds, Edwin and I had been best friends from the moment we met three years ago.

I found him in the crowd that Thursday surrounded by a flock of pretty eighth-grade girls. They collectively made a face as I joined the group. I assumed it was partly because I smelled like a mixture of salted pork shank and Icelandic bog (yeah, so my dad made his own organic soaps and forced me to use them). Either way, I ignored the girls' annoyed stares as they dispersed—like they always did when I showed up.

"Hey, Greg," Edwin said with a huge grin. "Did your dad find anything cool on his trip? Any extinct Norwegian tree saps? Or a new strain of peat moss? Maybe he finally tracked down the rare and elusive Arconian button mushroom?"

Part of my dad's job as an *artisanal craftsman* (his words, not mine) involved traveling all over the world in search of new ingredients to use in his soaps and teas and other natural health products.

He'd been in Norway all week on the hunt.

"I don't know, he gets back tomorrow," I said. "Why? Are you really that anxious to try his newest tea?"

Edwin looked at me like I had asked him to put his finger in my left nostril.

"Uh, not after last time," he said with a laugh. "His last batch of tea almost caused my face to explode, remember?"

"To be fair, he had no idea you were allergic to shale," I reminded him.

"That's because shale is rock," Edwin said, grinning. "I never ate it before, because, generally speaking, people *don't eat rocks.*"

"Hey, you're the one who asked him for a sample. My dad never *makes* you try anything. *I'm* usually the guinea pig."

"I know, but I can't help it, I really like your dad," Edwin said. "He makes me laugh. Guy is hilarious."

"I'm glad one of us finds him funny," I muttered.

Deep down I also loved my dad's quirks, but I hated to show it.

"Anyway," Edwin said with a cheesy smile, "are you ready for the *breathtaking* world of the Lincoln Park Zoo?"

I rolled my eyes.

That was the thing about being as rich as Edwin: when you could afford to do literally anything you wanted, most normal things became boring. Just last winter his parents flew him in a helicopter over a Siberian nature reserve in eastern Russia— there was no way a trip to the zoo could live up to that. That was probably why he loved my dad so much: one of the few things money couldn't buy you was a kooky, eccentric, and (debatably) hilarious father.

"Hey, you never know," I said. "Maybe watching depressed animals lay around in a cage is more exciting than it sounds?"

Edwin laughed. He got a kick out of my bizarrely gloomy optimism. I blamed my dad for that trait.

"Don't be such a gwint," he said.

Edwin called me a gwint when he thought I was being too *pessimistic.* I had no idea what *gwint* meant, but it'd always seemed oddly fitting. Edwin had a knack for making up strangely appropriate nicknames. Like Hot Sauce, for example. He was one of the PEE's English teachers and field trip chaperones. His real name was Mr. Worchestenshire, and of course we all knew that Worcestershire sauce wasn't technically hot sauce, but when Edwin coined the nickname, he didn't know exactly what kind of sauce Worcestershire was. Plus, Hot Sauce was just a way better nickname than Miscellaneous Food Condiment. So it stuck.

"Whatever," I said. "It's your move, by the way. Or are you stalling, hoping that I will forget what my Master Plan is?"

Edwin scoffed and took out his phone.

One of the things we realized we had in common right away was chess. Not many kids played chess. In fact, I'd only met one other kid who played chess: Danny Ipsento. He used to live down the street from me. Turned out, in addition to playing chess, his other hobbies included starting fires and throwing shoes at pigeons. So we never really became friends—I was too unlucky to have a friend with such dangerous hobbies—it'd be hazardous to my health.

But the point was: the rarity of chess players made it seem almost too perfect the first time I saw Edwin open the Chess With Friends app on his phone. I only started playing because my dad was obsessed with the game and taught me when I was three. My dad never stopped talking about chess's *perfections*: how ancient it was, how it was the *only* game in existence where luck played absolutely no factor, and how you completely controlled your own destiny. Every move, every win, every loss was entirely in your own hands, something that life never offered (especially to Belmonts). Which was also why I grew to love it, despite the fact that I rarely won. Every new game, the possibility of success was limited only by my own actions. Which was immensely comforting for someone from a family cursed with terrible luck.

I was still nowhere near as good as my dad. Or even Edwin, for that matter. I beat Edwin probably once every ten or fifteen games, and even then I figured he only let me win to keep me interested. He loved chess partially for the same reason as me: he grew up learning. His dad, in addition to being obscenely wealthy, also happened to be a former world chess champion. And Edwin had always idolized his dad, so much that he used to try to emulate his movements so he would one day walk and talk and act just like him. But Edwin also loved chess on an even deeper level, maybe for the same reason he was able to make so many friends: he loved deciphering people's inner thoughts.

Edwin finally made his move as Hot Sauce, our chaperone, led our group down a concrete path.

"Oh, man, I don't even want to know what you're up to," I said.

I didn't have a phone myself (a long story). So I'd have to wait to see his move until later when I could get to the computer lab.

"Try not to worry about it too much," Edwin taunted. "Just enjoy this spectacular trip that the PEE has arranged for our delights and amusements."

I laughed.

We started the tour with the Big Bears Exhibit—as if there was any other kind of bear. We entered an area surrounded on three sides by European buckthorn trees (yeah, so I kind of have a thing for trees) and low wooden fences. In front of us, a thick pane of clear viewing glass separated the zoo patrons from this portion of the bear exhibit. It consisted of a sloping stone cliff scattered with rocks. Several massive polar bears lounged on the rocky slope in front of us.

The other kids oohed and aahed as the giant bear heads turned to stare at us.

The hairs on my arms stood on end as the largest of all the bears locked eyes with me. He let out a roar so intense we could all hear it through multiple layers of safety glass.

I'd never really been much of an animal person. Other people's pets usually avoided me like I was diseased. Which was embarrassing since dogs had literally evolved over thousands of years to *love* human beings.

But as I stood there and stared in shock at the large bear roaring at me inside the Lincoln Park Zoo, this felt entirely different from dogs and cats not liking me. It's hard to explain, but I definitely knew something was off right away. It was clear in that moment that the bear hated *me* more than anything else in the world.

Everybody watched in awed silence as the polar bear took a few steps toward us. On two legs, he was easily three times my height. With paws large enough to hack off my whole face in a single swipe.

The bear's lips parted into another snarl.

Then he bent over and picked up a boulder with his front paws. The other kids gasped. A few laughed as the bear shuffled closer toward us with the giant rock squeezed between his claws.

"Dude, did that bear really just pick up a boulder?" Edwin asked.

A young employee with a name tag (*Lexi*) stepped in front of our group of stunned students.

"There's no need to be alarmed," Lexi said with a proud smile. "Wilbur and several of the other adult bears *love* playing with the rocks. They do it all the time. Bears, like dogs and cats, can be surprisingly playful animals."

Wilbur let out another savage roar.

Lexi was still smiling, but her eyes flicked nervously back toward the bears. Wilbur took a few more steps forward, the boulder in his grasp. He was now directly on the other side of the viewing glass.

And still staring right at me.

The polar bear raised the rock and smashed it into the safety glass.

THUD.

The crowd gasped and took a collective step backward as the pane vibrated. But it did not break, or even crack. Lexi's smile was gone, but she was doing her best to reassure us that everything was okay.

"There are five separate panes of reinforced laminated safety glass," she said, her voice shaking. "No need to worry."

Wilbur let out another roar and smashed the rock into the glass again.

THUD.

The innermost pane of the glass splintered like a spiderweb. The crowd's nervous murmurs turned into something much closer to panic.

Bears do not shatter unbreakable safety glass.

I knew that as much as I knew that Goblins did not exist and my dad's soap really did smell terrible—they were facts. Yet all I could do was watch in horror as this particular bear, worked into an unearthly rage by my presence, smashed the thick viewing glass yet again with the boulder.

THUD.

Shards of glass fell around the bear inside the pen. He'd just easily shattered several more layers of the viewing glass. The crowd backed up steadily. Some people were already running away. Any traces of calm that had remained on Lexi's face were gone as she spoke rapidly into a walkie-talkie.

Wilbur the polar bear reared back with the rock and then thrust it forward a final time.

CRASH!

The final two layers of glass shattered, spilling onto the floor in a million little pieces.

Kids and other zoo patrons screamed as they dove for cover. Wilbur rushed past them as if they weren't even there. He had a very specific target in mind and nothing would get in his way.

Wilbur the twelve-foot-tall polar bear was charging right toward *me*.

CHAPTER 2

❖

Wilbur Makes It Known That My Dad's Organic Soaps Offend Him Greatly

F rothy white goo trailing from Wilbur's snarling mouth splattered softly onto the pavement behind him as he lunged forward.

It nearly distracted me into just standing there dumbly while he mauled me into a pile of human hash. But at the last second, I snapped to my senses and dove out of the way of the charging polar bear.

I quickly scrambled to my feet, knowing that the frenzied bear wasn't going to just give up. A massive set of claws whisking by, inches from my face, confirmed this.

Wilbur roared again.

People screamed.

I ran.

Weaving through the dispersing crowd, I heard myself panting words between huffing breaths.

"Bear, bear, bear, bear," I said, since apparently my

subconscious felt that some of the onlookers didn't see the twelve-foot-tall beast chasing me. "Bear, bear, bear!"

I ran around a large wooden sign informing people that Wilbur was the oldest and largest polar bear in captivity (well, *formerly* in captivity). I ducked behind the thick wooden placard like it was a fortress.

Wilbur shattered it easily with one swipe of his paw.

A hail of splinters showered onto my head and I took off in a full sprint. But I didn't make it very far. My foot clipped the corner of a food vendor's abandoned cart. I stumbled, fell, and rolled to a stop in front of a bench, crushing someone's dropped hot dog in the process.

Wilbur slowed, continuing his pursuit at a steady walk—knowing that I was trapped with nowhere to go (and now also amply seasoned with mustard).

I sat up in terror and watched the bear move in for the kill, his raging eyes empty and black against his white fur. At least three tranquilizer darts were lodged in his back, the drugs having no effect on his fury-fueled state.

Two zoo employees in tan outfits flanked him, one on either side. They crept forward, one reloading a tranquilizer gun, the other holding a pole with a noose on the end. Wilbur easily swiped one of the employees away with his paw. The guy flew up into a nearby tree (an American elm). The other employee hesitated. Wilbur turned and roared at him. The guy scampered away after shooting me a sympathetic and apologetic glance.

I faced the bear . . . and my own certain death.

But then suddenly someone was standing in front of me—shielding me from the furious animal. It was Edwin. Standing tall and confident as he stared down a polar bear that likely regarded us both as light snacks.

"What are you doing?" I asked, terrified that the last thing I'd ever see was my only friend getting eaten as an appetizer.

Edwin ignored me and continued facing down the bear. Wilbur stood to his full height and snarled viciously. Edwin said nothing—just stared.

After a few moments, Wilbur's eyes glazed over. Now completely vacant. He wobbled slightly on his hind legs for a moment and then collapsed onto the pavement with a soft THUMP. Zoo employees with animal-handling equipment rushed in to secure the unconscious animal.

Edwin spun around with a stunned look on his face. He put a shaking hand to his chest. The total lack of fear he'd shown seconds before now seemed to be hitting him all at once as his knees trembled.

"Dude, how—how did you—" I stammered, still too shocked to speak coherently.

"I—I don't know," Edwin said, shaking his head, clearly in shock himself. "I . . . I just . . ."

But he never got the chance to finish, because the other kids swarmed him. They patted him on the back, congratulating him for being a hero. They stopped just short of dumping a bucket of Gatorade over his head and hoisting him onto their shoulders. Edwin kept insisting that the tranquilizer darts must have finally kicked in and it had been pure luck, but everybody ignored his modesty and showered him with praise.

I slowly climbed to my feet.

A long shadow crossed my face, and for a second I thought perhaps more bears had followed Wilbur through the opening in the pen. But then I looked up and saw Hot Sauce scowling at me.

It was no secret that Hot Sauce didn't like me.

"What have you done now, Mr. Belmont?" Hot Sauce demanded.

"Nothing," I said desperately. "You can't think that I caused this . . ."

"No doubt the scent of that dreadful so-called soap your father peddles has upset the animals," Hot Sauce said, eyeing me like I was a carton of spoiled milk.

"Hey, I know my dad's soaps are a little robust, but . . ."

My words got caught in my throat and I couldn't finish. The truth was, I still hadn't really considered what had just happened. I'd been too busy running for my life to stop and ask: *Why?* Why had the bear chosen *me?* Why had I made a polar bear so angry that he shattered supposedly unbreakable glass just to show me in person how much he didn't like me?

Did my dad's soaps really smell *that* bad?

———•I•———

During the bus ride back to school, the other kids hummed with excitement.

I didn't talk to anyone since Edwin ended up on a separate bus during the post-attack chaos. But I heard plenty of kids around me whispering feverishly:

"Edwin's a hero, dude."

". . . *hypnotized* the bear somehow!"

"Greg really is a freak . . . Did you see how badly that bear wanted to eat him?"

". . . must've looked like a thick Human double cheeseburger to it . . ."

"I can't wait to post my video of the attack, it's gonna go viral . . ."

"I'm *definitely* going to make out with Edwin this weekend . . ."

Once we were back at the PEE, I pushed through the crowded hallways toward my locker. I was anxious to get to my dad's store before my shift started at 4:00 p.m. Working at Earthen Goods and Organic Harmony Shop (which I called Egohs) was usually really boring. Exactly what I needed at that moment: a quiet, bear-free setting to clear my head and make sense of everything.

My classmates looked at me like I was a ghost as I passed them. And that's probably what I *should* have been: a kid who died in a horrific field trip incident, now cursed to spend a tortured eternity haunting the PEE's privileged students.

A few minutes later, I rounded a corner near the PEE's north exit, anxious to get out of the school before one more kid gaped at me like I was a zombie. But a wall of angry muscle stepped into my path.

"Can't go this way, Fatmont," said the hulking figure. "Not without first paying the tariff."

Fatmont was one of my nicknames at the PEE (you know, because I was fat and my last name was Belmont). Others included Roly-McBowly (because I resembled a Human bowling ball) and Gravy Dumpster (because presumably fat people loved gravy, which, to be fair, I really did love gravy).

The gargantuan shoulders towering over my head belonged to Perry Sharpe, an eighth grader who could have easily been mistaken for a small rhinoceros. His real name was Periwinkle, but only someone with a death wish would ever call him that. He was the cruelest kid at the PEE. Most bullies stuck to harmless basics like name-calling or ear-flicking, but Perry found it more satisfying to explore the more creative forms of torment. Such as dunking my head into the Souper Bowl, or booby-trapping my backpack by jamming sharp pencils faceup inside it when I wasn't looking.

"Did you hear me, Fatmont?" Perry said. "You can't pass without paying the tariff."

One of his meaty fingers rammed into my shoulder and I nearly fell, but managed to catch myself.

I wanted to inform Perry that a tariff technically referred to an import/export tax on international trade and wouldn't apply to this situation. That the word he likely intended to use was *toll*, which was more commonly used to describe a right-of-passage fee.

But I didn't say those things. Instead, I merely said:

"I could just go another way . . ."

Perry laughed.

"That's where you've got a problem, Fatmont," he said. "The tariff is comprehensive. You gotta pay either way. And it's pretty steep, so steep I can guarantee that you can't afford it, not with the measly profit margins of your dad's dumb hippie store. And so instead you'll have to face the penalty for non-payment. Which is that I get to punch you in the arm as hard as I can. And you can't flinch or else I get to do it again, and you can't flinch again, or else I get to do it again, and on and on like such in perpetuity."

I swallowed hard, nearly choking on my own tongue.

"You know what that means? In *perpetuity*?" Perry asked, as if he was the one who got into the PEE on an academic scholarship and not me.

Just for the record:

per·pe·tu·i·ty
noun

1. the state of lasting forever or for an indefinite period,
   in particular

To narrowly escape a polar bear attack on a Thursday as a Belmont was a minor miracle in itself. But the law of random happenstance would not save me twice. I'd been a Belmont long enough (thirteen years) to know that.

I sighed in defeat.

At least getting dismembered by a bear would have been mostly quick and painless.

CHAPTER 3

Super-Dark-Gray Thursday Is Terrifyingly Only Half Over

I n time, I would come to refer to that particular Thursday as Super-Dark-Gray Thursday.

Black Thursday was already taken by something almost as bad: the huge stock market crash that caused the Great Depression—which also led me to suspect that a Belmont must have somehow been involved.

Resigned to my fate, I turned my shoulder toward Perry.

Being a Belmont made me exceptionally good at taking my lumps in stride, however painful they may have been. Life wasn't fair, I understood that already. Changing such universal certainties was impossible. Merely dealing with the unfairness with some semblance of dignity and poise was much easier.

I closed my eyes and waited for the pain.

But a familiar voice hit me first.

"*There* you are, Greg!"

I opened my eyes—Edwin was standing between an obviously annoyed Perry and me.

"You ran off so quickly, man," Edwin said to me. "You must have forgotten about that *thing* we have to do. You know, the *thing*? Unless you're busy here?"

I shook my head.

Perry scowled. He'd never cared much for Edwin (likely the only kid at the PEE who felt that way). But he never bullied him the way he did all the other kids. It was almost as if he was afraid of Edwin for some reason, despite being twice his size.

"Whatever," Perry said, stalking away. "I'll see you later, *Greg*."

"Thanks," I said to Edwin, finally breathing again. "Twice in one day. One, a horrible, hairy beast with rotting breath and a brain the size of a grape . . . and then also the polar bear earlier."

"Such a comedian!" Edwin joked. "Come on, I'll ride with you to the store. It's Thursday, after all, so you'll be a lot safer if you stick with me. Clearly."

I grinned and nodded.

"Yeah, I think we both *bear* witness to that," I said.

"Nice one!" Edwin laughed. "Even with the tense discrepancy."

He wasn't laughing at how clever my pun was (it wasn't), but at how bad it was (*very* bad). We had this thing with lame puns. Don't ask me to explain why we both found them so funny, because I don't know. Last year in Math class, we would pass pun notes back and forth until our faces were red and trembling because we could barely hold in the laughter anymore. We'd even conspired to one day try to establish a new U.S. federal law requiring any person about to make a bad pun to first stand up on a chair and formally declare that a pun is forthcoming with their index finger raised high into the air. The funny thing was that Edwin's parents were probably rich and powerful enough to actually make that happen if they wanted.

Edwin and I headed out of the school and walked the few blocks to the Clark/Division CTA station. We crammed onto a crowded train and found a few open seats in a back corner. I almost always rode the train to and from school, my apartment, and my dad's store. They weren't close to one another, but were all along the same train line, which made it pretty easy. Edwin rode with me on the few days he didn't have after-school activities. He actually had his own personal chauffeur, but for some reason I've never fully understood Edwin used his services as little as possible.

"You should come over tonight after work," Edwin said as the train lurched forward. "I already told my parents what happened and they're throwing me a party to celebrate being a hero. The president might even show up to award me a Medal of Honor . . . that's the rumor anyway . . ."

I laughed.

Edwin frequently poked fun at the perception that he was perfect—it was his way of making it all less awkward. The praise kids and teachers frequently lavished on him made him uncomfortable. He once told me I was the one person he could admit that to. Anyone else would either get jealous and then annoyed, or simply think he was being ungrateful. He said I was the only one he knew who understood that perception wasn't actually the same thing as reality.

"All my parents' friends," he'd said when explaining what he meant. "They give a lot of money to charities at fund-raisers and stuff. But they wouldn't do it unless other people knew about it. Well, also the tax breaks . . . But the point is, they'd never even consider anonymously going to a soup kitchen and helping out.

Their generosity is perceived well, which is the whole point, and though it still helps, it's not *genuine*."

The more I got to know Edwin and his parents, the more I understood exactly what he'd meant.

"I think I'll pass on the party tonight," I said.

Edwin rolled his eyes dramatically.

"Come on, Greg!" he said. "You know how much the other kids at the PEE bore me. My parents are getting a DJ and ordering a full spread of Chicago's finest pizzas. I *know* you love pizza. And I promise: no bears will be admitted."

I laughed again.

The free pizza *was* pretty tempting.*

"I'll think about it," I said. "Maybe I could *bear* it for an hour or two. If I can *claws* the store early enough."

This time Edwin laughed.

"Nice ones."

"But seriously, *what happened* today at the zoo?" I finally asked.

Edwin's smile disappeared. He looked at me for a moment and then out the window across from us. The tops of tall Chicago greystones whizzed by. It was a rare time when that natural glow in his eyes was absent.

"Well, besides your awesome juke moves avoiding the bear, I have no idea," he finally said. "I was hoping *you* could tell *me*. You're the one who somehow provoked a polar bear into a psychopathic rage!"

---

* A quick side note about how much me and my dad loved pizza: we once accidentally put our favorite pizza place out of business on their now infamous first (and last) All-You-Can-Eat Wednesday. That was another thing about Belmonts: we really, really loved eating. No fewer than four Belmonts have been crowned world champion eaters in competitions.

I shook my head in disbelief.

"You can't possibly think that I—"

"Relax," Edwin said, grinning again. "I'm kidding. I heard Hot Sauce try to blame you afterward. The nerve of that guy."

"Yeah," I agreed. "He did eventually ask if I was okay . . ."

"Probably just to cover his own butt, legally," Edwin said. "To protect the PEE's huge endowment."

"But how did you get the bear to back down and pass out just by *staring* at him?"

Edwin shrugged.

"I have no idea, probably just perfect timing with the tranquilizer darts," he said. "I knew I had to *do* something. I wasn't about to stand there and watch a polar bear fillet my best friend like a salmon. I mean, I'm sure you were terrified, but ultimately I think watching you get eaten would have been so much worse than just getting eaten myself."

"Well, you saved my life today," I said. "Twice."

"*Maybe*," Edwin said.

"No, I mean it," I insisted, not letting it go. "You could have *died*. Should have died, probably. Right now we both should be fusing into each other inside the bear's fecal matter . . ."

"*Gross*, Greg," Edwin said.

An older lady sitting next to us on the train shot me a nasty look and then scooted a few inches farther away. Not an uncommon occurrence for us. The longer we hung out, the more messed up our jokes tended to get. We laughed at things nobody else seemed to understand were actually funny.

"My point is," I said, lowering my voice, "thank you."

"Hey, what are friends for," Edwin said, "if not for keeping their best buddies from turning into bear poop?"

He said the last part extra loudly, eliciting another nasty glance from the old lady. I tried not to smirk.

"Well, I guess we just got lucky the bear *pooped out* when he did," I said.

"Yeah, that could have been a real *grizzly* mess," Edwin said.

We were both laughing now and the old lady looked positively disgusted at the state of today's youth.

"Yeah, it certainly wasn't a very a-*moose*-ing situation," I added.

We both frowned at the last one, which of course didn't even work. That's how our string of lame puns always ended, when one of us came up with one *so* bad that we couldn't even fake it.

"So you really have no idea why the bear was chasing you like that?" Edwin asked a few moments later. "Were you stashing bacon in your pockets again?"*

I shook my head, but couldn't help a smile.

"No . . . but maybe, *maybe* Hot Sauce was right?" I suggested. "Maybe the bear just really hated the smell of my dad's soap as much as everyone else? He *has* been making me try even more of his products lately. And he's getting kind of weird about it."

"*Getting* weird?" Edwin joked.

"Okay, weirder than usual," I clarified.

"I guess it's *possible* the soaps and teas or whatever had something to do with it," Edwin mused thoughtfully.

"Yeah, but that'd be ridiculous, right?" I asked. "Then again, so is a bear smashing unbreakable glass with a rock . . ."

---

* Okay, so yes, one time I went to school with my pockets full of bacon. Partially as a joke (fat kid smells like bacon! ha-ha!), and partially because I frequently get hungry at school and bacon makes the best snack. Either way, let's just say it was not a great idea for a myriad of reasons.

For a moment I considered what some people said about animals being able to see into the true nature of a Human soul. Like the theory that dogs could sense a sociopath, or recognize true evil within seemingly nice people. If that was the case today, then maybe I was destined to become some sort of sick serial killer with a collection of Human thumbs that I would use to construct a model replica of Houston in my basement, which I'd then rename Thumbston.

"Hey," Edwin said mischievously. "Be honest: I bet when that bear was chasing you around, you still took the time to identify all the trees you were running past, right? Right? Tell me I'm right . . ."

I shook my head, trying to pretend that it'd be absurd to be aware of such things while running for your life. But he nudged me with his elbow, letting me know he'd find it hilarious like he always did, not weird like most kids would.

"Yeah, I was," I said, trying to keep from laughing. "I could even tell that the sign Wilbur shattered was made from Atlantic white cedar."

Edwin laughed uncontrollably and shook his head.

"You're incredible," he said.

I shrugged as the train arrived at my stop.

"Thanks," I said, standing up. "For everything today, I mean."

Edwin lifted a shoulder and grinned.

"Think about coming over later," he said. "The party will probably last until nine or ten. It's sure to be an un*bear*ably good time."

I smirked and shook my head at him as the train doors slid closed.

A few minutes later, as I walked the last few blocks to Egohs, all I could think about was the bear's vicious, uncompromising eyes as it had moved in to eat my face. I distracted myself by identifying the various trees I passed (even though I'd done so dozens of times before already):

Box elder
Maidenhair
Sassafras
Green ash
Box elder
Box elder with an angry bird flying from the branches
An angry bird flying right toward my face

I ducked and broke into a run. The small bird narrowly missed spearing my cheek with its tiny beak. I figured it was another freak Thursday occurrence, but then it squawked at me and circled around for another pass. A few other people on the street stepped out of my way as I ran with my arms waving frantically over my head.

What was going on?

Half a block from Egohs, the little bird finally called off its attack. But as I walked through the front door, all I could wonder was whether I was stepping into a stifling vat of world-class bear and bird irritants merely posing as organic soaps and teas, or if something else bigger and even more implausible and insane was happening.

"What's wrong?" Mr. Olsen asked from behind the front counter.

"A bird just attacked me outside!" I said breathlessly as I headed toward the back room. "What a day!"

"Well, it is Thursday," Mr. Olsen noted.

As Egohs' only other employee besides my dad and me, Mr.

25

Olsen had spent enough time around us to hear all about our family curse. I wasn't sure if he entirely bought in to the theory, but he humored us either way.

I flashed him an exasperated look as I entered the small office behind the front counter.

Earthen Goods and Organic Harmony Shop was a little hole-in-the-wall-type place in Lincoln Park, where most of our wealthy, health-minded customers resided. It wasn't much larger than a school classroom and was cluttered with aisles of handmade soaps and tonics and other health products. Bins of organic grains and other earthy ingredients lined the outer walls. The place was rarely completely empty, but never busy. Which meant between the three of us, we always had it covered. Even when my dad was away on one of his trips.

I stashed my backpack in the office and grabbed my Egohs apron before joining Mr. Olsen behind the cash register.

"Getting attacked by a bear at the zoo seemed like enough bad luck for one Thursday," I said as I tied on my apron.

"What do you mean?" he asked.

Mr. Olsen was in his late forties or early fifties and always wore a mismatched vintage suit. He had a trimmed gray-and-white beard and had been a close family friend since well before I was born. He supposedly even did the eulogy at my mom's funeral, but I'd been way too young to remember that.

As I told him what had happened at the zoo, his eyes grew wider and wider. But he didn't seem shocked and horrified, as you'd expect. Instead, it was almost a look of concerned recognition. As if he'd heard of such a thing happening before—like it *wasn't unusual* for zoo bears to randomly go berserk on a kid.

"That's quite a story, Greg," he finally said. "You kids are too soft these days. Back in my day, I'd have wrestled the bear to his death. Skinned him right then and there and turned him into a rug."

I nodded, trying to smile politely.

Mr. Olsen was a nice enough guy once you got to know him, but on the surface he was sort of a crotchety old man. Always rambling about the decaying state of today's world. It was one of the reasons my dad and him were buddies. They held *old-fashioned* in such high regard, you'd think their personal gods were literally named Traditional and Handmade, the quirky odd-couple deities who lived in the clouds and bickered constantly.

I know this is hard to believe but my dad didn't even have a cell phone. Nor did I. Whenever I asked my dad about it, he always made up some excuse or other:

They give you brain cancer.

It's not good for your eyes.

Kids are too disconnected with the earth and life around them these days.

They're too expensive.

Uncle Melvin's phone exploded one night while charging and burned their whole house down. (A Thursday, of course.)

You've done just fine without one for thirteen years.

The only reason I even had an email account was because of the PEE's computer lab and free computer usage at various Chicago Public Library branches. I kept telling my dad that the store could do a lot more business if he at least got a website of some sort. But he stubbornly refused every time.

But the point is: My dad could be hard to reach when he traveled. He was basically off the grid. So he probably wouldn't even find out I almost got killed by a bear until the next morning, when he returned home from Norway. Which meant I'd have to wait until then to see if he reacted to the news as bizarrely as Mr. Olsen had.

⸻✦⸻

Later that night, after closing down the store, I skipped Edwin's party just like we both knew I would.

That's not to say I didn't like video games or movies, or swimming in his rooftop pool or anything like that. But I always found playing chess, or making lame puns, or talking about astronomy and space junk a lot more fun. And we couldn't do those things when Edwin's other friends were around—they found them too boring and nerdy. They'd rather fantasize about what type of luxury car their parents were going to buy them when they turned sixteen, or obsess over how many Instagram followers they had.

It might seem strange that a kid like Edwin would choose someone like me as his best friend. But Edwin isn't actually like most people think. Plus, it makes more sense if you know how we met.

My first ever day at the PEE was over three years ago. I'd gone to Chicago Public Schools through grade five, but then my dad insisted I take something called the Rittenhouse Intelligence Gradient Graduate Equivalent Determination exam (or, the RIGGED test). It was developed specifically for private school placement. After scoring high enough to land a full scholarship at the PEE, I was excited about starting sixth grade at some fancy private school where none of the kids knew me. It could be a fresh start, since I hadn't exactly been a friend magnet at my old school either.

I'd expected private school to be full of polite kids wearing blazers walking around with chessboards tucked under their arms. Of course I found out pretty quickly that chess was just as unpopular at the PEE as it had been in public school. And also that private school kids (though dressed in required blazers) were not at all polite—and maybe even meaner than public school kids in their own bizarrely urbane way.

The first time I ever saw Edwin, he was covered in blood.

He stumbled into the school hallway completely soaked from his face to his feet. Like he'd been dunked into the waste bucket at a slaughterhouse. He looked dazed.

A girl nearby shrieked before fainting.

My first thought had been: *zombie!*

But I eventually realized the blood wasn't his. Or even real.

I found out later that the PEE's theater department was somewhat famous locally for staging elaborate and expensive and controversial plays. In fact, even the *Chicago Reader* and *Time Out Chicago* would sometimes review them. After all, not many middle schools staged $10,000 musical versions of classic movies like *Platoon* and *Star Wars*. Edwin was involved in at least one school play every year.

At that time, they'd been working on their own stage version of an old horror movie called *The Evil Dead*. Part of the "fun" was drenching the first few rows of the audience in fake blood—like they did when it was Off Broadway in New York. The audience was even instructed to wear white for maximum effect. Anyway, they'd been in the middle of rehearsals when one of the blood sprayers malfunctioned and exploded all over Edwin, who played the lead character, Ash.

After everyone in the hallway was finished freaking out, Edwin calmly said: "Well, I'm never popping a zit that big ever again."

The few kids left in the hallway (who hadn't run screaming

when he burst onto the scene looking like a slasher-movie victim) laughed until their faces were red.

"Want to trade shirts, anyone?" Edwin asked. "I can't finish rehearsal in this thing."

I'm still not sure why I did what I did next. I took off my own shirt and held it out to him. This was a big deal for me. In addition to having a pretty round stomach, I also had the most bizarrely hairy back probably ever seen on a sixth grader. For someone trying to make a good impression at a new school, this was about the dumbest thing I could have done on my first day.

The other kids snickered as Edwin accepted the offer and grabbed my T-shirt.

"You're all right, new kid," he said, looking genuinely relieved. "But I really wouldn't expect you to have to wear mine all day . . ."

"It's okay," I said, unzipping my backpack. "I have a backup."

Edwin raised his eyebrows.

"I'm a messy eater," I explained. *

When Edwin saw I really did have a backup shirt in my backpack, he began to laugh. He laughed so hard I thought he might pass out. When he was finally able to stop, he insisted I come over to his house after school to eat pizza and play video games. He said he had to hang out with someone cool enough to need to carry around a spare shirt. I wasn't sure if he was messing with me or not, but I accepted his offer either way.

It didn't take long for us to discover our shared love of chess, making fun of especially bad YouTube channels, astronomy, and the very *idea* of terrible puns, among other things. Who else

---

* Which was true. So I always carried a spare shirt. If you came to just one of our huge Belmont family holiday dinners you'd understand why this became a habit.

could laugh with me at an unintentionally funny TV show, then play a game of chess while discussing the finer points of whether or not the growing masses of space junk in orbit were eventually going to doom us all (me: absolutely; Edwin: no way, humanity would find a way to fix the problem).

It also didn't take me long to realize how genuinely *nice* Edwin was—probably the nicest middle school kid I'd ever met. I never once, in three years, had seen him be cruel to anyone. Plus, he routinely gave away whatever cash he had on him to homeless people we passed in the streets or on the CTA.

But I think the real core of it all was how much we respected each other, even above our shared interests, as weird as that sounds.

About a year into our friendship, he told me that he admired the way I never let the bullies at school get to me. (Which was nice of him to say, of course, but the truth was that they *did* get to me . . . sometimes.)

And another time, he randomly said:

"You know what I like best about you, Greg?"

"Um, that I always have snacks on me?"

"No, it's that I never have to pretend around you," he'd said.

"What do you mean?"

"You're like a fern plant," he'd said. "Leafy and unassuming."

This, of course, had made me laugh, and his eyes lit up.

"See what I mean!" he said. "Nobody else would have laughed so hard at that. I can say almost anything to you, and you'll either laugh or have something equally interesting or funny to say back. With all my other friends, I have to spend too much time and effort pretending to care as much as they do about the Bulls, or superhero movies, or fast cars. I mean, that stuff is okay, but it consumes their whole lives. Whereas I know you'd do anything for your friends and family. You'd give me the shirt off your own back if I needed it. I mean, how many times have you literally done that for me now? Five? Six?"

It was true. Another thing we had in common was a penchant for destroying our own clothes in freak accidents. Me from frequent food spills and things like storing bacon in my pockets. And Edwin from always getting involved in crazy stunts for school plays and other more adventurous endeavors.

Edwin saying these things to me had almost made me cry. But instead I made a lame pun and we'd both laughed. Because I don't cry. Seriously, I never have. One of my dad's very few household rules was: *Belmonts never cry. Ever.* Even the medical staff at the hospital where I was born had apparently remarked at how bizarre it was to see a baby that didn't cry. To which my dad had nodded, smiling proudly. One time I even asked my dad about his no-crying rule, because it seemed so counterintuitive to his generally gentle demeanor. He told me simply that there was never a reason to cry. Because when things seem bleakest, that's when your future couldn't possibly look any better, any more hopeful. There might be a Thursday every week, but it's always followed by six non-Thursdays.

But, anyway, the point is: Edwin and I could always rely on each other. Which is why the more I thought about what he'd done for me at the zoo earlier that day, the less shocking it was. After all, I'd have done the same thing for him. I'd have stepped in front of an angry polar bear (or twenty) without a second thought.

I fell asleep pretty quickly after getting home that night. Especially for a day that had involved getting attacked by a polar bear, a small bird, and a huge psychopath named Perry.

But knowing Edwin was my best friend made it all feel a lot less dangerous than it probably was.

Then again, I also fell asleep never suspecting that the next day (a Friday) was going to be forty thousand times worse than every terrible Thursday in my whole life combined.

CHAPTER 4

I Eat Those Goats Covered in Bee Vomit for Breakfast

M y dad got home from Norway the next morning more giddy and excited than I'd ever seen him—and for my dad that's saying something.

It didn't take much to excite Trevor Belmont. And despite believing that every endeavor would end in failure, he still attempted them all with the vigor of someone certain they'd succeed. My dad was probably the happiest, most enthusiastic and motivated pessimist you could ever meet.

And it was now Friday—my dad's favorite day of the week because it was the furthest away from the next Thursday. He usually tried his craziest, most ambitious stunts on Fridays.

In some ways, I wished I could be more like him. Not exactly like him, though. He was still, by all accounts, one letter short of certifiably insane, after all. A man who spent every last dime he had searching the world's most isolated forests for things most people didn't even believe existed. Even Mr. Olsen didn't seem to fully understand my dad's bizarre obsession with what he majestically called *My Quest*.

But years of trying to make things better, only to make them worse, had left me incapable of action. My dad, however, just kept on going, trying one new zany thing after another, ignoring the usually disastrous results (and the onlookers who frequently called him a fool). Like two summers ago when he tried to build an indoor stone hot tub in our living room and unwittingly caused the whole floor to cave in.

Even then, he'd merely grimaced and said, "I guess next summer I'll try it out on the patio!"

He was so convinced of his own failure that it eliminated all fear and disappointment. He was incapable of self-pity.

My dad once told me this: "Greg, tragedy requires optimism. Always expecting the worst makes you invincible to heartbreak."

———◆I◆———

"Greg!" my dad shouted that Friday morning, poking his head into my room at least an hour before I would normally be awake. "Come to the kitchen! I've got new tea and the board all set up!"

Normally, getting up an hour early on a school day would have made me groan miserably. But that morning was different. I shot out of bed and threw on some clothes as if I hadn't been sleeping at all.

This was my favorite part of his trips.

Ever since I was four, it'd been a ritual. Every time he got home from a trip, it didn't matter what time of day, even at three in the morning, he'd brew up some tea and we'd play at least one game of chess, usually more. It was such a big deal that if he got home in the middle of a school day, he'd stop by the PEE and get me out of class for an impromptu game at a nearby coffee shop.

Before I had barely put a single foot into our small eat-in kitchen, my dad rushed over and gave me a bear hug (ha-ha!) that momentarily left me gasping for air.

"I'm so relieved you're okay," he gushed. "I had a strange feeling *something* might happen to you while I was away, especially *yesterday* of all days. But I never considered a polar bear attack!"

"Yeah, it was really weird," I gasped as he finally released me. "And scary."

"Thursdays are unrelenting devils," he said. "Well, come on."

He motioned to the small table next to the fridge. He'd already poured two cups of organic tea and the chessboard was ready to go. This time I played black—we alternated sides with every game.

"I can't wait for you to try this new blend I concocted in Norway!" my dad said, so worked up his hands were practically vibrating as he pushed one of the rattling cups on a saucer toward me. "It's made with this new ingredient I found there, something the locals call *barberhøvelblad*, which roughly translates to razorleaf."

His behavior wasn't unusual—he was always excited beyond reason for me to try any of his newest products. Sometimes it seemed like he made them just for me and not for the store's customers at all.

This newest tea was slightly brown and smelled of foliage and burned wood. Not unlike a lot of his blends. He tended to make them richer and earthier than the garbage most commercial coffee shops sold.

The tea in front of my dad was different from mine. Like

no tea I'd ever seen before. It had a vibrant, almost purple hue. The steam seemed to float above the hot liquid like some kind of mystical fog.

"Yours is different?" I asked.

"Yes, well, this one I made using an extra-special, very rare ingredient I found in Norway," he said. "I've been hunting for it a long time. A *very long* time. Since well before you were born—"

"Dad," I interrupted, as he stared at the ceiling dramatically. "It's way too early for this."

"It's *never* too early for stories about tea, Greg," he said with a grin that was hard to not acknowledge with a smile of my own.

"Can I try yours, too?" I asked.

"*No,*" he said quickly. He seemed to realize how suspicious that sounded because then he smiled. "Sorry, I mean . . . It's just that this new ingredient is rumored to have some side effects. I just—I don't want to risk you drinking it yet. Let me test it out. If it's safe, you can have some tomorrow, okay?"

I shrugged and nodded as I went over to the pantry and dug out a box of Thatcher's Holistic Organic Stone Ground Oats and Tasty Spelt (or as I liked to call them, Thos[e] Goats—because they tasted how I imagined raw goat hide would). The ridiculously long name of the cereal took up so much space on the box that there wasn't even room for a silly cartoon character.

I sat back down at the table with a bowl of cereal doused in organic honey (aka bee vomit—seriously, look it up) and organic whole milk.

My dad sipped from his cup as he made his usual opening move: e4. As white, my dad *always* opened with e4. It was a very common opening. At least it used to be prior to the 1990s. Opening with the queen's pawn was way more usual in modern chess. But my dad had never opened with anything but e4 in over forty years of playing chess. He always said it was better to master one single variation rather than be mediocre at many.

It was hard to argue with that logic.

I choked through my first bite of dried grains, washing it down with a sip of tea. It tasted pretty much like all the other teas he made (a combination of dried ditch weeds, moldy fruit rinds, and sifted gravel). Which surprisingly isn't as bad as it probably sounds.

My dad stared into his own cup. He swirled it and took another sip, then leaned back expectantly, as if he thought the tea might suddenly turn him into an eagle or something.

"How is it?" he asked.

"It's fine," I said as I made my first move: d5, the Scandinavian Defense.

My dad grinned, seeming to understand that I'd made the play specifically to acknowledge his trip to Norway. Edwin would also have loved my pun-themed opening.

"You know, Greg," my dad said, "that bear at the zoo yesterday didn't ever stand a chance against you. Not a Belmont. My great-great-great-great-great-great-granddad wasn't known by his whole village as Borin the Bear Butcher Belmont because he liked to feed bears treats and then tuck them in at night with bedtime stories. He didn't have a wardrobe made up entirely of bearskins because he let bears best him in battle. He didn't have a huge necklace made from bear skulls because he was best pals with grizzlies. He didn't—"

"I think I get the picture, Dad," I interrupted. "Besides, didn't you once tell me that Borin was eventually eaten by a family of bears somewhere deep in the Siberian forest?"

"That's beside the point," my dad said.

"Is all that other stuff really true?"

"Well, yeah, *mostly* true . . ." my dad said, making his next chess move. "They did call him Borin the Bear Butcher Belmont, but it was his trade, after all. He sold bear pelts and furs. This was back before bears were semi-endangered, mind you. Back when they were actually considered somewhat of a dangerous nuisance to rural villages."

I took another sip of my bitter tea.

My dad took another drink of his. Then frowned. Whether from the poor flavor or an apparent lack of pizzazz was unclear. He continued frowning as he made his next move.

"So you really think I could have taken on that bear?" I asked.

"Well, probably not," he admitted. "At least not unarmed. Even the highly skilled Borin the Bear Butcher eventually met his match."

It wasn't unusual for my dad to be blunt or brutally honest. I was used to it. He almost never lied (not even about small stuff), partly because he was terrible at it.

I nodded and made another move in the game.

As I took another sip of my tea, waiting for him to counter, I noticed a large duffel bag in the hallway near the door. It bulged unnaturally on two sides and had an intricately carved wooden handle with metal inlay sticking out of the zipper. It looked expensive. There was something more about it that I couldn't put my finger on. This will sound insane, but it almost felt like the strange handle was taunting me, beckoning me to walk over and pull it free from the duffel bag—whatever *it* actually was.

Do it, said a voice in my ear.

"What?" I said.

"What?" my dad said back, confused.

"What did you just say?"

He shrugged. "I didn't say anything, Greg."

"Just now, you didn't say anything at all?" I asked.

He shook his head, looking very concerned.

I chalked up the voice to a stress-induced hallucination. But I kept staring at the strange object in my dad's bag.

"What's that?" I asked.

"What's what?"

I pointed at the duffel bag in the hallway behind him.

"Oh, that!" my dad said, startled. He hopped to his feet. "That's nothing, just a cheap replica for store decoration . . ."

He rushed over and quickly shoved the bag into his bedroom with his foot.

Like I said: he was a terrible liar.

"It didn't *look* fake," I said, which was true even though I still had no idea what the object was.

"Well, it's a really good reproduction," my dad mumbled as he sat back down and took another drink of his purple tea. I could tell there was something more he wanted to tell me, but he didn't. Instead, he said: "Have some more tea, Greg."

I'd suspected my dad had been keeping something important from me since I was eight. That was when I started noticing all the times he'd say *Greg*, and then pause dramatically with a sharp inhale like he was about to tell me I was actually a robot he had built in his basement or something. But then he'd either think better of it or chicken out, because instead he'd usually just finish the thought with something like: "Hey, I'll make schnitzel for dinner tonight." My two leading theories on whatever it was he was keeping a secret were either that I had a long-lost twin brother who died under mysterious circumstances, or that my grandfather had a secret past as a bloodthirsty psycho killer who terrorized teenagers every summer at some remote lake camp downstate.

I never really pressed him in those moments, because with my dad it was usually best to let these things go. The one time I really pushed him for an answer was back when I was nine and begging him to tell me the "secret ingredient" (with my dad there was *always* a secret ingredient) in his stew. He eventually gave in and told me I had just eaten calcified lizard tongues fermented in whale stools. And ever since, I wished I'd just accepted my dad's cryptic secrecy for what it was. It wasn't lying, exactly—I'd call it selective omission. He was a terrible liar, but a great selective omitter.

"So the new tea is good?" he asked. "Calming? Too exciting? Too boring?"

"Too boring for what?" I said. "Dad, it's *tea*, of course it's boring."

He swirled his own tea around in his cup as if it could somehow whisper to him the secret of how to make it taste better.

Then he made another chess move.

It was a good one. In fact, I was pretty much in zugzwang already. Which, if you don't play chess (and I'll assume you don't since you're probably a normal kid), means a loss was inevitable even though we were still several moves away from an official checkmate. It was good chess etiquette (and not considered quitting) to simply resign once a game was out of reach.

"Well, that's it," I said, laying down my king. "I'd better start getting ready for school."

My dad nodded thoughtfully.

"You almost pushed to an endgame this time," he said. "Your Scandinavian Defense, though an amusing pun, likely did you in. You know I always defend that well."

"Dad, you defend *everything* well," I said. "Am I ever going to beat you?"

"Yeah, of course," he said. "Someday every Belmont eventually beats their father. I was nineteen when I first beat your grandpa. It was a big day for me—a Friday of course."

I drained the rest of my tea in a few swallows.

"I wish you could play Edwin sometime," I said. "It'd be quite a match."

"I'm sure it would be," he said.

My dad had always liked Edwin as much as Edwin liked him. Which made sense since Edwin was the only person I knew who found my dad's *Quest* for new health product ingredients as interesting as he did. He was always asking my dad about them, which my dad ate up.

You should drink your dad's tea, a voice suddenly said into my ear.

"What?" I said, startled.

My dad raised an eyebrow.

"Are you okay, Greg?"

"Yeah, I . . . well, I don't know," I said. "I'm just hearing stuff this morning is all. Too early I guess."

My dad nodded thoughtfully, staring down at his purple tea. I knew the voice was only in my head. And I believed my dad when he said the side effects of the new ingredient might be dangerous, because it'd happened before. (One time, a new soap he made turned my face green for a whole week.) Plus, as much as I usually enjoyed my dad's tea, it wasn't like I couldn't live without trying them all or anything. And so I'm still not entirely sure why I did what I did next. Maybe the voice in my head was just that convincing. Or maybe it was that none of his teas had ever been bright purple before. Either way, I "accidentally"

42

pushed my king too hard, knocking over some of my dad's chess pieces, causing several to roll off the board and onto the floor.

"Oh, sorry," I said.

"No worries," my dad said as he leaned down to retrieve them.

I quickly grabbed his cup and took two huge swallows, then set it back just as he sat up again.

The tea exploded in my mouth.

Not literally, of course. But it was unlike any tea I'd ever had. It was tangy and sour, almost funky, and it instantly made my whole mouth numb. I regretted stealing those gulps already. But it was too late to undo it now.

"I need," I mumbled, trying to speak over my numb, clumsy tongue. "Go get ready for school."

My dad smiled and nodded. Had I known it would be one of the last times I'd ever see his smile, I would have smiled back. I would have paused and stared so I would remember it more clearly.

I certainly wouldn't have just slunk guiltily off to my room like a gwint.

CHAPTER 5

Greg and Edwin Prance and Frolic in a Flowery Meadow

A photo printed on 8x10 paper was taped to my locker.

It was a frame from a YouTube video of me frantically running from Wilbur the polar bear. In the picture, my mouth was twisted into an ugly grimace that made it look like I was trying to digest an active beehive.

There were dozens more posted all over the school.

I found it amusing that someone took so much time and effort to print that many pictures, and then come to school early enough to hang them everywhere. It was *almost* flattering. Besides, there was nothing else to do but grin and ignore it. Plus, to be fair, some of the other kids had valid reasons to dislike me.

I'd been told (mostly by Edwin), that I had a certain bluntness that a lot of people found rude. My whole family had this problem, including my aunts and uncles. Even my mom was supposedly like that before she died. Belmonts were not good liars (as I said before) and so we usually just said what was on our minds, for better or worse.

For instance: I probably should not have told überpopu-lar eighth grader Jenny Allen that her YouTube channel (about the importance of makeup and always looking pretty) was in-herently demeaning and undercut her own ability to realize a valid sense of self-respect. Looking back, I can sort of see why this had made her cry, but at the time, I was just being honest.

At any rate, it wasn't until later that Friday—third period, to be precise—that I noticed something was wrong with me.

At first I wasn't sure if it was residual shock from the bear attack the day before, or something else entirely—like maybe I was just really, really hungry. Which wouldn't be unusual. Sometimes I got so hungry I seriously considered eating the tis-sues on the teacher's desk. And once, I actually ate the wood off my lead pencil (it didn't taste as bad as you'd think).

Third period was Ancient Humanities, and we were read-ing about Dante Alighieri's *Comedy*. Our teacher, Dr. Tufnell (I called him *Mr.* Tufnell once and got an automatic hour of deten-tion), refused to refer to the work as *The Divine Comedy*. He was trying to explain why doing so was an egregious academic error, but I wasn't paying attention. I was way too busy trying to figure out if I needed to start gnawing on my own arm to satiate an otherworldly hunger, or if I was merely developing sudden-onset superpowers.

Because that was the funny part: I didn't feel *bad* strange. It was more like . . . *powerful* strange, as dumb as that probably sounds. I felt invincible. Like I could wrestle a hippopotamus on a Thursday and win. Make that two hippopotamuses. Armed with nunchucks.

By lunchtime, the feeling had grown so intense that I was convinced it had to be hunger. If it wasn't, then I would conquer the school, raise a Belmont flag, and sit up in the old minaret and occupy the PEE as its one true Lord and Ruler. I felt *that* powerful.

But first I would eat, just in case I was only hungry.

Edwin was always inviting me to sit at his table during lunch. But it was usually filled with sparkly girls and flawless guys who made sure I knew I didn't belong there. I'd sat with them once in sixth grade and it hadn't gone well. Even when they weren't being directly malicious, I still felt out of place.

So I usually ate lunch in a quiet section of the cafeteria, away from the other tables. Away from where the other kids sat and joked around with their friends. My spot was behind a few ceiling-support columns where a sofa, chair, and coffee table were tucked neatly away in a nook of the massive room.

Nobody else ate over there except Froggy.

Froggy was the only kid at the PEE who somehow had a worse social standing than I did. Part of it was because he came to school without pants one day—I can only assume by mistake. Also, he was always mumbling things to himself. Strange things. Such as on that particular Friday, when I got to my spot, he was mumbling something about putting hamsters in balloons and tying them to your belt.

I'm not kidding.

"When you have balloons full of hamsters you're going to be happy. You tie the balloons to your belt and walk around with a bunch of hamsters in balloons hanging off your belt . . ."

I could go on, because he certainly did, but the rest was even more confusing. Actually listening to Froggy's rambling only led to mysterious questions that would never be answered. The few times I'd asked him what he was talking about, he always responded with shorter, even more cryptic answers, such as:

King Missile.

Pedro the Lion.

Say Hi.

To which I'd raise an eyebrow. And then he'd grin at me and just go back to his rambling.

I'd tried talking to him about other stuff a few times. But he never seemed interested. The most normal thing he ever said to me over the span of three years was to reveal that his stepdad had created one of the most popular video game franchises in history. Which was funny, because that would probably have catapulted him to the top of the social order if the other kids at the PEE knew. But I suspected that was exactly what Froggy *didn't* want for some reason.

As he sat down on the couch, still talking about hamsters (apparently having the correct *number* of hamsters tied to your belt is crucial), I examined my meal. It was a relatively pedestrian lunch by the PEE's standards: pan-seared sole with a white wine butter sauce and fresh arugula salad. I looked at the tiny portions, wishing desperately that I had more food. The school served insanely small portions compared to what I was used to at home.

That bizarre "conquer the world" feeling in my gut kicked in again. Suddenly (and illogically) I *knew* that I could have more food if I wanted. I didn't know where the thought came from, but I *believed it*.

And then something utterly impossible happened.

A green plant began to sprout under my feet.

Little tendrils poked up from the cracks in the marble-tiled floor. They rose slowly, an inch every few seconds. And then they sprouted leaves. And after several more seconds, I was staring at two perfectly beautiful patches of arugula growing directly from the floor.

"Froggy, check this out," I said.

He glanced over, but either didn't notice the plant or didn't find it strange. He went back to his own world, staring vacantly at the ceiling and munching slowly on a sardine-and-Vegemite sandwich he'd brought from home.

I reached down and gently grabbed one of the leaves sprouting between my feet. I pulled it free and slowly put it on my tongue without even thinking. I needed to make sure this was really happening before I commenced with a total meltdown.

The arugula leaf tasted slightly peppery and fresh.

And very real.

My lunch tray fell from my hands and landed facedown on the floor. Froggy glanced at it before once again dissolving back into his own thoughts. I rushed around the corner into the regular section of the school cafeteria.

Edwin was at his usual table, surrounded by hordes of friends. They snickered as I approached. But Edwin shushed them.

"Can I talk to you?" I asked.

"Sure, Greg, what's up?"

"Not here," I said. "It's important."

Edwin stood up and made some joke about me and him going off to prance and frolic in a flowery meadow. The whole table laughed. If I had tried to make that joke, it would have been met with an uncomfortable silence. But then again, Edwin had a way of making anything funny. He could tell you your grandma just died and you'd be in stitches for some reason you couldn't begin to comprehend.

He followed me into an empty hallway adjacent to the cafeteria, looking genuinely concerned.

"What's wrong, buddy?" he asked. "Look, I know the kids

have been really hard on you today. I've personally torn down every one of those photos I've seen hanging on the walls—"

"It's not that," I interrupted. "Something weird is happening to me. *Has* happened. And I feel . . . *different*. Like, I don't know, like I'm actually good at stuff for once. I know this will sound lame, but it's like I have . . . I don't know . . . *powers* or something."

"Ohhhh . . ." Edwin said slowly. "Greg, dude, that's just called *confidence!* Something you always had deep down."

He reached out to jab me jokingly with his finger. I slapped his hand away.

"I'm being serious, this isn't a joke!" I said.

"Okay, just calm down," Edwin said, his grin fading. "Maybe it's the adrenaline of realizing you survived a near-death experience yesterday? Like, *If I can survive a bear attack, then what can't I do?* That sort of thing?"

"Yeah, maybe," I admitted. "But . . . I'm a *Belmont!*"

"So?"

"So you know that means I've already survived a bunch of near-death moments," I said. "Like last summer, when my dad and I got into that car accident caused by an exploding cow." (Yes, for real. It's a long story.) "Or three years ago, when my dad nearly burned down our apartment building trying to make boiled goose for lunch. Or how—"

"Okay, yeah, I get it," Edwin said.

It always bothered him when I talked about the Belmont family's penchant for disastrous failure. He thought our own belief in the superstition was what actually caused all the bad luck—*a self-fulfilling prophecy* was what he'd called it.

"Let's play a quick game of chess," Edwin suggested, taking out his phone. "If you really are developing powers, then you might stand a chance at beating me. It's the only way you ever could, after all."

"Dude, not funny."

"I'm not joking," Edwin said.

I nodded, but then remembered a test wasn't even necessary.

"Actually, I already have proof that something strange is happening," I said. "Follow me."

I led Edwin around to the other side of the cafeteria. Froggy was still there, eating his sandwich, but he ignored both of us. I pointed at the arugula plant sticking up from the tiles next to the sofa.

"I made this grow here, just now," I said. "*With my mind.* I don't know how I did it, but *I* did it, I'm sure of it."

And then the strangest thing happened. Edwin's expression completely changed. But not to a look of confusion or shock. Or disbelief. Or even amusement. He suddenly looked worried. As if seeing these plants was more troubling news to him than finding out his parents had lost their entire family fortune betting on the Chicago Bears to finally win another Super Bowl.

"Wow," Edwin finally said. "You weren't *leafing* me on, were you?"

"Really, right now with the puns?" I said, but couldn't hold back a grin.

"No, I a-*green* with you," he said. "This isn't a time for puns, it's truly bizarre."

I laughed in spite of my growing concern for my own mental health—likely the whole point behind him making the puns: to calm me down. I was just glad he wasn't calling the school psychiatrist on me.

"What should I do?" I asked.

"I don't know, Greg," Edwin said. "Maybe try your best to

not do anything more like this, okay? Just fight that weird feeling and don't bring any more attention to yourself."

"Why? Do you know something?"

"No, of course not!" he said. "I'm as baffled by this as you are. But I do know that most teachers would assume it's some sort of elaborate prank or something. So just try to keep your cool and get out of here as soon as you can after school. We'll talk about this more later, okay?"

"Okay . . . okay, yeah," I said, thankful he was being so calm.

"All right," he said, turning away. "Lie low with this stuff . . . seriously."

I nodded as he left, still finding his reaction both comforting and odd. It definitely seemed like he knew *something* I didn't. But with Edwin it was always hard to tell—it was why he was so good at chess and making friends. He *always* knew something you didn't. He was just that smart.

As I stood there by the arugula plant that I had somehow grown telepathically, I became aware that Froggy was staring at me intently. He stood and faced me.

"You're more than you think you are," he said.

"What?"

He didn't answer and instead quickly picked up his backpack and walked away before I could ask a second time what he'd meant.

CHAPTER 6

I Discover a New Talent: Breaking Bones with My Face

N othing else strange happened the rest of that school day. But this was partially because I'd been so determined not to let it—per Edwin's advice. After eighth period, my goal was simply to get out of the building before anything else happened. Before I accidentally grew a corn patch in the hallway or made it rain inside the gym or something.

I grabbed my backpack from my locker and bolted for the nearest exit.

But while descending the back stairwell, I ran into a mass of kids. They were circled around the cramped second-floor landing. From the third step I easily saw what they were watching:

Perry and Froggy.

And they weren't engaged in a secret handshake.

Perry was holding Froggy upside down by his ankles. The poor kid's long, greasy hair hung down over his face.

"Come on," Perry said with a laugh as he lifted and lowered Froggy several times, his head nauseatingly close to hitting the polished marble floor each time. "I want to see you bounce like a little toad."

Remarkably, the kids gathered around giggled as if this were funny instead of horrifically sadistic. I wanted to believe they were merely afraid of the repercussions of not laughing, but at least half of them were Perry's equally demented friends. So they were probably genuinely enjoying it for reasons only a fellow deplorable would understand.

On any other day, I know exactly what I would have done. I wish I could tell you that I would have intervened and saved the day and then taken the inevitable pummeling for it. But the truth was I would have simply fled like a coward. Because past experience had taught me that fighting back in the face of crisis usually only made things worse—especially with my luck. It was better to just minimize the damage and let one kid get beat up instead of two.

But it *wasn't* a normal day.

It didn't take long, perhaps a second or two, for me to decide that Perry would not get away with this. The decision to actually *do something* felt so foreign that I was becoming increasingly convinced it was probably just indigestion. Which is why I opened my mouth before I could back out.

"Hey Periwinkle!" I shouted.

Everyone's head turned.

Nobody got away with using Perry's full name.

"Just because you're jealous that Froggy's mom didn't abandon him doesn't give you the right to torture the poor kid," I said.

The crowd collectively gasped. Everybody knew that Perry's mom ran out on him when he was two years old. And he was still broken up about it, as evidenced by the six Mom-themed tattoos that his professional UFC–fighter dad had let him get.

I instantly regretted what I'd said. Not interfering, but doing it in such a foolhardy way. I could probably have just politely asked him to stop. That might have ended better.

"Roly-McBowly Fatmont," Perry said slowly, enunciating each word carefully.

He dropped Froggy onto the ground in a crumpled heap.

At some point, I'd descended the final three steps onto the landing. The group of kids encircled me, essentially blocking any escape routes. Froggy uneasily climbed to his feet and grabbed his backpack. He shot me a grateful glance and then squeezed through the crowd and ran down the final set of stairs.

Perry was now just inches from my face, so close that his hot breath was practically melting my eyebrows.

"You really must be a masochist or something," Perry said (that was the funny thing about entitled private school bullies— they had oddly huge vocabularies). "First taunting a polar bear and then insulting my mom. It's just . . . well, it's *rude*. You're *mean* for a fat kid, you know that? At least apologize before I smash your face in. Maybe I'll make it quick if you actually sound sincere."

"Uh, I'm *sorry*?" I said, realizing just how empty the words sounded as they left my mouth.

"Yeah, you definitely will be," Perry said slowly, almost regretfully—as if he didn't actually *want* to pound my face into dust but was merely obligated to do so by some ancient Code of Machismo.

Whatever courage I'd mustered before was gone. The super-power feeling I'd had all day suddenly felt totally imaginary. I cowered farther back into the corner, like an exhausted boxer hitting the ropes, praying for the end of the round.

Perry was done talking.

He'd decided to finish our conversation with his cinder block–size fists. He grabbed my shirt with his left hand and pulled back his right with agonizingly slow consideration.

I closed my eyes and waited for the cheek-shattering blow.

In an instant I felt a gust of wind on my face as his fist zoomed forward at an incredible velocity. I was vaguely aware that an impact followed shortly after, but it was strange—I *felt* nothing. There was no pain, my head didn't jerk backward, there wasn't even any pressure on my face—it was almost as if his fist had just bounced off me like rubber.

Perry's bloodcurdling scream prompted me to finally open my eyes again. He was hunched over, holding his arm. His face contorted in pain as he cradled several crooked and swollen fingers dangling from his right hand. He looked at me and flinched, taking a step back.

"Freak," he sneered.

All the kids gathered in the stairwell stared at me in stunned silence. I had no idea what had just happened, but I knew these facts:

1. My face felt fine.
2. I'd somehow broken Perry's hand.

Kids whispered as I moved to squeeze past them. As I approached, they parted on their own like a set of automatic doors, or a magical sea in an old fable.

Then I heard whispers that I knew simply couldn't be true:

"*Was I seeing things, or did Greg Fatmont just turn into stone?*"

CHAPTER 7

How to Get Your Lats Juiced

M y dad was behind the counter in his Egohs apron when I
stepped into the store.

He glanced at me briefly, and then went back to explaining
to a customer what made his handcrafted soaps so special: *It
comes from the quality, rarity, and harmonic, synergetic integrity of
our raw ingredients. And the process itself, which is done in an ancient
timeworn manner from back before the idea of "organic" had even been
created. The holistic, handcrafted properties of . . . blah, blah, blah, etc.,
etc., etc.*

I'd heard him make the same impassioned pitch hundreds
of times. But he wasn't just selling products. He really *believed* in
them. He sincerely thought that his products connected people
with the earth and nature in ways nothing else could.

I put on my apron and joined my dad behind the counter.
He rang up the customer's purchase and then finally turned
toward me.

"How was school?" he asked.

"Um . . ." I said, not sure where to begin.

How was I supposed to rationally explain everything that had happened (i.e., me apparently turning into stone and also telepathically growing plants through the tiled floor) in a way that wouldn't make him want to have my head examined?

"Well," I finally continued. "Actually, something really *weird* happened . . ."

He raised his eyebrows slightly.

"But, I mean . . . I just . . ."

"Greg, you can tell me *anything*, you know," my dad said.

"I'm just—I'm not sure you'll believe me," I said.

"Try me."

"Okay, well, I . . . uh . . . Dad, I think I telepathically made a plant grow right through a second-story marble-tile floor. Am I going crazy?"

I expected my dad to laugh. I expected him to scoff and tell me I was imagining things. I expected some mixture of disbelief and concern. I certainly didn't expect his eyes to light up like a string of supercharged Christmas lights. He leaned forward as if he'd just won the lottery but needed me to tell him where I had hidden the winning ticket.

"Greg, I need you to be honest with me," my dad said. "It's very important that you tell me the truth. I won't be mad either way . . ."

"Okay . . ."

"Did you sneak a drink of my tea this morning?"

I sighed and nodded, expecting his weird excitement to turn into anger. Or at the very least disappointment. But instead he nearly leaped into the air in celebration. He actually grinned and threw a fist into the air.

"I knew it!" he said smugly at nobody in particular.

"Dad, what's going on?" I asked. "What do you know?"

"Did anyone else see you do this?" he asked, ignoring my questions.

"Dad, what is happening to me? What was in the tea?"

"Greg, this is important," he said firmly. "Did *anyone else* see what happened today?"

In that moment, I thought about Froggy and Edwin. They had seen the arugula plant. But then my mind shifted to the twenty or thirty kids who had witnessed me turning into stone. The obvious answer was: yes. Lots of kids saw what happened. But in that moment something inside me finally snapped. My dad *knew* what was going on. It was clearly related to his strange purple misty tea. And the weird object in the duffel bag. And all the other secrets he'd obviously been keeping from me his whole life. I'd been okay looking the other way in the past when I'd thought it was mostly just stuff like not telling me that I was eating fried bird brain fritters or pickled duck tongues or pureed worm guts. But now that I was getting attacked by bears and birds and turning into stone, I *deserved* to know the truth.

"I'm not going to tell you anything more until you tell me what's going on," I said. "What was in your tea? What was that weird thing in the duffel bag? Why did a bear attack me yesterday? *What is happening, Dad?* Please."

My dad leaned back as if I'd slapped him. He hadn't been expecting this. I think he'd assumed I'd just take the cryptic weirdness in stride like I always did. Then he shook his head and I knew he wasn't going to tell me anything.

"We can talk about all that *later*," he said breathlessly. "I promise. But this is vitally important. My whole life's work depends on it: What else happened at school? Did anyone witness it?"

"Your *life's work?*" I nearly shouted. "Listen, Dad. I'm really tired of hearing about your life's work. Especially since you never actually share it with me. Don't you think I'd have liked to go on some of your *Quests* with you? We could have done it together. Instead, you keep secrets from me! And now your son is having a crisis, either losing his mind or something perhaps even worse, and all you're worried about is your life's work! Gee, thanks for caring, Dad."

I saw a look on my dad's face then that I'd never seen before: I'd actually hurt his feelings. In a lot of ways he was like a puppy—always happy, impossible to discourage. But I saw genuine pain in his eyes. That usual spark of joy was gone.

"I know you think all I do is worry about work, and hunt for ingredients, and keep secrets," my dad said, his voice shaking slightly. "But there's more. I mean . . . it's difficult to explain now, but . . ."

He stared vacantly at the cash register, unable to look at me.

My gaze drifted to the windows. It was unusually dark for 4:30 p.m., nearly pitch-black, and I wondered if it was going to storm. The weather seemed like the only reasonable thing to think about after a day in which I may or may not have turned into stone and then hurt my dad's feelings—both things I would have thought impossible before that moment. As if to answer me, rain began pouring onto the sidewalks outside. People popped umbrellas and rushed past our doors. Part of me wanted to stammer some sort of halfhearted apology, mostly out of the shock of seeing my dad so miserable. The only other times I'd ever seen him look that way were once a year on the anniversary of my mom's death.

But I didn't say anything more, because he *deserved* to feel bad. Even after my blowup, he was still just sitting there. He still hadn't expressed any concern for me beyond who saw what. So if he was going to be stubborn, then so would I. Even though I was starting to feel a little guilty.

"Dad, can't you just . . ."

"Forget it, Greg," my dad said, not looking up. "We can talk about this later. I need to go make a phone call. What happened today is . . . well, it has greater ramifications than you'll ever know."

"I *would know* if you'd only tell me—" I started, but he cut me off.

"Greg, I'm done with this conversation, I don't have time," he said firmly. "Now go greet those customers who just stepped inside and see if they need help. We'll talk later."

I paused, not wanting to let this go again—like I always did. But he was already holding the store's ancient telephone to his ear and dialing a number. So I peeled myself away from the counter to welcome the customers, who were likely just escaping the rain.

The first patrons I approached were an odd pair.

Two guys. One was massive and hulking, struggling to squeeze past the narrow rows of products. He wore a tan trench coat and gray sweatpants and had short buzzed hair like a soldier. He was at least six foot seven and weighed probably close to three hundred pounds, solid muscle. His sleeves pulled at his bulging arms as if he were wearing spandex instead of a coat. His buddy was nearly as short as me, but a lot skinnier, literally less than half the size of his counterpart. He had sand-colored hair that hung down past his ears, and a lean face.

"Can I help you guys?" I asked.

They spun around, startled by my voice.

"Oh, hey, bro," the big guy said. "Is this place, uh, Earthen Goods Shop, like, the . . . uh, the one run by Trevor Belmont?"

He had a slight accent that I couldn't quite place, but thought might be either Canadian or Californian.

"Yeah," I said, still feeling tense from my conversation with my dad. "That's what it said on the front door last time I checked."

"Hey, kid, watch your mouth," the smaller guy said, but not like he was scolding me—more like he was offering me an insider tip. "You really don't want to make my friend mad, bro. Trust me."

"What, is he, like, the Incredible Hulk or something?" I asked.

The bigger guy cocked his head, not seeming to understand the reference. The smaller guy laughed, but it sounded nervous. Uneasy. Almost as if he was saying: *Yes, that's exactly what I meant.*

"Well, sorry about that," I said. "Trevor is my dad. This is our store. Looking for something in particular?"

The Little Bro glanced toward the door like he was checking for the nearest exit. The (ample) hairs on my arms stood on end, and I suddenly had a bad feeling about these guys. But then he finally grinned again. Big Bro followed suit, and although it was crooked, and his teeth were stained and uneven, there was a certain dumb charm to it that put me at ease.

"Yes, actually we are," the Little Bro said. "Our lifting buddy said he got some sick all-natural supplements that are *totally legit and legal* for competition from this place."

"And it totally worked, bro!" Big Bro chimed in. "Our bud Marlon is more jacked than I've ever seen him. He's just flat swole. I mean, his lats alone are juiced! He deadlifts seven hundo."

I cringed at his description of his lifting buddy's lats, whatever those were.

"Sounds like you've found the right place," I said. "The mind and body enhancement supplements are two aisles over, near the back, facing this way. They are *all* organic and completely natural, which I figure probably makes them legal for, uh, competitions, or whatever."

"Cool, bro, thanks," the Little Bro said.

I backed up out of the aisle and stood near the register so there was room for Big Bro to get by. He gave me a quick look from head to toe as he passed.

"Hit me up if you want any workout tips," Big Bro added. "You look like you could stand to crush the weights some, bro. Know what I mean?"

"Yeah, well, you look like you could stand to crush the weights a little less, *bro*," I mumbled. "Know what I mean?"

Big Bro scowled at me, his face turning red. I quickly retreated around to the next aisle where I saw another customer, an older lady, carefully picking through our selection of organic tree oils.

Just as I reached her, the power went out.

The lights snapped off with an electric crackle, casting the whole store into darkness. I was only a few feet away, but all I could see now was the lady's frail and tiny silhouette.

She gasped.

"It's okay, ma'am," I said. "It's probably just the storm. Plus, you know how ComEd is—"

Then the old lady inhaled sharply as if to scream.

"It will be okay, we have flashlights . . ."

But as my eyes adjusted to the dark, I finally saw her face. She wasn't worried about the lights going out. She was too busy gaping wide-eyed at something behind me.

"I told you not to make him mad, bro!" Little Bro shouted.

I spun around. And then let loose the very scream that the old lady had somehow managed to hold back.

CHAPTER 8

My Dad's All-Natural Weight Gain Supplements Are Apparently Highly Effective

T he Big Bro loomed in front of the cash register.

I could only make out his huge silhouette in the dark, the square shape of his head and billowing trench coat. But it wasn't just the Big Bro standing there in the dark.

He was *growing*.

Like the Incredible Hulk, the Big Bro grew larger by the second in front of my very eyes. His head expanded and bulged, rising at least three or four feet higher, nearly touching the ceiling. His shoulders ballooned and the trench coat ripped away from his inhumanly large torso. His already obscenely muscular arms were now so massive that I could have fit completely inside of his biceps with enough room to host a small tea party. His balled-up fists were almost the size of small Volvos.

Little Bro had run for cover.

I realized I was screaming, so I closed my mouth. For a glorious moment there was nothing but dark silence in the store. Lightning cracked outside as Bro Monster took a step toward me. His brown, crooked teeth looked almost fluorescent in the flash.

He took several more thundering steps, easily smashing aside two shelves. I glanced back to reassure the old lady that I could protect her, but she was no longer standing there. She'd been smart enough to flee while I'd been screaming like a frightened three-year-old.

The Bro Monster towered over me.

I finally saw more than just his silhouette and slimy teeth. He'd not only grown, but also seemingly transformed into something else completely. Not quite the Incredible Hulk like I'd joked—but something else even less Human.

His skin was pale gray and rough, like it was made from shark hide. His head was knobby and misshapen, and the rest of his features, the nose in particular, seemed to have grown to match his squared jaw. His eyes were glowing golden rings, like a wild animal's, set back underneath a cliff of a forehead.

Bro Monster growled.

His teeth seemed sharper than they were before.

"Wow, our supplements worked a lot faster than I bet you expected," I said, mostly because I couldn't think of anything else appropriate to say.

Then the Bro Monster roared. His breath was sour like Chinese takeout left in the sun. He raised a hand above his head and it smashed a crater into the old tin ceiling. Drywall and ancient plaster sprinkled onto his shoulders like dandruff. His unearthly roar intensified as he swung his fist down with clear intent to crush me like a bug.

I cowered and my knees buckled.

Even if I did somehow turn to stone like I had a few hours ago at school, I doubted it would have helped. Bro Monster seemed perfectly capable of pulverizing a small, pudgy rock into crumbles.

But just before the impact, my dad came flying in out of the darkness behind the monster. He was wildly swinging a large object at the monster's approaching fist. Whatever it was connected with the Bro Monster's wrist, deflecting it slightly. The huge hand crashed down just inches to my left, smashing apart the old tiled floor like brittle wood.

I stumbled into the crater as he reared his fist back to strike again.

My dad jumped in front of him. That's when I realized the object in his hands was a huge battle-ax. He wielded it like an action movie hero. Except not quite like in an action movie, more like a slapstick comedy, to be perfectly honest. In reality, my dad was just clumsily swinging the heavy ax in all directions with no grace and very little coordination or design. But what he lacked in skill, he made up for with pure panicked effort.

The ax blade blindly grazed the monster's knee.

He bellowed in pain before stumbling back and falling into our front counter, obliterating it instantly. The Bro Monster quickly began climbing to his feet, but the fall bought my dad enough time to grab my arm and pull me around the corner.

"Greg, run!" he yelled. "Get out of here. I'll distract it . . ."

"Dad, no!" I protested, but it was too late either way.

The Bro Monster had recovered from the fall much faster than I expected. He lumbered over and flung my dad away with a quick backhanded swipe like he was made of tissue paper.

My dad crashed into the giant plastic bins of organic grains hanging from the wall in the back of the store. Steel-cut oats spilled all over him as he slumped to the floor.

I dove quickly out of the way of the monster's other fist as it came smashing down toward me.

The store looked less like a store now, and more like the site of a recent tornado. My dad had told me to run, but I couldn't just leave him there to be bench-pressed into oblivion by the Bro Monster. I was feeling something I'd never felt before—it was similar to the way I felt at school earlier when I'd stood up to Perry, but also different—this felt more real. More like *me*.

I suddenly wanted to fight this thing. I felt like I could go pick up the ax and actually stand a chance of fending off the beast. The strange voice in my head from earlier that morning even came back and told me so as clear as if there was a little person sitting on my shoulder with a tiny megaphone:

You can, Greg. You can stop this attack. Don't run!

I dashed over to where my dad was slumped and covered in whole grains. He groaned uneasily and reached around for the ax. He finally found the handle and used it to push himself back to his feet.

"Greg, I told you to get out of here," he said.

"I'm not leaving without—" But I didn't get to finish.

My dad shoved me out of the way as the Bro Monster charged again. He barreled right in between us and smashed headfirst into the brick wall. It partially caved in as the monster groaned in pain.

Panic ripped into my guts. Whatever inner strength I'd mustered up a second ago was completely gone. I was back to being Greg Belmont, Überchicken, The World's Foremost Coward, Spineless Fat Kid. Besides, all I'd accomplished so far was distracting my dad enough to almost get him killed twice. He'd be better off fighting this fight without me.

My dad swung the ax around in wild pinwheels as he clambered toward the huge monster.

I turned and ran, heading toward the rubble that used to be the cashier counter. I opened the door to our office and scrambled inside, taking one last look into the store.

The Bro Monster spun toward my dad, easily smashing the ax from his grip. As my dad stumbled to the floor with a stunned expression on his face, the Bro Monster roared with rage and raised both of his massive fists into the air, ready to bring them down with enough force to crush a tank.

I cowered backward and slammed the office door closed.

CHAPTER 9

A Future Contractor Finds a Big-Boned Skeleton Inside a Wall

I realized immediately that I'd made a grave mistake.

I'd abandoned my dad. Turned my back on him as he struggled to fight off some sort of horrible creature—the world's most grotesque gym rat. I grabbed the door handle and pulled. But it wouldn't budge. It was either locked or jammed—maybe from structural damage sustained during the attack.

Panic flooded my throat and chest. I'd possibly just witnessed my dad's demise and I had done nothing to help. But there was still another way I could get back into the store. It might not be too late.

I ran into the alley, intending to circle around the block toward the front entrance.

But as soon as I stepped out into the damp alley, a man was standing in my way. The rain had stopped, but there was a biting chill in the air and I could see my own exhalations rising up in front of me as they came out in shallow bursts.

"Mr. Olsen?" I said uncertainly. "You're not supposed to be working tonight. The store . . . there's—there's been an attack . . ."

"I know, Greg," Mr. Olsen said calmly. "But you can't go back. You must follow me. It's urgent that we hurry, there may be more of them lurking . . ."

His eyes darted around nervously. He wasn't kidding, this wasn't a strange and elaborate and expensive practical joke. This was really happening and Mr. Olsen was terrified to be standing in that dark alley.

"But, my dad—"

"It's too late, Greg," he said. "Don't worry, your father is stronger than he seems. We must go now. We can't risk losing you both."

"What's . . . what's going on, Mr. Olsen?" I asked.

"My name isn't Mr. Olsen," he said. "It's Fynric Grufftrack."

"But . . . *what?*"

"There isn't time," he said, grabbing my arm and pulling me down the alley. "We'll explain later. Now we must hurry away from here. The Council will meet soon."

"Council . . . ?" I managed as I stumbled along after him.

"Yes," Fynric said. "The Council has much to discuss. There hasn't been a verified Mountain Troll sighting in almost five thousand years . . ."

I was vaguely aware that Fynric had just told me the creature presently attacking our store was a Mountain Troll. But I could barely walk as he led me through another dark alley, let alone consider the possibility that Trolls were real. All I could think about was that final look on my dad's face before . . . well, before I'd fled like a coward.

"This way, hurry," Fynric said. "We're almost there."

It was obvious that Mr. Olsen, aka Fynric Grufftrack, wasn't just some family friend who worked at Egohs. He was clearly in on all the secrets my dad had been keeping from me. And somehow that hurt almost as much as knowing I'd just run out on him. That he'd trusted a friend with his weird secrets more than his own son.

Fynric stopped near the end of a particularly dark alley and nodded at a small crevice between two adjacent buildings.

"After you," he said.

I blinked. This guy must have forgotten what I looked like in the light—there was no way I would fit into the twelve-inch gap between the buildings.

"We don't have all night, come on," Fynric urged me.

When working at Egohs, Mr. Olsen was normally such a calm man, if not a tad grouchy. But now he seemed downright frantic. His eyes flickered with unnerving anxiety—which was about as soothing as chewing on a mouthful of rusty nails.

"I can't—I mean, I'll never fit," I said. "My nickname at school isn't Fatmont because—"

"Just try," he interrupted, frustrated. "Now! We must hurry!"

I decided to humor him. Once Fynric saw I wouldn't fit, then he'd stop hassling me and we could find a door like normal people. I pressed up against the space between the buildings. The brick edges dug into my gut.

"Oh, for Landrick the Wanderer's sake, turn sideways, boy," he said impatiently.

I rotated and pressed my hip against the wall. At first, as I suspected, it accomplished nothing since my stomach was still nearly double the size of the small crevice. But then something remarkable happened. I felt myself slowly squeezing into the space.

I *did* fit!

But just barely.

The crunchy texture of the old bricks scraped my skin and clothes as I pressed inward. Fynric gave me a shove and then I was entirely inside the crevice, so squeezed that there wasn't room for my chest to heave as I breathed in a fierce, rising panic. And I wondered: Why on earth did I just let a dude with a name like Fynric Grufftrack trap me in between two solid-brick walls?

Was I insane or just that stupid?

"Come on, keep moving," Fynric said.

He was behind me in the crevice now, still pushing me forward. I scooted farther in using stilted sideways shuffle steps, my feet and head twisted unnaturally to the side like a ballerina. The space narrowed and after a few more steps I couldn't go any farther.

"I'm stuck," I said. "We have to go back."

There was no reply.

Panic welled inside my throat. I somehow managed to turn my head around, scraping my nose and forehead against the rough bricks.

Fynric was gone, as if he'd just vanished.

I began to ease my way out, but the passage seemed too narrow. I couldn't go any farther toward the alley. Which was impossible. Brick walls didn't expand and contract like living things.

And yet the walls seemed to be narrowing even more as I stood there panicking. I suddenly knew that decades from now some construction contractor with a blue plaid shirt and impeccable gray mustache was going to find my bones amid a pile of rubble.

"Man," the guy would say with a perfect Chicago accent, running a finger along his mustache. "This kid sure was big-boned."

I was praying that rats wouldn't start nibbling on my ankles when I finally heard Fynric's voice again.

It was hollow and seemed to be coming from below me.

"Keep moving."

I didn't see how that was possible since my arms and legs were essentially trapped, crammed into the walls like ground meat inside sausage casings. But I obliged him anyway and slowly tried to shuffle farther in.

This time my foot found nothing but air—as if the dirty pavement beneath me had disappeared. I tried to use the walls to steady myself, but it was too late. I tumbled forward (or sideways, technically) into the void.

I should have landed on the ground, folded up like a pretzel. But instead, I kept falling. The walls were gone and I was soaring through a dark cave or tunnel. I was too shocked to even scream or yell, though I was grateful that it was dark enough to censor the gory mess I'd inevitably make at the bottom of whatever pit I was falling into.

But my landing was softer than expected. I thudded onto a damp and soggy wooden panel, knocking the wind from my lungs. After a few seconds, it slowly gave way underneath me and I fell through what seemed to be a trapdoor, landing again with a solid THUMP on hard, wet concrete.

Lying on the cold surface, I stared hazily up at a stone ceiling. The dim glow of the Chicago streetlights was still visible impossibly far above me through the trapdoor. Then it swung slowly closed and it was so dark that I may as well have been dead. Stars from the pain in my aching butt, head, and back were all I could see until a small light danced to life next to me.

It was Fynric snapping on a Zippo.

He smiled.

The flickering orange light made his face look ghoulish.

"That wasn't so bad," Fynric said. "Was it?"

He helped me to my feet. By all accounts I should have had at least a broken bone or two after that fall. But I was fine aside from a few aches and bruises. Fynric seemed entirely unconcerned—as if a serious injury was never even a possibility.

We were in a small concrete chamber with a few dark tunnels branching off in several directions. The floor and walls seemed to be man-made—poured concrete or smoothed cinder blocks. Water trickled and dripped slowly somewhere nearby, but otherwise there was only silence.

"Where are we?"

"Deep beneath the city," Fynric said.

"Like in the old Prohibition tunnels?" I asked.

Every kid who grew up near Chicago learned about the secret network of tunnels underneath the city once used to smuggle illegal booze during Prohibition.

"No, no." Fynric laughed. "Though we certainly helped Al build them."

"What? You *knew* Al Capone?"

"Well, not me personally," he said. "But my grandpa did. He was one of us, after all."

"What does that mean?"

Fynric didn't answer the new question. He just offered a wry grin and finished answering my first question.

"We're *far below* those old Prohibition tunnels," he said. "We call this the *Underground*. Come, we must continue on."

14

"How is that even possible?" I asked, sure this was all a dream now. And I hoped dearly that it was, because then I would wake up and find our store in one piece and my dad definitely still alive. "We just squeezed . . . I mean, the crevice in an alley . . . the fall alone should have killed us both . . ."

Fynric did not answer any of my questions.

"This way," he said, motioning me to follow.

Fynric led me through a network of narrow concrete hallways lined with wooden doors. Small, dim electric lights hung from the walls and stretched on seemingly forever down the passageways. They crackled and flickered as if they were moments from shorting out.

"How did you know?" I asked, after we'd walked for some time.

"Know what?"

"That there was an attack at Egohs?"

Fynric finally stopped next to a large wooden door on the right. He turned to face me, frowning, as if mulling over the best way to explain something I definitely wouldn't understand.

"Your dad always knew something like this was a possibility," he said. "Especially if he ever found it . . . finally *proved* it was real. Which I still can't believe he did myself, that kooky genius . . . But, anyway, we're still obviously surprised the attack happened so quickly afterward . . . and *how* it did . . ." Fynric stopped his nearly incoherent babbling and shook his head sadly. "Dunmor will explain all of this better than I can."

Without offering anything more, he opened the door and motioned for me to step inside.

There was an older man seated at a large wooden table inside a room the size of the principal's office at the PEE. The walls were made of large stones, like we were inside an old castle. The man had a long red beard, bushy eyebrows, and thick stalks of hair poking out from his ears. He was short and thick. Not fat. Just . . . *thick*. Almost like he'd been carved from a giant tree.

Red Beard motioned for me to sit across from him.

I fidgeted nervously in the hard wooden chair. Fynric Grufftrack left, closing the door behind him. I looked at it anxiously.

"Greg, my name is Ben," Red Beard said. "Well, that was once my *Commoner* name, long ago. My *real* name is Dunmor Beardbreaker."

"Uhhh . . . okay," I said, not sure what he meant or how to respond (or how he knew my name for that matter). "What . . . what is this place?"

"In time," Dunmor said, waving his hand dismissively. "We first have more important things to discuss. I will have to be brief, as I have much to do before the Council meets. The past few days have been . . . well, quite frenetic."

I waited for him to tell me what in the world was going on.

"There's no easy way to tell you this," Dunmor began, stroking his obscenely huge and tangled red beard. "So I'm just going to say it. Greg . . . you're a Dwarf."

CHAPTER 10

The Lord of the Rings Is Extremely Offensive

W ell, sir," I said calmly. "That is not a very nice thing to say. I think they prefer to be called Little People. And furthermore, I don't really think I'm *that* short . . ."

"No, no, no," Dunmor said. "You misunderstand me. You're a *Dwarf,* Dwarf. Like from *Lord of the Rings.*"

"But I never saw those movies," I said, my mind racing. "Fantasy stuff is *really* lame. The people all have stupid names like Aragrood the Impeccable or Gandorff the Great. And even the weapons have silly names like the Sword of Seven Galaxy Stones . . . and jewelry always plays a weird role in the plot, plus there's *always* some lame prophecy . . ."

"*How* do you know of Gandorff the Great?" Dunmor interrupted, looking both confused and annoyed.

"I—I *don't,*" I said slowly. "I just made that up right now, but . . . uh, I . . . this is . . . Look, I gotta go . . ." I needed to get away from this crazy, hairy guy as quickly as possible.

"*Sit,*" Dunmor said in a way that made me plop back into

my chair immediately. "It's actually *good* that you're not familiar with *The Lord of the Rings*. Because despite being based on several poor translations of old historical Separate Earth texts, they're full of inaccurate and misleading details. And they're quite offensive, I should say. Like this preposterous notion that Dwarves love gold. Heh, quite offensive indeed! Amusingly misguided *at best*."

"Okay, sure . . ." I blindly agreed, suddenly worried that if I angered this insane guy, he would try to make a purse out of my skin or something. "But what does that have to do with *me*?"

Dunmor Beardbreaker rubbed his eyes as if he was trying to explain the essence of quantum mechanics to a horse.

"I already told you," he said. "You. Are. A. Dwarf."

"I know, but—"

"We are an ancient people, Greg," he interrupted. "Born from the earth itself upon the dawn of its very inception, created from the rocks and dirt and plants and water. There are many other Dwarves living among us. They might be your neighbor, or mailman, or favorite athlete or musician. And soon enough, thanks to your father, we will truly rediscover our heritage. We will be revealed to the world once again. You're the son of a Council Elder, Greg. A Council Elder who . . . well, we always thought Trevor was a bit of a nut with all his conspiracy theories—some even called him a joke—but I guess the joke is on us, ha-ha! But anyway, perhaps I'm getting ahead of myself a bit."

I sat there stunned.

His words were hard to digest. I mean, it's not shocking to hear anyone call my dad a nut. But a *Council Elder*? I didn't know what that meant, but it sounded *important*, which is the opposite of anything my dad would want to be involved in. Everything this guy said was almost as impossible as the insane things I'd witnessed since the polar bear attack.

Dunmor clasped his hands thoughtfully under his beard. I spotted a chunk of turkey stuck in the tangled mess of red hair under his chin, but I didn't say anything. Being told you're part of a supposedly mythological race tended to make such things seem trivial.

"Perhaps I should start from the beginning," Dunmor finally said in a soothing tone. "I'm sure this is all somewhat confusing. Let me elaborate: A long time ago, back before there were computers, or skyscrapers, or cars, or even the pyramids, there existed a Separate Earth. It occupied the same planet as our own, but it was hardly the same world. Separate Earth is gone now, buried deep beneath the ruins of other lost 'ancient' civilizations, beneath layers of geothermal shifting, and volcanic eruptions, and meteoric impacts.

"Separate Earth was a place in constant turmoil. A never-ending struggle for power plagued the world as the two original peoples, Dwarves and Elves, battled each other for dominance. Over many generations, the war escalated. Both sides began using magic so powerful that the total destruction of the planet seemed inevitable. Which is why the Fairies finally interceded."

"Fairies?" I asked.

"Yes, well, don't be so self-centered as to assume Dwarves and Elves remained the *only* races," Dunmor said. "Others eventually emerged. In fact, back then there were thousands of creatures that no longer exist today."

I nodded, even though I was pretty sure I didn't believe *any* of this. Not that I was a Dwarf, or that my dad was gone, or that a Troll had just attacked our store. It all felt like some kind of dream. I hoped desperately that it was.

"Anyway," Dunmor continued, "foreseeing the impending destruction of the planet, the Fairies devised a way to bury the very essence of all magic deep within the earth—where it could no longer be accessed by any of the ancient races of Separate Earth, including the Fairies themselves. So dire was the threat of the escalating war that they even gave up their own magic, which they knew would eventually cause them to be erased from existence. But they succeeded in their sacrifice, and the entire world was suddenly stripped of all magic. Without it, both sides slowly lost their bloodlust, and many species of people and creatures dependent on magic (including the Fairies) vanished as if they'd never existed. The violence dwindled and a truce between Elves and Dwarves was uneasily forged. This tense promise of peace remains intact to this day.

"Lacking the magic that had once enhanced their unique abilities and traits, the Elves, Dwarves, Trolls, Goblins, and other remaining mystical races slowly blended with a changing world—one that saw a new species growing rapidly and taking over: Humans. Over the span of thousands of generations, the distinguishing physical characteristics of our races softened, and by the start of the first Roman Empire most individuals with 'mythical' lineage were virtually indistinguishable from Humans by appearance alone. But the true spirit of Elves and Dwarves has remained in the form of various separatist groups around the globe—existing in a hidden realm just beneath the surface, behind the walls, floors, and secret doors of the modern world."

"Um, okay, then . . ." I said cautiously.

Dunmor was stroking his red beard now and his fingers finally found the piece of turkey stuck in the red tangles. He plucked it out neatly and popped it into his mouth. I resisted the urge to gag.

I'd already convinced myself that none of this could be true; in spite of everything impossible I'd already seen that day. I was about to tell him so when the door burst open, interrupting us.

It was Fynric Grufftrack/Mr. Olsen, holding a huge battle-ax. He rushed over to Dunmor and whispered something into his ear. Dunmor nodded solemnly as he listened, shooting a few nervous glances my way.

I recognized the ax. It was the same one my dad had been using to try to fend off the Troll. Seeing it now in somewhat less stressful circumstances, I also recognized it as the mysterious object I'd seen in my dad's duffel bag earlier that morning. The object that I'd sworn might have spoken to me somehow.

"What happened?" I asked, panic constricting my throat. "Is my dad okay?"

They ignored me as Fynric finished speaking. Eventually Dunmor nodded a final time and then turned to face me.

"He's still alive," Dunmor said.

Relief flooded my chest, allowing me to breathe again.

"At least, he was when the Troll carried him away," Fynric added. "Several witnesses saw him being dragged from the store by the Troll and a smaller man. He was badly hurt, but still alive."

Dunmor shook his head slowly and slumped back against his chair, distraught, stressed, and broken.

"What can you do to find my dad?" I asked. "You will try to rescue him, right?"

"Yes, certainly," Dunmor said. "But we must first discover who is responsible for such a brutal and unprovoked attack!"

"Surely it was Elves," Fynric said.

"Can we be *sure*, though?" Dunmor challenged. "Would they really risk another war by breaking the peace treaty? They're the ones with everything to lose, after all."

Fynric hesitated, clearly not certain about anything at all.

"Perhaps that is a hasty conclusion to draw just yet," he admitted.

"But your suspicions are not entirely unwarranted," Dunmor said. "Who else could it be? The Goblins are all but extinct. And most of the other remaining ancient species have never shown any interest in our old war. The matter will surely need a full investigation."

Fynric nodded solemnly. Neither of them would look at me, and I sat there growing frustrated. What were they going to do to rescue my dad from the Troll? I didn't care who was responsible, or about their ancient war, I just wanted them to do something, *anything* to start looking for him.

"At least you've recovered the Bloodletter," Dunmor said after a moment of doomed silence, reaching toward the large battle-ax. "The attackers likely didn't know of its importance or they surely would have taken it, too."

I wanted to interject and tell him how offensive it was that he would deem some dumb ax more important than my dad. But I said nothing because I was distracted again by the strange feeling from earlier that morning—that the ax was reaching out to me, calling for me.

Then a voice said:

I AM calling out to you, Greg. Don't ignore me this time.

I looked around, startled. The voice had sounded real, like a man with a deep baritone had been speaking directly into my ear. But nobody else in the room had reacted. I'd been the only one to hear it.

Could an ax really be talking to me? I shook my head.

Fynric handed it to Dunmor.

"Can we use this to avenge Trevor?" Fynric asked. "Isn't that its purpose?"

"That's a matter for the Council to decide," Dunmor said somberly as he examined the ax.

Fynric nodded.

"Speaking of, I'm afraid we must cut this meeting short in light of the news," Dunmor said. "I'm sorry, Greg, there was so much more to cover, but I'm afraid it will have to wait for later. We have more pressing issues for now, including finding your dad."

I still had so many more questions:

Why and how had I turned into stone that day?

Why had a bear attacked me and did it have anything to do with all of this?

What was up with a Troll attacking my family?

Was this all related to me (allegedly) being a Dwarf?

What was this place?

How had I survived the fall?

Could Dwarves and Elves actually be real and still exist?

Were Fairies really an extinct group of suicidal martyrs?

But Dunmor had said something that trumped all those concerns: *finding your dad*. And so I merely nodded, anxious to let him and this Council get started on figuring out what had happened to my dad and how to get him back.

"We will meet again tomorrow," Dunmor said, rising from the table with the ax they'd called Bloodletter still in his hand.

"For now, Fynric will look after you. Please do whatever he says . . . for your own safety."

I nodded as Dunmor headed for the door, my eyes locked onto the axe.

We will meet again, Grey, the strange voice said into my ear.

I shook my head. It couldn't be real.

Of course I'm real! Otherwise, you're obviously going crazy. Which of those options sounds more fun to you?

Dunmor hurried off with the chatty Bloodletter tucked nervously under an arm, looking far more frantic and disheveled than when I'd first entered the room.

Fynric stared at me sympathetically. I looked down at the floor, struggling to dismiss all of this as the nonsense it surely was. Me, a Dwarf? Talking axes? Ancient wars with Elves and long-lost magic? Mountain Trolls? It was all so absurd.

Even then, though, I think I knew that I was struggling to ignore the truth. But just the same, there was one thing I wasn't ever going to turn my back on: finding out what had happened to my dad and getting him back.

Whether I actually believed any of this or not.

CHAPTER 11

There's Bad Weather Brewing in My Guts

As Fynric led me through more narrow and dark tunnels beneath the city, all I could think about was my dad.

How I never got to apologize for our last conversation. How he might be getting tortured by Trolls at that very moment, remembering how hurtful his only son's last words to him had been. Well, I was thinking about all of that, and also about how hungry I was. I hadn't eaten since my fifth-period snack almost seven hours ago. Which for a Belmont was like three days without food.

We rounded a corner and entered a massive underground hallway—like an old subway tunnel with no tracks. There were still doors on both sides, but they were becoming less frequent. The tunnel looked like it stretched ahead forever. The ground under our feet became rougher, more like a naturally formed cave floor.

Fynric finally stopped at a large pair of wooden doors. They were thick and damp and very old, crisscrossed with cast-iron support bars. He grunted as he pulled one of the doors open. The hinges creaked loudly, but it was barely audible above the raucous noise that greeted us on the other side.

The doorway led to a massive underground cavern so huge that Wrigley Field could have fit entirely inside of it with space to spare. The vast space had several small alcoves branching out from a larger central chamber. Each separate section had a high, uneven stone ceiling that danced with shadows from the dim glow of burning torches affixed along the outer rock walls.

The cavern buzzed with activity from hundreds of kids of all ages. Their excited voices echoed off the grotto's deep and weathered walls like in a concert hall.

The little alcove nearest to the door was decked out in modern furniture. Chairs and leather couches surrounded a huge wooden coffee table. Ping-Pong, pool, and foosball tables occupied the back half. Kids swarmed around the games, rooting for one another loudly. Several others sat on the couches chatting excitedly.

The other subdivisions of the cavern were anything but a modern playroom. There was a considerable opening to an actual cave in the far corner, partially filled with clear spring-water and groups of kids gathered around with ropes, pickaxes, and helmets. They smiled and laughed like spelunking was no different from a casual board game.

Another section of the cavern contained a small metallurgy workshop—complete with stone vats of glowing molten metals on pulleys and several iron anvils with hammers and other racks of tools. A kid no more than ten years old showered the floor with sparks as he pounded on a glowing strip of metal with a hammer. I realized, with a mixture of amazement and surprising jealousy, that he was making a sword.

There was also a corner of the cavern with alchemy equipment—beakers and vials and dozens of bottles and pouches holding a variety of colorful chemicals and powders—and a small section where several kids were blowing glass into random shapes.

Everyone seemed to be having fun, either unaware or unconcerned that a Troll had attacked a fellow Dwarf less than an hour ago.

"What is this?" I asked Fynric.

"This is where many Dwarven children spend a great deal of their free time," he said. "I believe they call it the Arena these days. It's a place where, for many generations, Dwarven youth have grown accustomed to what it means to actually *be a Dwarf*. It's where they go when the modern world disappoints them, which it usually does. Anyway, I'll be back to get you once the Council meeting is over."

Fynric closed the door behind him as he left.

Most of the kids hadn't noticed my arrival—the whole cavern was so expansive I wouldn't have expected them to. But three kids sitting on a worn leather sofa near the front door smiled and waved like we were old friends.

I hesitated, assuming they had mistaken me for someone else. But they continued to wave, so I uneasily wandered over, wiping my sweating palms on my pants. It'd been at least two years since a kid other than Edwin had randomly been nice to me. It felt completely foreign.

There was a girl and two boys, all around my age. They looked like normal kids. And I supposed they *were* normal kids—despite (allegedly) being Dwarves.

"You must have *just* found out," the girl said. "You have that look on your face . . ."

"It's easier to handle when you're eighteen," one of the boys added. "That's what they tell us—that's why some parents wait. But we've all known since we were little."

I plopped down on the couch across from them, still too dazed and exhausted to say much. They seemed to understand this and let me sit there and take it all in.

The girl had silvery-purple hair that was buzzed on one side and short and messy on the other. She looked more like she belonged in a cool punk rock band rather than hanging out in a damp cave with a bunch of Dwarves. One of the boys looked a lot like her and I figured they must be twins. His hair was splayed around his head in long, rigid tangles like a mad scientist and he was wearing a homemade-looking tunic with frayed edges, a rope cord for a belt, thick wool pants, and soft, worn leather boots. The third kid was the tallest and thinnest of us—though still no taller than average. He had short black hair and sharp features that made him look solemn and intelligent. He looked less like a Dwarf and more like a brooding teen movie star.

"Wherefore art thyne origins, fledgling *Commoner*?" the kid with messy hair and rustic clothes said. "Eke, which kinfolk appellation hath befallen thyne bloodlyne?"

I stared at the kid with my mouth hanging open trying to decide if he was making fun of me in some weird Dwarven way.

"Don't mind my brother," the girl said quickly. "He's just wondering where you're from and who your family is."

"Why did he say it like that?" I asked.

"Tis ye fundamental dialect, lest nay stricken from thyne mem'ry," the kid said, puffing out his chest.

"Traditional Dwarven speak," the girl explained. "Or at least as close to an English translation as we think it would be. There's very little record of our original Dwarven language left—most of what does exist is two or three times removed from the source materials."

"Why use a forgotten language?" I asked.

"Our family is . . . well . . ." she said, stopping as if embarrassed. "My dad is a *Traditional* Dwarf, which basically means he thinks we need to be doing things as close to the way Dwarves did back in Separate Earth as possible. He wants Dwarves to live separately, our own way."

"But *you're* . . ." I said, and stopped, looking at her modern hair and clothes.

She laughed. It was probably the most charming laugh I'd ever heard. It was somewhere between a giggle and an uncivilized guffaw and it made me want to laugh along with her.

"Yeah, well, I haven't bought into what my dad has been beating into our heads the way my brother has," she said. "It's why I refuse to eat *any* meat or animal byproducts at all, for that matter—much to *my father's* extreme embarrassment and shame . . ."

"To be fair, who has ever heard of a *vegan* Dwarf?" the kid with dark hair asked with a laugh. "I mean, how many more plants have to needlessly suffer and die for your beliefs . . ."

The girl grinned defiantly and then rolled her eyes. She clearly wasn't going to apologize for her stance on the matter.

"What about it, though?" the kid with dark hair asked me. "Where are you from and what family?"

"I live here . . . well, uh, in Bridgeport, I mean," I said, my voice shaking. I was surprised at how anxious I felt—at just how much I really wanted these kids to like me. "My dad . . . my dad is Trevor Belmont."

"Oh . . ."

Their collective facial expressions told me that they somehow already knew about the attack on the store.

"So sorry," the girl said. "Your dad is a truly amazing Dwarf."

I didn't respond because it was such a bizarre thing to hear anyone say about my dad. Not even the Dwarf part, but the reverence with which she referred to him as *amazing*. Even Edwin, who by all accounts was my dad's biggest fan, viewed him as more of a hilarious and endearing curiosity than anyone particularly remarkable or distinguished. Hearing her refer to my dad like that made his sudden absence all the more painful—so gut-wrenching it felt like my heart was slowing to a stop.

"Well, I don't have a *Commoner* name," the girl said. "You know, because of my dad's beliefs and all—"

"Commoner name?" I interrupted.

"Oh, yeah, sorry," she said. "I keep forgetting you just found out. A lot of Dwarves have two names, their real name from their original Dwarven heritage, and then a *Commoner* name their family has been using ever since to help them blend in with modern society."

"None of us have a Commoner name," the kid with dark hair added. "My parents are also Traditional Dwarves—they have never believed in trying to blend with modern society. It's why we knew we were Dwarves from birth as opposed to only finding out when we turned eighteen. Which is around when you would have found out had things . . . well . . ."

I waited while he struggled to figure out a nice way to say *Had your dad not just been attacked and taken hostage by a terrible creature thought to be extinct.*

"The three of us have never gone to Commoner schools like you," the girl said. "Or interacted with many Human kids.

We've spent most of our lives here in the Underground, learning the old ways of Dwarves. We've been, uh, *homeschooled*, I guess you would say?"

"So Greg Belmont isn't my *real* name?" I asked, feeling sick to my stomach.

It seemed to cement the fact that my whole life thus far had been a lie.

"Right," the girl said. "Your father's real Dwarven surname is Stormbelly. You're Greggdroule Stormbelly. And you come from one of the most courageous Dwarven families ever known to exist."

CHAPTER 12

Brightsmashers, Mooncharms, and Stormbellys

After a moment of me trying to *digest* (ha-ha!!!) being a Stormbelly (with a real first name like Greggdroule no less), they finished the introductions.

The girl's name was Ariyna (Ari) Brightsmasher. Her strange brother was Lakeland (Lake) Brightsmasher. The tall, dark-haired kid was Eagan Mooncharm. They told me that all Traditional Dwarven names were symbolic of a family's ancient skill or trade.

Ari and Lake Brightsmasher came from a line of Dwarves rumored to be among the best weapon makers of Separate Earth.

"The name Brightsmasher was born from the pure, glowing light my family created when pounding out the finest weapons any man, Dwarf, or god would ever hold," Ari explained. "It is said that a Brightsmasher created sparks so vibrant it was as if they were pounding on the sun itself. Our ancestor Caiseal Brightsmasher forged Poseidon's trident from a single slab of iron ore laced with veins of natural gold."

"What about Mooncharm?" I asked Eagan.

"My ancestors were among the best Dwarven communicators," Eagan said, taking on a different tone, sounding more like a professional narrator than a kid. "We're political leaders. My family has traditionally filled out the highest ranks of ancient Dwarven governments. Charisma and charm are foreign qualities to most Dwarves. So much so that it was often said back in Separate Earth that even the most persuasive Dwarf could not manage to sell a flagon of fresh water to a rich man dying of thirst in a desert. My name comes from a fable retold to children for thousands of generations. Once, long ago, my ancestor Makgrumlin held council with a shy moon. A moon that only provided its glowing silver light in the darkness but twice a year. Makgrumlin convinced the moon to instead emerge from hiding twelve times per year in exchange for the heads of twelve mountain goats, two boiled geese, and a mincemeat pie . . . an agreement it has honored ever since."

I nodded thoughtfully, trying to ignore the implausible nature of what they were telling me. But I was sitting in an underground cavern where kids were crafting weapons, brewing potions, and spelunking just for fun. That made it easier to simply nod and go along with everything. I still wasn't sure how much I really *believed* any of this. But it surprised me how much I *wanted to*. Suddenly I was kind of excited about possibly being a part of something huge and cool—knowing that I wasn't just some kid from a loser family so cursed that we all accepted our bad luck with big, dumb smiles on our faces. Here was a whole new world for me to explore, a world where I'd finally belong, and it apparently came with built-in (potential) friends.

"What about my family name?" I asked, wondering how on

earth I had ended up with the least cool Dwarven name imaginable. "Uh . . . Thunderguts, was it?"

"*Stormbelly*," Lake corrected.

"There was a legend told to the children of Separate Earth since the beginning of recorded time," Ari said. "The legend of your oldest-known ancestor, Maddog Stormbelly."

She turned to Eagan, clearly the best storyteller among them.

"It was said," Eagan began with a distinguished smile, "that Maddog Stormbelly was so fierce in battle, so courageous taking on much larger, stronger armies that far outnumbered his own, that he created fire in the bellies of his foes. And storms in those of his allies. Like thunder in their guts pressing them into action, his fellow Dwarves could not stand idly by and watch him take on whole armies by himself with no regard for his own safety. He led dozens of battalions into battles during which they were far outmatched, yet emerged victorious."

The idea that my family came from a long line of courageous warriors seemed downright laughable. I'd seen my dad handling an ax earlier that very night and he'd looked anything but legendary. More like he'd been trying to swat a fly with an old truck tire. He was probably lucky he hadn't accidentally chopped off his own head.

"Then again," Eagan continued, "there's also the rumor that the name actually came from the, uh, *potency* of Maddog's devastating flatulence. It was said there was a toxic storm constantly brewing in his belly. One legend says it was so bad that he once wilted an entire field of oats after a meal of poached ham and beans that—"

Ari slapped his arm.

"But, you know," Eagan hastily added, "regardless of where the name specifically came from, there's no disputing his prowess in battle."

"So do you guys know what my mom's real name was before she became a Stormbelly?" I asked.

"*What?*" Ari snapped. "Do you think of her as a piece of property that your father purchased?"

"Huh?" I asked, startled and confused.

Eagan grinned at me and then explained:

"Dwarven women do not take a new name when they marry. Dwarves have long celebrated a woman's strength and individual identity. We have never, going all the way back to Separate Earth, treated them as property to be conquered, won, sold, or *labeled* as do Humans, historically. Changing your name upon finding a life partner is such a vulgar, unsophisticated tradition. Dwarven women actually have honor and self-respect in who they are."

"Your name is part of your identity," Ari added. "It's one of the few things nobody can ever take away from you. Of course we never met your mom, but we heard stories about her."

"According to my dad, your mom came from a long line of weapon enhancers," Eagan said. "Dwarves who concocted potions and cast charms on weapons and warriors to enhance their abilities in combat, among other things. Her Dwarven name was Danaerra Axebrew."

I nodded, trying to get over the fact that nobody in my family was actually a Belmont at all. A name I'd long thought to be cursed.

There was a small explosion from the back section of the cavern, in the alchemy alcove. I looked up, worried another attack might be in progress. But it was just an embarrassed kid covered in black soot, holding a shattered beaker, getting laughed at by his friends.

"My dad always used to tell me that Belmonts were cursed," I said. "He was making it all up?"

This made the three of them laugh. It surprised me how good it felt to have these kids laughing with me, rather than at me. Saying something so (apparently) ignorant at the PEE would have been met with snide jeers and snickers.

"Not necessarily," Eagan said. "Your family *is* cursed. In a way."

"Huh?"

"We *all* are," Ari said with a grin.

"Aha!" Lake shouted, throwing a declarative finger into the air. "Thyne populace doth fashioned historical allegiances with ye throes of defeats and failures."

"Dwarves lose," Eagan translated. "It's what we do. As a race, we're prone to unspeakable bouts of . . . well, for a lack of a more nuanced term: *bad luck*."

I thought about some of the defeatist things Dunmor had said to me just a little while ago, the way he had seemed so demoralized after finding out my dad had been taken hostage. It should have frightened me that I was now part of a large group of people who always failed and always expected to. Instead, I found it bizarrely comforting.

"But our luck seems to be changing lately," Ari added excitedly.

"What do you mean?" I asked, not pointing out that my dad was a hostage of Trolls, possibly even dead—which still seemed wholly fitting, given the bad luck I'd always lived with.

"Ye glorious sparth christened Bloodletter hath hereunto

96

doth unearthed from ye ruins of bygone epochs," Lake said. "Thee hath unveiled thyself three fortnyghts past in ye Nederlands—submerged, sayeth do ye elders, ye dust and bones of thyne ancient vanquished brethren."

I raised my eyebrows.

"Dwarven miners recently rediscovered the long-lost Bloodletter," Eagan translated. "It's one of the most powerful ancient Dwarven axes ever created. It's said to be indestructible, despite also being cursed. According to legend it calls out to whomever it has chosen to be its new owner . . ."

"The Bloodletter," I said slowly, the name finally clicking into place—it was what Dunmor had called the ax my dad had used to fight off the Troll. "My dad brought it home with him yesterday."

"You've *seen* the Bloodletter!" Eagan asked. "In person? For real!?"

They all leaned forward excitedly.

"Yeah, I saw it a few times, I guess," I said.

They burst into excited gasps and whispers. I sat there and thought about the ax. About how it had *spoken to me* telepathically. Several times. Just like Eagan had said the legends foretold.

Suddenly I felt like I could no longer breathe.

Only then did I realize how much I'd sort of wanted this all to be untrue. And until that moment, I'm pretty sure I hadn't fully believed any of it. I'd been drifting along, listening to everyone, nodding as if I was merely playing out a dream. I'd been focusing on the cool parts, and the idea of making new friends, and not what it all actually meant: that my dad really had been abducted by a giant Troll.

And right then I knew I wasn't dreaming.

This was *real*. As real as the Bloodletter's voice in my head.

As real as me somehow turning into stone earlier that day. As real as the Troll that had destroyed Egohs. Which meant I wouldn't be "waking up" anytime soon, and the only way out of this insanity was to run.

"Is there, um, like, an exit?" I asked

Ari pointed at the door.

"No, I mean, out of here . . . the Underground," I said. "I just need some fresh air."

Eagan nodded.

"Take a right and follow the tunnel to the end," he said. "You'll find some old stone stairs. From that point it should be self-explanatory."

"Okay, thanks," I said, standing up. "Thanks for, you know, talking to me and everything. I'll, uh, be right back."

Of course I had no intention of coming back. Even if I really was a Dwarf, I couldn't just sit underground and obsess over talking axes while my dad was still out there somewhere possibly being tortured by a Mountain Troll at that very moment.

One way or another, I was going to get him back.

CHAPTER 13

I Fail to Execute an Act of Comedic Genius

There was one place in the world I could go at a time like this: Edwin's house.

Or, as I liked to call it: the Château Aldaron, because it was more like a royal palace complex that just happened to occupy a double lot on one of Chicago's most prominent boulevards than it was a simple house. My whole apartment could have fit inside Edwin's gymnasium-size bedroom.

It was probably close to midnight by the time I reached the huge oak doors at the top of the front steps. So I was relieved when Edwin answered the front door and not one of his parents or their live-in staff.

"Greg . . ." Edwin said, clearly surprised. "I tried calling the store and your house a bunch of times, but there was no answer. What happened?"

I tried to put together some sort of coherent answer, but all that came out was a shaky sigh. Edwin quickly shook his head and stepped back.

"Come on, let's go to my room," he said.

"Are your parents home?" I whispered, following him inside.

"No," he said. "They were only here for an hour last night to pay the caterers and DJ for my party. Otherwise, they've mostly been at the penthouse downtown lately, working long hours."

Edwin's parents owned three residences in the Chicago area: this mansion on the Northwest Side, a huge penthouse in the Gold Coast neighborhood, and a massive lakeside estate in Evanston. But Edwin had always claimed they spent more time working than they did at all three of their houses combined.

I followed Edwin to his bedroom, which occupied nearly half of Château Aldaron's massive fourth floor. His cat arched its back and hissed at me as we passed it on the stairs. Edwin's room had a closet large enough to house a thousand people, and two full sets of stairs. The first led to a loft area with a guest room, where I slept when I spent the night. The other led to a rooftop deck and pool.

"Sorry if I woke you," I said.

"I wasn't sleeping," he said. "I was actually up worrying about you. After what happened at school and then not being able to reach you tonight . . ."

I shook my head, not sure how much to tell him. Mostly because I only had this one friend, and I was afraid that him thinking I was totally insane was probably the one way to ensure I had none going forward. But also because the longer I was away from the Underground, the less I was convinced that any of it had been real. Even though I knew better.

I realized then that I'd been rambling something the whole time. Speaking actual words. But I had no clue what I'd just said.

"Greg, calm down," Edwin said. "I can't even understand what you're saying. What happened at the store? There was an attack? Did Egohs get robbed? Did you say something about a . . . a Troll?"

The worried look on his face calmed me. Edwin and I could say anything to each other. It was part of what made our friend-ship work. And so I decided to just get right to the point.

"Edwin, I'm a Dwarf," I said.

He blinked a few times.

I expected him to say: *Come on, you're not that short, Greg!*

Or I expected him to laugh at me for coming over late at night acting all harried and upset and then in a most serious moment of reveal deadpanning a joke so random that it was nothing short of comedic genius.

But instead, Edwin simply said:

"Greg, I know you're a Dwarf. I've always known."

"What?" I managed to say. It was not remotely close to a worthy response. And so I tried again: "Wait, what . . . I mean, like . . . *huh?*"

"Greg," Edwin said calmly. "I'm an Elf. That's how I knew."

Of all the things I'd expected him to say, this was not on the list.

"Why didn't you tell me?" I asked angrily. "How could you keep something like that from me? All this time you knew the truth and I had no clue!"

"I didn't think it was my place," Edwin said. "It's common for Dwarves and Elves not to find out their reality until later in life, either sixteen or eighteen for most. And every family is different with that stuff. I thought I'd respect your dad's wishes, you know? I didn't want to ruin anything between you."

"*Ruin* anything?" I asked, exasperated. "I mean—I—he's my dad, you're my best friend, why would you take *his* side?"

"I wasn't taking *any* sides," Edwin insisted, staying calm but speaking with passion. "There *are* no sides. Tons of kids don't find out until they're older. It's not that big of a deal. It'd have been like telling a little kid Santa Claus isn't real, you know?"

"No," I said. "I don't know, because nobody told me!"

Edwin just shrugged helplessly. Clearly, from his perspective he'd done nothing wrong. And maybe he hadn't? Maybe I was overreacting. After all, even my own father had kept the truth from me. Besides, a new realization was making all of that seem entirely insignificant.

"Edwin . . . you *can't* be an Elf," I said quietly.

"Yes I can," Edwin said. "You can't come in here and tell me you're a Dwarf and then say I can't be an Elf. It doesn't work like that."

"No, I mean," I said, trying to rein in the dread blooming in my guts (in my Stormbelly), "if you're an Elf and I'm a Dwarf . . . then we can't be friends."

"Says who?" Edwin asked defiantly.

I reminded him that Elves and Dwarves were apparently involved in some ancient war that was merely on pause at the moment. And also that a Troll had kidnapped my dad earlier that night and that some of the other Dwarves thought Elves might be responsible. So if he was an Elf, then *his people* had destroyed our store and taken my dad hostage.

"That's impossible," Edwin said calmly. "Trolls are extinct. Everyone knows that."

"Edwin, I *saw* it with my own eyes."

He sat there shaking his head. But for the first time maybe ever, he looked uncertain of what he thought he knew. It was an odd expression to see on his face, wholly unfitting of the Edwin I was friends with.

"Everyone thinks *Elves* were behind the attack," I reminded him, since he had apparently missed the most important part. "So it doesn't matter if they used a Troll or a rocket launcher. The Elves . . . *You* attacked us."

I felt anger bubbling up again even though I was convinced Edwin had had nothing to do with the attack. There was no way he'd do that. I'd bet my life on it, even on a Thursday.

"No," Edwin finally said. "No way. We'd never do that. Elves had nothing to do with whatever happened at Egohs."

"How do you *know* that?"

"Because I'm not just any old Elf, Greg," Edwin said. "My father is the Elf Lord. Which means I'm preordained to become the next Elf Lord—it's my birthright. It means I *know* Elves better than anyone, and we simply wouldn't do that."

It suddenly felt as if every refuge I'd ever had was being pulled out from under me. My dad was missing, Egohs was destroyed, my family curse was not only real but also part of something even bigger, and my only friend was the heir apparent to the throne of an entire "mythical" race of people. People supposedly destined to be at war with Dwarves . . . with *me*. But he was still my best friend and I still trusted him more than anybody.

Edwin must have mistaken my brief, stunned silence for disbelief because a few seconds later he continued making his impassioned case. "I mean, *why would we want* to do something like that?" he asked. "The Elves want nothing more than to keep the peace. We have so much to lose if the conflict between us grows. But in the unlikely event that we *did* have something to do with the attack on Egohs and your dad, I'll find out. I'm going to help you figure out who's responsible. I love your dad, you know that. I'm probably almost as devastated by what happened as you are. Let me help you, I have resources you don't."

He was right. Not just because he already ran in mythological circles of important mythological beings surely more well suited to finding things out than me. But there was also the money thing. Money could still get you pretty much anything, including information. Edwin probably *could* help find out what had happened to my dad.

"Okay, yeah," I finally said. "Thank you."

Edwin nodded, tears welling in his eyes.

I had to look away to keep from breaking my dad's only rule: *Belmonts/Stormbellys never cry. Ever.*

"Don't worry, Greg, we'll find him," Edwin said. "I promise."

CHAPTER 14

Cronenberg's Offal Delicatessen and Rotary Telephone Repair Shop

I t was nearly 1:00 a.m. by the time I got home to find Fynric Grufftrack sitting at my kitchen table.

I began mentally running through excuses as to why I'd run away from the Underground, but after the day I'd just had, all I could manage was a tired sigh.

"Go pack a bag," Fynric said. "You're moving to the Underground."

"Why?" I asked, though I wasn't entirely sure I wanted to stay in this place alone and be constantly reminded of what I'd lost. "This is my home."

"It's too dangerous here," he said. "In fact, you already endangered yourself running off like you did. Whoever was behind the attack specifically targeted your father. So it's reasonable to assume they might come after you next. It was irresponsible to even come back here at all."

I nodded. It seemed as good a reason as any to move into a series of tunnels deep beneath Chicago's sewage system.

"Plus, it's where you belong," Fynric added. "Where you've always belonged. You have family there."

I tilted my head at him.

"All Dwarves are family," he explained. "Maybe not in the traditional sense, but our collective bond is as strong as blood, if not stronger."

I nodded and then went to my room to pack clothes and a few essentials. As I stuffed things into my small suitcase, I thought of what Fynric had just said about Dwarves and family. I'd never really had much of a family, aside from a dad who was gone a lot and some aunts, uncles, and cousins who I saw once or twice a year. As sad as it was to be leaving the apartment I'd considered home most of my life, I was sort of excited about moving to a place where I'd have an instant connection, at least one big thing in common with virtually everyone there. I'd already gotten a hint of what that felt like in the Arena with Ari, Lake, and Eagan. Sure, I'd fled in a panic, but talking about all of this with Edwin had calmed me down again—like it usually did.

The one thing still missing, of course, was my dad. The biggest thing. And so leaving still didn't feel entirely right. What if he escaped and came back here looking for me? Plus, what would become of my friendship with Edwin if I moved into a secret underground lair? I had already lost my dad, I was certain I could not handle losing my best friend as well. Not to mention that him being an Elf would surely make the other Dwarves wary of the friendship at the very least. But I forced my doubts from my mind.

A short time later, Fynric and I were on an empty CTA train heading back to the north side. The lights flickered as the train thundered on the tracks, passing mostly empty city streets.

"Greg, where were you tonight?" Fynric asked with a bigger frown than usual.

"Edwin's," I said.

"Greg, he's—"

"An Elf," I finished. "Yeah, I know that now. He assured me Elves had nothing to do with the attack, by the way."

"You can't trust anything he says, Greg," Fynric said abruptly. "In fact, it'd be best if you stayed away from him completely from now on."

"I can't do that," I said. "He's my only friend."

"You *must*," Fynric said firmly. "Don't worry, you'll make new friends. I still can't believe your father ever allowed that to happen at all. I was always against your friendship with Edwin. It was irresponsible . . . dangerous even. But your father can be so stubborn."

"You just don't know Edwin," I said. "He's the only kid who's ever been nice to me at the PEE. What am I supposed to do now?"

Fynric frowned so deeply, it was almost a pout. "That won't be a problem," he said. "Since you will not be returning to that school."

"But it's like three months until graduation!"

"Irrelevant now, I'm afraid," Fynric said with little sympathy. "It's simply too dangerous."

"Too dangerous? Fynric, it's a *school*."

"Not just any school," he said. "Isaacson Preparatory Empowerment Establishment is an Elven school. Well, it's not *entirely* Elves—some of the students are merely rich Humans. But Elves have always had the money and power to ensure their kids go to the best of the best schools and are placed in an advantageous position in life from the start. Your father told me that you're the first Dwarf to ever score high enough on the placement test to go there. He saw it as an opportunity—an opportunity to use you to help bridge the gap between Elves and Dwarves. He thought by sending you to an Elven school, he could show that the tensions leftover from the ancient war were silly, that Elves and Dwarves and Humans could all coexist just fine. It's partially, I think, why he was so keen to see your friendship with Edwin develop."

I wanted to be angry with my dad for sending me to a school where he knew I wouldn't fit in. *Using me* for his own social experimentations and political agendas. Keeping me from the truth, from making friends with other Dwarves like Ari, Lake, and Eagan. And yet, without the PEE, I wouldn't have met my best friend. So it was hard to be *too mad*—especially considering what had just happened to him.

"Well, I'm glad my dad sent me there," I said. "Because of it, I'm *best friends* with the next Elf Lord, which—"

"What did you just say?" Fynric hissed, his dark eyes burning more intensely than I'd ever seen them. "Edwin is the next Elf Lord?"

"You didn't know that?" I asked weakly.

"We have long speculated on the true identity of the Elf Lord," Fynric admitted. "There have been many theories, many rumors. This, like the others, may prove to be false—but it will surely need to be investigated."

"Yeah, okay," I said. "But my real point was that my friendship with him offers us a greater chance of finding my dad."

"Enlighten me," Fynric said.

"Edwin can enlist the Elves to help us find out what happened at the store," I said. "He *wants* to help."

I expected Fynric to take this news with hope. Though

I'm not sure why, given what I'd found out about the nature of Dwarves (and what I already knew about the nature of Fynric/ Mr. Olsen as a grouchier, more cynical version of my dad). And true to form, he frowned skeptically.

"I doubt the Council will share your faith in your friend," he said.

"We have to *try*," I said. "It's better than ignoring the offer."

"Perhaps," Fynric said. "I'll speak to Dunmor in the morning. If he's intrigued, he will present your case to the Council, and then perhaps even at the upcoming Global Session. I certainly *hope* you're right . . . for your father's sake."

The train finally lurched to a stop at the Addison station.

Fynric got up and ushered me off. After a few minutes of walking, we turned onto one of Chicago's alley-streets: a street that looked like an alley (stacked with garbage cans and rats), but actually had a real street name and houses lining one side. We stopped in front of a small house that had been converted into a store. It was set toward the very back of a the lot, almost like it didn't want to be seen. A hand-painted sign hung above the front door, under the peaked roof.

The words were barely visible in the glow of the nearby streetlights:

CRONENBERG'S OFFAL DELICATESSEN AND ROTARY TELEPHONE REPAIR SHOP

"What is this?" I asked.

"The Underground's front entrance," Fynric said, leading me up to the front door of the dark store. "You didn't really think every Dwarf went in and out through that dirty alley, did you? That was just one of many hidden emergency entrances."

He fished out a huge key ring from his pockets.

"What's offal?" I asked.

"It's pronounced oh-full," he said. "It's a name Humans gave to animal organs and other . . . *unconventional* cuts of meat. They're generally too afraid to eat them, though I have no idea why. It's the same thing as the overpriced hunks of muscle they pay for. *Everything* on this earth is composed of the same basic materials—"

"So this is an organ deli plus a phone repair shop?" I asked incredulously. "What's a rotary phone, anyway?"

"It doesn't matter, Greg," Fynric said impatiently, while unlocking the front door. "The whole point is to keep non-Dwarves from coming in here."

Inside the dark store smelled like a weird combination of musty plastic and boiled hot dogs. It was small, containing only a classic curved glass deli display case and, across the room, a small wooden desk surrounded by piles of old telephones with curly cords and circular dials on their faces.

We went around the deli counter and into a kitchen. A dim emergency light by the back door illuminated the space in a soft yellow glow. Fynric stopped near a huge walk-in fridge.

"Open it," he said with a sly grin.

I grabbed the slim metal handle and pulled. The lock clicked and the door swung open, revealing shelves stacked with meats covered in plastic wrap. It was the strangest array I'd ever seen: pans of gooey eyeballs, a mound of small hearts, long and skinny bird tongues, various unrecognizable organs, and a whole tray of small brains. Of course I was used to eating these sorts of things. One of my favorite meals was beef-lung-and-liver stew every Sunday night. My dad made awesome lung stew.

I still didn't get why we were looking into a fridge, though.

"Now close the door," Fynric said.

I did, more confused than ever.

"Open it again," he said. "But this time pull straight down on the handle, then twist it to the right."

I did as instructed and as I pulled it, the handle slid several inches down the door. When I twisted it, the entire bracket rotated on hidden hinges and locked into a sideways position. I pulled back on the lever and the door clicked open once again. We weren't looking at a fridge full of offal anymore. Instead it was a small and rickety wooden elevator.

Fynric stepped inside and motioned for me to join him.

"How?"

"Another example of Dwarven ingenuity," Fynric said with a rare grin.

The elevator descended slowly. Eventually it stopped and the old wooden doors creaked open. The hallways of the Dwarven Underground were still aglow with faint electric wall lights. But otherwise deserted. Which made sense: it was close to 3:00 a.m.

I followed Fynric through another maze of tunnels.

"Don't worry," he whispered after at least our third turn. "Dwarves have a great natural sense of direction. You'll learn the layout a lot sooner than you think."

"How many Dwarves live down here?" I asked.

"Just over five thousand," he said. "There are many more in Chicago living topside like you and your father."

I was shocked. All along there was an entire community of Dwarves living right here, underground, beneath one of the largest cities in the country.

Eventually we stopped in front of a wooden door that looked

identical to the hundreds of others we'd passed. But instead of asking Fynric how I was ever supposed to find my new front door, I trusted that he was right about our innate sense of direction. Now that I thought about it, I'd *never* gotten lost. And that's in a city the size of Chicago, without a smartphone, Google Maps, or a GPS.

Fynric opened the door and flicked on a light switch. The room was tiny. It contained just two twin beds, a small wooden table with two chairs, and a very basic kitchenette in the corner. A small door next to a half fridge led to a cramped bathroom.

"Welcome home," Fynric said drily. "We're going to be roommates . . . for now. At least until you get accustomed to life down here."

I nodded, flinging my suitcase onto one of the beds. This didn't seem so bad.

"One last thing," Fynric said softly, holding out several sheets of thick parchment paper. "Your father . . . well, if anything ever happened to him, he wanted me to give you this."

My shaking hand grabbed the sheets of parchment and I instantly recognized the handwriting hastily scrawled across the pages. I'd spent my whole life in his store, where every item was meticulously labeled in that same sloppy, yet somehow always legible handwriting. I took several deep breaths, fighting back tears (Belmonts/Stormbellys *never* cry. Ever. It was the last thing my dad would want me to do at that moment), and began reading:

For my son, Greg, in case I die too soon—before I can tell you about the world and the way it really is:

There is a lot you don't know about the true history of the earth. I chose to keep it secret from you, to protect you. In the event my theory is wrong, I wanted you to have a good life in the modern world, blissfully ignorant of your complicated true heritage. I must beg your forgiveness for all the years of secrecy—I never intended to hurt you.

I only wanted the best for you.

But in all fairness, even I do not understand our full history. Our real past, what makes us unique, has been lost for thousands upon thousands of years. But we are finding out more every day and I fear that I may not survive long enough to tell you all I've discovered. I know what you're thinking right now: You always say that, Dad. That you'll die too early. It is true, I have unsuccessfully predicted my early demise far too many times to count—even just last holiday season when I was convinced I would perish trying to hang lights from our apartment balcony (why I attempted that on a Thursday is still a mystery, even to me). But this time is different.

I have devoted my life to finding something special. My Quest. The true nature of which is to find the long-lost essence of magic that once made Dwarves special. Many—MOST—have said my pursuits were foolish, impossible, and a waste of time. That magic is gone forever and never coming back. That I'm crazy for thinking I can find it. And I certainly hope this is not the case. For then I will have sacrificed so much lost time with you for nothing.

But if I'm right, if I can find the lost magic of Separate Earth, it will have been worth it. For it's the only way to return our race to what we once were. And more than just us: we can bring the entire world back to that magical place. Most important of all, though, I believe that magic can be used to finally bring a lasting peace to this world. That magic can be used in ways never before considered to unite all living creatures into a kind of mystical symbiotic harmony. It can end the war between Dwarves and Elves peacefully—EVERY war for that matter—once and for all. It will be hard, there will be dangers, but together we can help every creature on this earth adapt to the new world.

And if I'm dead, know that it was for a cause bigger than me. Bigger than all of us. And I did it for you and everyone else. I did it to make the world a better place. And please forgive me for not telling you any of this sooner.

I love you, Greg.

I know you'll make me proud and do the right things even if I am no longer there to guide you. (And please do not cry. Dwarves never cry.)

CHAPTER 15

◆ ─── ❖ ─── ◆

The Grand Spectacle of
Borin Woodlogger's Big Toe

I slept like a slab of granite that night.

Which I was very grateful for, given all that had happened. I fully expected to have nightmares of my dad getting munched on like beef jerky by a huge family of Trolls. But there were no dreams, just sleep that was probably too close to being dead for comfort. It was especially surprising having read my dad's letter right before going to bed—discovering that my dad's *Quest*, as he'd called it, had never been about teas and organic soaps at all, but rather had been a lifelong search for the lost magic of Separate Earth. Not only that, but considering he had meant those to be his parting words meant I had to accept the possibility that they just might be. Something I was not ready to do.

I couldn't.

Fynric's bed was already made by the time I woke. But he had left me a light breakfast on the small table: six fried eggs, five links of blood sausage, six strips of bacon, one piece of toast, and a small pot of tea.

There was a knock on the door shortly after I finished eating.

"Ah, young Stormbelly!" Dunmor said with a grin as he brushed past me through the small doorway. "I trust you find your accommodations here acceptable."

I nodded.

"Good. Good, then," he said. "Well, I hope you don't mind my unexpected visit. But our meeting was cut rather short last night and—"

"Any news on my dad?" I interrupted.

Dunmor inhaled sharply and then shook his head slowly.

"I'm afraid not," he said. "But Fynric told me about your little friend. The supposed Elf Lord heir. And his *offer*. The Council discussed it last night and voted overwhelmingly against accepting. Plus, I must tell you this, Greg: you are not to speak to Edwin Aldaron any further. Even if you think you can trust him, there's simply no way we can ever know that for certain. We will look into your father's disappearance on our own—we are quite capable, I assure you."

I wanted to argue, to yell at him that we should explore every option we had for finding out what had happened to my dad. But I knew this wasn't the time or place. Besides, just because Dunmor said I couldn't talk to Edwin and that he couldn't help me find my dad, didn't mean I had to obey. It didn't mean Edwin had to obey either. He could easily still help me find my dad, with or without the Council's approval.

So I nodded.

"Good, good," Dunmor said. "The real reason I'm here, though, is to finish discussing what we started last night. If you'll please follow me, I have quite a lot to show you."

I followed Dunmor out into the hallway. He nodded at several Dwarves hurrying by. They smiled back and gaped like they were passing a celebrity. As we moved through the Underground labyrinth, I noticed that the hallways were bursting with chaotic energy. Dwarves were running this way and that as if they all had urgent deadlines they were in danger of missing. Dunmor was stopped several times to sign a parchment or approve something or other.

"I must apologize for the distractions," he said to me after one interruption. "You dad's discovery has caused quite a stir around here, as I'm sure you've noticed. Turned our whole world upside down, in fact."

"What discovery?"

"You'll see, my boy," Dunmor said with a grin. "You'll see. We're nearly there now."

"Where?"

"The doorway to our true past," he said.

I gave him a look that I hoped he understood meant: *Stop being so vague and cryptic.* He seemed to understand because he smiled at me patiently.

"I keep forgetting just how little I was able to share with you last night," he said. "Greg, the entire history of Elves and Dwarves has been lost to time. But that doesn't mean we've stopped influencing the world in powerful ways. Elves and Dwarves have orchestrated many important historical events. Bill Gates, both President Roosevelts, Alexander the Great, Genghis Kahn, Picasso, Queen Elizabeth II, Mark Zuckerberg, Joan of Arc, and Tom Brady are just a few among many famous and important Elves or Dwarves—though some of them weren't even aware of their true identity."

"Tom Brady?" I said dubiously.

"Yes, well, he's an Elf, unsurprisingly," Dunmor said as we

finally came to a stop outside a pair of huge wooden doors. "He has wealth and power, after all . . . and height."

"Why would wealth automatically mean he's an Elf?"

"By nature Elves are shrewd and charismatic—they can easily manipulate and control the minds of lesser beings, including Humans," Dunmor explained as he plunged an old key into a huge lock on the door. "As the world progressed, these were far more important traits than knowing how to weld or frame a house or install plumbing. Elves also accept technology more so than Dwarves. These things, coupled with their more innate desires for material goods and status have helped them amass most of the world's money. Whereas we Dwarves tend to have different proclivities . . . such as physical strength, dexterity, earnestness, engineering prowess, and a close connection to the earth. Characteristics that no longer have much value in a modern world dominated by technological development, fame, and money. We've become a mere afterthought in this world, Greg."

Dunmor frowned, muttering to himself as he struggled with the large handles on the massive wooden doors.

"How many Dwarves are left in the world?" I asked.

"Hard to say," Dunmor said. "There are nine officially recognized sects of Dwarves. The largest and most powerful, and the one that rules the Dwarven Council, is us, right here, in Chicago. Our Council alone governs the organized actions of the entire species."

"So you mean to tell me that Chicago is, like . . . the *world capital* for all Dwarves?"

"Yes, of course," Dunmor said. "At least those of us who actively choose to *live* as Dwarves, outside the modern world as much as possible. Instead of letting our culture die, we choose to promote the celebration of old Dwarven artifacts, texts, and customs. But there are many Dwarves out there who either don't know their heritage or simply choose to ignore it and live as Humans."

Dunmor finally pulled open the ancient wooden doors. They creaked loudly. The room inside was completely dark.

"There are many other sects of Legacy Dwarves, of course, and a whole history lesson of how we came to be and where we all live and so on and so forth," Dunmor continued. "But all of that is modern history—we can discuss it later. What we really care about is how we lived back in Separate Earth. And so: I'm quite proud to welcome you to our *Grand Hall of Dwarven Artifacts!*"

Dunmor hit an old electrical switch and several lights flickered to life on the walls. The room was much larger than I had expected, practically the size of a school gymnasium. Which seemed like overkill since it was mostly empty. Several large tables were scattered throughout the space, heaped with ancient junk. A dozen or so pedestals held pieces of crumbling statues. The mostly bare walls were dotted by a few faded banners and scraps of old scrolls. Despite the room's impressive size, I would hardly have called the sparse and disorganized contents *grand*.

But Dunmor beamed with pride as we stepped inside.

"Your father was . . . *is* a standing Council Elder," Dunmor said. "And also the director of mining operations. That's what he's been doing on his recent travels: guiding our search efforts for lost Dwarven armaments, texts, and artifacts. The very elements that once breathed real life into our culture. Come, see some of what we've found so far."

"This is *all* there is?" I asked, my voice echoing inside the huge chamber as I followed him into the center of the room. "*This* is the *entire* history of Dwarves?"

"Yes, well, most everything has been destroyed by time," Dunmor said defensively. "Buried deep within the earth along with our ancient cities. A few original texts remain, as do some poorly translated newer editions, but mostly we only have the stories spoken aloud among families, passed down for generations. That's why we're searching for the primary-source histories of our ancestors. Not to mention old weapons and other artifacts. We're digging farther into the depths of the earth and finding more every day." He must have seen I was unconvinced because he hastily added: "It's a work in progress, you know . . . plus, there's much more that merely hasn't been cataloged yet."

We walked past a few tables scattered with old pots and chunks of metal. Dunmor pointed at a tattered and stained book, hand-bound with thick leather strips that looked to be one sneeze away from turning to dust.

"An old cookbook!" he said gleefully. "Finally, we have found the *original* recipe for traditional horse stew. Turns out, you have to boil halved hooves to make the broth!"

I tried not to let my horror show.

"You . . . *eat* horses?" I asked.

"Of course not!" he said. "But our ancestors did. Dwarves are creatures of the earth. We believe in utilizing everything it has to offer. It created life to sustain life, after all. Some would have us feel badly about our meat-heavy diet, but why should we? It's certainly not like animals show *us* any favor."

"What do you mean?" I asked.

"Well, I heard about the incident at the zoo the other day," Dunmor said with a wry grin. "Animals have a long history of hating Dwarves, you see. Many of our original Dwarven fables were founded on this inexplicable and perplexing hatred and the countless random attacks we've suffered from animal species of all kinds. Many Dwarven historians have tried to explain the phenomenon. Perhaps it's our natural odor? Whatever the case, this natural revulsion seems to have intensified in recent days. Dwarves across the globe have been reporting incidents similar to your polar bear encounter. We suspect it has something to do with your father's recent discovery . . . but I'm getting off track. Come now, let us move on."

I sighed under my breath, despite finally getting an answer (of sorts) to the question of why Wilbur had tried to eat me. But did this mean I would spend the rest of my life dodging random attacks from animals everywhere simply because I was born a Dwarf? The illogical nature of it all was the most frustrating part.

"And here"—Dunmor beamed as he paused in front of a small pedestal—"is a statue of one of the greatest Dwarven leaders of all time: Borin Woodlogger. It was said that he defeated an entire army of Orcs with nothing but a spoon—since they had come upon him during lunchtime, whence his weapons were stowed far from where he sat."

"Okay . . ." I said, eyeing the nearly empty pedestal.

"Well?" Dunmor asked—clearly waiting for some kind of reaction.

The only thing on the podium at all was a small lump of stone, barely the size of a peanut. I finally recognized it as a toe. Not a real toe, of course, but carved from rock.

"Isn't it wonderful!" Dunmor said. "As heroic as the tales speak of!"

"Um, is that his, uh, pinkie toe?" I asked, looking at the lumpy piece of stone.

"No, it's his big toe!" Dunmor said.

"How do you know it came from a statue of Born Woodsman or whatever his name was?" I asked.

Dunmor sighed in frustration.

"Because unquestionably a toe reflecting such prominence and supremacy could not be from a statue of any ordinary Dwarf!" he exclaimed. "Come now, there is something even more important to show you."

"Clearly . . ." I mumbled as I followed him.

"Finally: your father's latest discovery, the one that has thrown this place into upheaval," Dunmor said as we arrived at the back of the huge chamber. "You know, Greg, it's sometimes hard to admit when you're as wrong as I was. For years your father was considered a fool by a great many Dwarves, a quack who spent his free time wearing a tinfoil hat spouting off wild theories about the return of the lost essence of magic, a substance he called *Galdervatn*. Most Legacy Dwarves believed him to be a nutcase, of course, since magic was long gone and never coming back. But your father persisted. He always said Galdervatn was the one missing element that could restore Dwarves to our true history and heritage. That it could bring balance back to the world. And, well, to our collective astonishment, he proved to have been correct all along!"

Dunmor gestured toward six Dwarves armed with swords and axes near the back of the room. They were guarding a display case containing several small vials, five in all, each filled with a vibrant, swirling fog-like substance that constantly changed color as it rolled and shifted inside the small tubes like a smoky, liquid rainbow.

Galdervatn.

"Your dad was right!" Dunmor hissed excitedly. But more

than excitement, there was uncertainty and fear behind his eyes. "Magic *does* still exist. And we suspect it's seeping closer to the surface of the earth as we speak! We don't yet fully know what this means, since so many had considered it impossible until recently. But we suspect the Dawn of a New Magical Age is coming. That one day soon, maybe in a few months, maybe years, the world as you, *all of us*, know it, will cease to exist."

CHAPTER 16

❖

An Arrow to the Eye, a Bullet to the Head, or a Sword to the Spine Are Just a Few of the Ways I Could Die

W ait," I said, struggling to decide which of my thousands of questions to ask first. "How would a return of magic change the world that much? I mean, the Internet would seem like really powerful magic to people just fifty years ago. Plus cars, smartphones, airplanes . . ."

"Well, partially because we suspect the return of magic will *end* the Technological Age," Dunmor said gravely. "There will likely be no more Internet. Or TVs, or planes . . . or even *electricity*. All the things you speak of will become nothing more than motionless relics of the past."

"How—how can that be?" I asked.

"Let me show you something we just discovered," Dunmor said. "Anyone have one of those intelligent cellular telephone devices I've heard so much about?"

The guards looked at one another and shrugged. Dunmor frowned.

"Come now, I'm not totally naïve to your penchant for contraband," he insisted.

Finally, one of the guards reluctantly pulled an iPhone from his pocket.

Dunmor examined the phone awkwardly. The screen lit up, prompting for a passcode. Dunmor walked over to the case of recently recovered Galdervatn—the supposed *essence of magic*. He held up the glowing phone so I could see the screen, and then moved it toward the vials. As soon as it was within a few feet, the screen went dark. Dunmor hit the Home button but nothing happened.

The iPhone was completely dead.

"Magic has a *physical* presence, Greg!" Dunmor said breathlessly, walking back over to me. "It has a material manifestation in this world, and it affects the quantum physics that guide our existence. Magic will short electrical currents, interfere with radio waves and satellite signals, render modern electronics blank and useless. Then, of course, there are also the Werewolves—"

"*Werewolves!?*"

"Yes, of course," Dunmor said. "They are quite real and still living among us. But stripped of magic, they have lost the ability to transform. It's likely that most of them have no idea they're Werewolves at all. But if Galdervatn does reach the surface of the earth, we suspect they'll once again change with the moon's cycles as of old. And . . . well, I'm sure you'll agree it's best not to imagine what our nights will look like with untold numbers of beasts roaming free, eating whatever or *whom*ever happens to fall into their path. The New Magical Age could be a very exhilarating and terrifying time . . ."

"*Could be?*" I said, almost afraid to ask anything more.

"Well, yes, we really don't *know* what will happen," Dunmor said. "We can only theorize based on old stories and what little we've discovered so far. For instance, we believe the looming return of magic may be what's responsible for the recent spate of animal attacks. It's as if the return of Galdervatn has awoken some long-dormant sixth sense in animals, their innate hatred of our species. But again, this is only a theory."

"No magic has existed for thousands of years?" I asked.

"That's correct," Dunmor said, nodding slowly. "Thousands upon thousands."

"So how did I watch a Human transform into a massive Troll last night?" I asked.

"Despite how that must have appeared, Trolls do not possess the ability to perform magic," Dunmor said. "Their transformation is a unique genetic trait that is purely biological. It's not so different from several animal species that exist today: puffer fish, rain frogs, or the mimic octopus—all creatures that can transform their appearance instantly, as if by *magic*. The real question is: How are there still pure-blooded Trolls around and we didn't know it? They're supposed to be extinct."

"Okay, but what about how I got down here last night?" I asked. "I mean, the trapdoor . . . falling all that way and escaping injury? That had to have been magic."

"No, no magic," Dunmor said, grinning proudly. "That was merely deceptive tricks on the mind's eye—a product of Dwarven ingenuity. We are masters of construction and design and engineering. We used to be the blacksmiths to the gods! We have no equals in manipulating the elements of the earth to do our will in ways that may seem supernatural, but are surely no more magical than the wonders of the construction of pyramids before the days of modern machinery—something which Dwarves actually played no small role in."

"But the fall should have killed me . . ." I said weakly.

"Let me ask you this, Greg," Dunmor said smugly. "Have you ever broken a bone in your life? Dislocated an elbow? Concussions?"

"Well, no, but "

"No," Dunmor repeated. "No, you haven't. Nor have I, or my children, or your father. That's because Dwarven bones are much stronger than the brittle twigs Humans call bones. We came from the earth itself; the gods themselves molded us from stone. The earliest Dwarves had skeletons made from granite, iron ore, and diamond. They were nearly invincible to mortal weapons. Even today, those of us who are still *mostly* of Dwarven lineage have much stronger bones than Humans . . . or even Elves."

"So . . . I'm *invincible?*"

"Hardly," Dunmor said, unable to hold back a laugh. "Our bones are strong, but our flesh and organs remain soft and vulnerable. An arrow through your eyeball would surely kill you in an instant. A properly sharpened Elven sword could open up your belly or pierce your heart with ease. Even bullets from Humans' savage firearms could irreparably damage your internal organs, plus there's—"

"Okay!" I interrupted. "I think I get the point. But how can you explain the magic *I myself* performed yesterday?"

All the color drained from Dunmor's ruddy face.

"What . . . what are you talking about?" he asked softly.

I explained to him how I had somehow caused a plant to grow out of a marble second-story floor, and then later had turned into pure stone for several seconds. As I spoke, he looked increasingly alarmed and then even angry. A dreadful sinking feeling tore into my guts.

"I told Trevor not to give you any Galdervatn!" Dunmor shouted. "And he ignored me as usual, that fool!"

It was hard to just sit there while he cursed out my dad. But I did, because I was so confused and afraid that I simply didn't know what else to do.

"Your father," Dunmor barked, shoving a finger in my face. "He begged us to let him take some of the recently unearthed Galdervatn home. And I told him that not a drop was allowed to leave the Underground! Dwarven magic is a relic—almost all knowledge of how it works has been lost. More trials need to be done, here, in a safe environment. But your father is just so—so—"

"Reckless and impulsive?" I suggested.

"Yes!" Dunmor nearly screamed, as he paced angrily. "He must have slipped you some . . ."

"No!" I said quickly. "He didn't . . . I mean, it was *me*, I did it."

Dunmor spun on his heels, glaring.

"What do you mean?"

"I—I didn't *know* I drank it . . ." I stammered. "He told me not to drink his tea. But I—I mean, had I known what was in it I wouldn't have . . . but I stole a drink when he wasn't looking."

Dunmor sighed loudly.

"This is why he shouldn't have brought it home at all," he said. "It's quite likely that several Elves witnessed your feats of magic. Which may very well explain the attack on the store. If they know we found Galdervatn, they'd surely want to know how and where. It's all making sense now . . ."

A devastating realization hit me just then: *It had been my fault.*

The attack on the store last night was my fault. If I had just walked away from Perry picking on Froggy, or had listened to my dad and not drunk his tea, then I wouldn't have been able to perform magic. And none of this would have happened—a Troll wouldn't have attacked the store that night and my dad would still be . . .

I couldn't finish the thought.

"Well, at least we know you have the Ability, if nothing else," Dunmor said with a frown.

"Ability?" I said.

"Yes," Dunmor said. "The ability to use magic. Not *all* Dwarves are capable of performing magic. Even back in Separate Earth, only a small percentage of Dwarves had the ability to use magic. We still don't know why or how those with the Ability acquire it—but regardless, it appears you are one of the few. But now I must once again excuse myself. You performing magic at an Elven school of all places . . . Well, it's disturbing news to say the least, the Council must hear about this development immediately. I trust you can find your own way back?"

I nodded.

But the truth was, I didn't care either way. Even as I stood there and watched Dunmor walk briskly from the room, all I could think about was my own role in my dad's violent abduction. I had just discovered I had a rare and special talent—the ability to perform magic! And yet all it had done so far was cause me grave misfortune and heartache.

Pretty typical for a Belmont.

Or I guess I mean for a *Stormbelly.*

CHAPTER 17

Mrs. O'Leary's Cow Is Finally Proven Innocent

The pretty Dwarven girl with short purple hair from the night before was standing outside my door when I got back.

"Hey, Greg!" Ari Brightsmasher said. "Welcome to the neighborhood!"

"Uhh . . . hi," I said, surprised she already knew where I lived, and that she wanted to come by at all since I'd bailed on them like a coward. "Um, thanks. I'm really sorry about ditching you guys last night."

Ari smiled and shrugged.

"No big deal," she said. "I totally understand. I mean this is all very exciting, the return of Galdervatn, the rediscovery of the Bloodletter, and everything. Dwarves finding our past. But it's also pretty overwhelming for you, I'm sure."

I nodded.

"Well, I came by to see if you want to come to the Arena with us?" Ari said. "Me, Lake, and Eagan, I mean."

At first I was too stunned to say anything. Was making

friends outside of the PEE really this easy? Or did this have more to do with our innate connection, being Dwarves living Underground and whatnot? I guessed it didn't matter either way; here was a group of kids inviting me to hang out even though I'd just met them.

"Yeah, that sounds fun," I said.

"Great!" Ari said with a huge smile. "This way."

I followed her down the hall, trying to take note of all the twists and turns we were making. It was true I had a great sense of direction, but the Underground was *huge*. Plus every hallway looked nearly identical.

"So I heard you've found a possible ally with the Elves?" Ari said after a few minutes. "That they want to help figure out what happened to your dad?"

Apparently there were no secrets in the Underground. But I didn't get a chance to ask her how she had found out, because she just kept on talking. Talking quite fast. She was almost giddy with excitement.

"I mean, I hope your Elven ally is for real," Ari said. "The Council will be skeptical, but they're skeptical of *everything*. They're Dwarves, after all. But maybe a new perspective is just the thing, right? I mean, fresh blood and all that. Too many of us are expecting the discovery of Galdervatn to lead to a new war with the Elves. Nobody *wants* that, I don't think. But it's as if they think there's nothing we can do to prevent it. They all think we should prepare for war—if not with Elves, then at least with monsters and such. But I think we should be focused more on the Humans. Helping them get through a crazy new world they're not going to understand. It's the new Riven. I'm just worried the other Dwarves don't really *get it*. You know?"

Ari stopped and took a few deep breaths.

"What's the Riven?" I asked, using the moment to get a word in.

"It's the long-standing rift among Dwarves," Ari said. "It changes every now and then, whatever our biggest issue is, I mean. For the last forty or fifty years, the Riven was all about isolationism—whether we should blend with modern society more or stay underground and keep pushing ourselves farther away from all that. But now that Galdervatn is apparently coming back, the Riven has shifted. Now the Riven is over how we should proceed with Humans and Elves during the Dawn of a New Magical Age."

"What do you mean?" I asked. "What does any of this have to do with Humans?"

"Well, some Dwarves want to use the magic we find to get ready for the chaos ahead," Ari said. "Not a completely terrible idea: to spend all our energy preparing to fight monsters and learning to defend ourselves from an Elven attack they see as inevitable. But they're only thinking about Dwarves first. They believe in taking care of our own kind and leaving everyone else to fend for themselves. They expect violence and aggression in the first stages of the New Magical Age, and think we need to train and prepare accordingly. Everyone for themselves. So where does that leave the Humans?"

I nodded, seeing her point.

All of this was certainly new and shocking to me as it was. I couldn't imagine what it would be like if I wasn't a Dwarf and didn't have this instant community down here where they all accepted me immediately. If they were right about the world descending into chaos, the Humans would be confused and lost and certainly would not fare well.

"Is that the side you're on?" I asked.

"Most Traditionalists, my parents included, are on this side of the Riven," Ari said. "But not me. I and your dad, and many others, believe the opposite. Of course we want to celebrate Dwarven culture and all that. But we also think it's irresponsible to just leave the Humans to fend for themselves. We want to use the Galdervatn to help prepare *everyone*, including Humans, for what lies ahead. Furthermore, we don't see this as a reason for the Elven War to resume, but quite the opposite. We see it as a way to make the bonds of peace even stronger. Can't we use the new world to unite Humans, Elves, and Dwarves? And make sure that chaos and violence don't win the day?"

Her green eyes burned intensely like a pot of melted gemstones. She reminded me so much of my dad—the way she got so worked up to do something insane because she felt it was right.

"So all Dwarves are on one side or the other?" I asked.

"No, of course not," Ari said with a laugh. "A lot of Dwarves are undecided or stuck somewhere in between the two extremes. This is all fairly new, after all. But in order for us to take any course of action, the Council must reach a majority vote. It's yet to come even close. So we're stuck doing nothing for now, like usual. But pretty soon they'll *have* to decide, what with the upcoming Global Session."

I nodded, trying to digest it all.

"So who's this Elven ally you supposedly have anyway?" she asked.

"My best friend is the heir apparent to be the next Elf Lord," I said.

Ari's mouth flopped open. Her already shining eyes widened

to impossibly bright levels. She gaped at me for several awkward moments.

"I mean, I had no idea who he was until last night," I explained. "But the good news is, he's on your . . . well, *our* side. He wants to work with us to find my dad. As the next Elf Lord, I'm guessing that means a lot."

Ari nodded thoughtfully.

"Well, you might be right," she said. "But unfortunately he's not the Elf Lord yet. All that really matters is what your buddy's dad thinks."

"Yeah, I suppose it doesn't matter anymore anyway," I said.

"How so?"

"Dunmor told me the Council already voted on the matter," I said. "They decided to basically ignore his offer to help."

I expected Ari to be shocked or disappointed, but she merely nodded with a wry grin.

"Of course they did," she said. "That's no surprise."

"Why do you say that?"

Ari laughed.

"You still have a lot to learn about Dwarves, Greg," she said as we finally reached the huge doors to the Arena. "Come on, I'll explain more inside."

———◆I◆———

The Arena was filled with kids excitedly chatting about Galdervatn and what its discovery might lead to.

Lake and Eagan greeted me with huge smiles—which was unexpected and, I have to admit, pretty comforting, all things considered. Being down here felt infinitely more relaxing than any time I'd spent around Human and Elven kids at the PEE (aside from time with Edwin) and at public school before that. But part of me wondered how much of that had to do with being a Dwarf among Dwarves, and how much was me just finally feeling comfortable and getting out of my own head—me feeling like I wasn't singled out and doomed with unusual bouts of terrible luck and family curses, but rather *all of us* were.

"The Council's inherent pessimism pushes them to inaction more often than not," Ari said, as the four of us started a game of pool. "Do you want to know how many measures have actually *passed* during the last ten years?"

"Twenty-five?" I guessed.

"No." Ari laughed. "Only *two*. Including the one that passed last night."

"The first was to increase Dwarven mining operations threefold," Eagan said. "Which happened about ten years ago."

Ari hit the cue ball and it slammed into the racked pool balls with a loud CLACK and they all spun everywhere across the table. The three kids clearly spent a lot of time down here playing these games—I was going to get annihilated. I'd only played pool a few times at Edwin's lakeshore mansion in the suburbs. And even then we'd just been fooling around, mostly scuffing the table trying to make insane trick shots.

"It's the main reason I'm worried about the Riven," Ari said. "Even if the Council eventually votes in favor of helping out the Humans, it will take so long to implement that it will probably be too late. But they're holding a special Global Session in the next few weeks to finally decide."

"Global Session?" I asked, remembering that Fynric had mentioned that as well.

"Yeah, it means members from smaller Dwarves sects all

over the globe will attend. It's pretty exciting, there hasn't been a Global Session in decades."

"Lest be thou that ye Dawn of Magic draws nigh!" Lake said excitedly.

He took a shot at the 2-ball and missed badly, giving me some hope that I wouldn't be the *worst* player there.

"Yeah, hopefully that will finally lead to *some* action," Eagan agreed.

"But it won't change the nature of Dwarves," Ari said. "There's always *something* pushing them into possible action that they never take. Before this it was the Goblin Revolt of '67. And then there was the Great Specter Scare in 1991. And don't forget about the Great Chicago Fire in 1871. *Now* it's the return of magic. It'll be the same either way: The Dwarves won't actually do anything. It's in our nature. Years of bad luck have pushed us into a haze of apathetic pessimism."

"What do you mean?" I asked.

"Let me guess, Greg," Ari said. "Your whole life you've been afraid to take drastic action for fear it will only make things worse?"

I stared at her in shock.

"Well, yeah, but . . . I mean, my dad isn't like that," I said. "He takes action *because* of the bad luck."

"Well, your dad is special, Greg," Ari said, her smile gone now. "There's a reason he became a Council Elder so young. One of the youngest in modern history, actually."

A heavy silence fell over the table. It was only broken by the sounds of other Dwarven kids playing games and working on projects all around us in the Arena. I had never considered that my dad was special before. I'd always looked up to him, but I'd never thought I looked up to him for the exact reason that set him apart from all other Dwarves. And from *me* as well, for that matter.

"You said the Great Chicago Fire?" I asked, wanting to change the subject. "Dwarves played a role in that?"

"No, not Dwarves, Elves!" Eagan said scornfully.

"Elves allegedly started the fire," Ari said. "They knew we had established Chicago as our unofficial modern capital. As it boomed, they became threatened by our growing power and influence. And so they sought to destroy the city while making it look like an accident. Not that we could ever prove it was them, of course."

"Wow," I said.

Among Humans, there was a lot of speculation over what had caused the fire that nearly destroyed the city—ranging from a cow kicking over a lantern in a barn to a simple brushfire gone wild. But the city had persevered and was rebuilt better than ever. Which seemed to be a theme in Dwarven history: keeping their heads down amid a string of terrible events and simply working to rebuild all that was lost.

"So Dwarves were the founders of Chicago?" I asked.

They all laughed.

"Isn't it obvious?" Eagan asked.

"Thyne characteristics nay doth befitting any other such creature but Dwarves!" Lake said.

"How would it be obvious?" I asked, clearly missing something.

"The blue-collar nature of the city, of the entire Midwest?" Ari said. "The core of this city has always been hard work. Not flash and status like Los Angeles and New York, two shallow, empty, mostly Elven cities."

"The meat-heavy menus of Chicago restaurants?" Eagan added. "The humongous portions? The wanton creation of deep-dish pizza? The abundant, gleeful consumption of hot dogs and sausages?"

"All the facial hair in Chicago?" Ari said with a huge grin.

"The ingenious, astounding engineering feat that was reversing the direction of an entire river?" Eagan said. "Take that, St. Louis."

"Until recently, the overwhelming inborn pessimism of Cubs fans?" Ari said. "I mean, a whole city of fans believed in a curse not unlike your supposed *family* curse."

"Lest nay dismember—" Lake started, but I interrupted him.

"Okay, okay," I said, laughing. "I think I get it. You're right. All of what Chicago is known for seems to fit perfectly with what I've learned about Dwarves."

We played pool for a little while longer, which seemed like a perfectly reasonable thing to do while talking about the history of Dwarves in the modern world. They told me about all the things throughout history that were actually related to Elves and Dwarves (and no Humans even had a clue), including NASA (an Elf thing), the overhunting of dinosaurs (an old Dwarven delicacy), and Napoleon Bonaparte (surprisingly an Elf, not a Dwarf), among many others.

Near the end of our last game, the subject of the Riven came up again. Ari was clearly very passionate about it, which again just reminded me of my dad. Listening to her made it seem all the more believable that she and my dad were on the same side.

"Plus, the Humans," Ari was saying. "We need to be ready to protect them. They will be scared and confused when the world turns . . . when magic comes back. They won't know how to defend themselves from a Werewolf or Alghoul, or even a

139

simple Hobgoblin. The first time a Wraith shows up in their attic they're going to think it's just a harmless ghost!"

"Well, that's to be determined," Eagan said. "I still suspect the Elves will use the return of magic to try and crush us once and for all. If that happens, protecting the Humans will be the least of our worries."

"Thyne ultimate skirmish rests ye golden-pronged crown upon thee dawn's horizon forthwith!" Lake said.

Ari rolled her eyes and shook her head.

"They're being dramatic," she said to me. "We still have no *idea* what will happen."

"Of course we do!" Eagan disagreed. "You really think Elves won't use the return of magic for personal gain? They take whatever they can, whenever they can. It's what they do. You don't see many Dwarven families living in six-thousand-square-foot homes when so many are homeless, or buying thousand-dollar dinners at fancy restaurants when so many are starving, do you? The Elves will use the Dawn of Magic for something selfish and possibly nefarious. It's in their nature."

"Well, we certainly agree on one thing: the Elves won't help out the Humans," Ari said.

"Hang on a second," I interrupted. "I *still* don't get why we'd need to help the Humans. I mean, they have armies and planes and tanks to fight the monsters . . ."

The only kind of war (with monsters or Elves or *anybody*) I could picture was one with machine guns and drones.

"No!" Eagan said, as if this was the most preposterous thing he'd ever heard. "Magic will render such things useless. That's the whole point. Protecting ourselves will have to be done with axes and swords and arrows and magic: the weapons of Separate Earth, the true weapons of our people. Plus, Dwarven weapons have powers that transcend anything the modern world could produce. Like the Bloodletter, one of the most powerful Dwarven axes ever created."

"I still don't get why an ax, even if it is *magical*, would be better than a drone or a tank," I said.

"It's complicated," Eagan said.

"Ghouls!" Lake said theatrically. "Specters, Wraiths, Alghouls, Orcs, Unicorns, Demons, Rock Trolls . . ."

"Unimaginable beasts that might return when magic does," Eagan said. "And only enchanted weapons can stop some of them."

"There's nothing we can do to stop magic from coming back?" I asked.

"Not if your dad's theory is correct," Ari said.

"And it looks more and more every day like it is," Eagan said. "The recent hostility of animals toward Dwarves is proof. I mean, look at what a tiny shih tzu did to me yesterday in the park!"

He pulled up his pant leg and revealed a nasty cut that looked like it came from a full-grown Doberman, not a small fuzz ball.

"Take heed, Commoner!" Lake said theatrically. "Thyne eyes hath not behest thyne creatures of enchantment—lest nay whence foregone enemies."

I wasn't sure what Lake meant, whether he intended to comfort me or scare me further. The thought of countless violent and terrible monsters and magical creatures roaming the world was more than I could handle.

"Well, no matter what happens," Eagan said, "it doesn't change how exciting last night's Council decision is."

"What actually passed last night?" I asked.

All I'd heard about the meeting was what Dunmor had told me: that my proposal to enlist Edwin to help find my dad had been defeated.

"Training," Eagan said with a huge grin.

I raised my eyebrows.

"The Council voted that it's to begin immediately," Ari said. "Tomorrow, all of us, including you, will officially start Dwarven combat training!"

CHAPTER 18

The Dwarven Anti-Mongoose-
and-Gerbil-Egg Society

T he next day began with total chaos.

And I'm not just referring to the current state of my life: losing my dad, suddenly being moved underground to live with a grouchy old man named Fynric Grufftrack, being told I'm a rare Dwarf with magical abilities. No, I mean the whole Underground was in chaos.

Hundreds of Dwarven kids and adults streamed this way and that throughout the Underground. Somewhere among the throng of disorder, Fynric ushered me into a line, at the end of which I was handed a small slip of paper that was so thick it almost felt like denim.

The words on the paper were hastily scrawled in barely legible cursive:

Greggdroule Stormbelly, your assigned classmates are:
    Ariyna Brightsmasher
    Lakeland Brightsmasher

Eagan Mooncharm
Glamenhilda Shadowpike
Please report for instructor assignment at the
DAMAGES Administration Offices at 1:12 p.m.

I couldn't help but smile that I had ended up in the same class as my new Dwarven friends (plus someone named Glamenhilda Shadowpike). I assumed this wasn't by chance.

A few minutes later, they greeted me with huge grins in the Arena.

"Thee doth christened to thyne fellowship of instruction!" Lake said excitedly.

"Yeah, I saw that," I said, holding up my little piece of parchment paper. "Who pulled the strings for that to happen?"

"My dad can be pretty persuasive when he needs to be," Eagan said with a smirk. "For a Dwarf."

"Plus he's on the BODE," Ari said.

"The what?" I asked.

"The Board of Dwarven Education," Ari said like it should have been obvious.

Dozens of other kids were pouring into the cavern, holding their little slips of parchment. They met up with their respective groups, some excitedly, and others disappointed and nervous. We overheard a rumor that Dwarven adults would also begin training today, in a secret catacomb deep beneath Soldier Field. The idea of a bunch of short and stout adults taking magic classes together would have made me laugh if I weren't so consumed with everything else.

"So you guys know this, uh, Glamenhilda Shadowpike person?" I asked.

"Ugh, *unfortunately*," Ari said. "The Shadowpikes are such a boorish family. They eat rats."

"They *eat* rats?!?!" I said.

"Hey, better that than destroying as many helpless vegetables as Ari does," Eagan said.

I'd forgotten that Ari was probably the world's only vegan Dwarf. Plenty of kids at the PEE were vegan, so that wasn't a big deal to me. But so far, all the Dwarves I'd met (including me and my dad and my extended family) were all voracious meat lovers.

"That's not mentioning the Shadowpikes' inability to not break something every hour," Ari added.

"You're just jealous of her immaculate mustache," Eagan said.

"Tis ye rarest of fine beauties doth fleeced upon thyne superior lip, nay but shy of forty years aged, mayhap less," Lake said.

"You did you say *her*, right?" I clarified.

"Oh, yeah, definitely," Eagan said. "You'll thank me later for getting her in our group. She's the hottest Dwarf in the Underground. Lake's right, too, she might be the first female Dwarf in centuries to grow a full stache before turning eighteen. Plus, she's strong as an ox already. Just wait till you see her—she's amazing."

"Hey, there's more to a Dwarf than her facial hair, you know," Ari scolded Eagan and Lake. "But . . . I can't deny that I *do* envy her mustache. It's *irrefutably* superb."

She touched her bare upper lip longingly.

"I think you look okay the way you are," I said, thinking I was being nice. (Only later did I realize how poor my word choice might have been.)

"Gee, thanks a lot, Greg," Ari said drily. "Come on, we'd better head to our assignment."

"Speaking of that," I said. "What is 'damages'?"

"You mean you haven't figured out that it's another acronym?" Eagan asked playfully.

"Oh, uh . . . is it the Dwarven Anti-Mongoose-and-Gerbil-Egg Society?"

The three of them laughed as we headed for the door.

"Close," Ari said. "Come on, we'll explain on the way."

———✦———

DAMAGES: the Dwarven Alchemy, Magic, and Arms Greater Educational School.

Which was why I was more confused than ever when we took the CTA train to the Ukrainian Village neighborhood and ended up outside a tiny storefront whose sign proclaimed:

JARMUSCH'S VCR/DVD REPAIRATORIUM

But I knew it was the right place because a steady stream of short and stoutish kids poured into and out of the small store. But more than that, Glamenhilda Shadowpike was already there. She looked angrily at a wristwatch that was nothing more than a small stone sundial attached to her meaty wrist by a rough hunk of leather.

"You guys were almost late!" she said. "Where have you been?"

Glamenhilda's voice was deep, like her throat was filled with coffee grounds. But I had to admit there was something rather sultry about it. It was obvious she was considered one of the "hotter" kids around based on the way that Eagan, Lake, and almost every other Dwarf nearby ogled her while trying (and mostly failing) to make it seem like they weren't.

She was a little taller than me, but nearly twice as big. Not fat, just . . . *large*. Her arms were muscular, her torso was like a block of concrete, and her legs looked like they belonged on a racehorse—I could see sharp muscle definition even through her clearly homemade leather pants. Her brown hair was pulled into several dozen braids that hung around her giant skull like she was a Medusa. And there, resting atop her upper lip, was the beginnings of a very fine, feathery mustache.

"But we *weren't* late," Ari said. "So relax."

"I'm just anxious to *crush* some Elven skulls," Glamenhilda said, slamming her fist into an open palm.

Lake laughed nervously. He was clearly intimidated by her beauty. And it was hard to ignore that her brutish confidence and domineering presence gave her a strange sort of allure.

"Well, I don't think we'll be doing any of that on the first day," Eagan said.

"Why not?" Glamenhilda demanded. "What more is there to learn? See Elf, bash Elf. See monster, bash monster. See, bash, see, bash."

"I think it will be more nuanced than that," Ari said.

"Pfft," Glamenhilda said, and then flicked her hard stare in my direction. "Who's the cute new guy?"

I was dumbfounded and momentarily unable to speak.

"This is Greg," Ari said. "Elder Stormbelly's son."

"Oh," Glamenhilda said. "Well, I certainly hope you have more backbone than your dad. You can call me Glam. Come on, it's our appointment time."

Without waiting, she turned around and entered the store. I would have been angrier about what she'd said about my dad if I wasn't so terrified of her.

As we followed Glam inside, Eagan nudged me with his elbow.

"She thinks you're cute," he whispered. *"Lucky."*

He meant it, too. But I didn't feel lucky. I was alarmed. Back in third grade, there was this girl who had a crush on me for a few weeks. She used to pinch me when I wasn't looking. I certainly hoped Glam expressed her feelings differently, because I couldn't even imagine what her version of pinching would be.

The inside of the store was even smaller than it looked from the outside. It didn't help that there were dozens of Dwarven kids crammed inside, waiting anxiously for their appointment time to be called out by a man with the hairiest ears and bushiest eyebrows I'd ever seen.

Every time the door opened and new kids entered, he would call out the same thing from behind the counter without even looking up:

"Welcome, I'm Headmaster Fozin Bookbridger, please wait for your assigned time to be called."

"So what is our instructor assignment anyway?" I whispered.

"Geez, cute kid is really dumb," Glam said loudly, perhaps incapable of whispering.

Several Dwarves nearby looked over and snickered.

"He's not dumb," Ari said defensively. "He just found out a few days ago. It's not like *you* know what exactly is going to happen—"

"Yeah, well—" Glam said, and then stopped, realizing Ari was right. "At least I don't look weak by asking so many questions."

"None of us really know what's happening, Greg," Eagan explained. "We've never done this before either. We always

148

knew DAMAGES existed and that we'd maybe train here some-day, but it's all been theoretical. Until now."

"Whence yore, thyne dreams doth become thy reality," Lake added excitedly.

"Thee doth speak nary a deceptive expression," Glam said to Lake, which made his grin spread even wider.

We waited the remaining few minutes in relative silence, except for Glam and Lake having a full conversation in old Dwarven.

Finally, it was our time. We stepped forward, pushing through the other waiting Dwarves. Headmaster Bookbridger looked up and glanced at each of our faces, one at a time, refer-encing something unseen on his wooden countertop.

"Welcome to the Dwarven training academy," he finally said. "I'm Headmaster Bookbridger. Your instructor assignment is Thufir Stonequarry Noblebeard. You will find him here."

He handed Ari a small square of parchment with an address on it. She looked at it uncertainly.

"Um, excuse me, sir," she said. "But why do we need to go elsewhere? Isn't *this* the school?"

Headmaster Bookbridger looked down at her and scratched the copious bundles of gray hair poking out from his ears. He looked around the tiny store theatrically, as if expecting to see something other than a low ceiling and bare walls. Then he looked back at Ari with a wry grin.

"You really think I could train thousands of Dwarves inside this small store?"

"Well, we, uh, sort of figured there'd be a secret passage to underground tunnels and chambers . . . like always," Eagan said before Ari could respond.

"Ah, I see," Headmaster Bookbridger said, still smiling. "Our schools are not like those of Humans, ones you may have seen in movies. We do not believe in large classes taught by an overworked, underpaid, and demoralized instructor. Dwarves believe in a more hands-on, personal, and realistic approach. This is merely the school's administration office. The whole city of Chicago, no, the *whole world*, is your classroom. You'll understand in time."

"Oh, okay," Ari said, looking down at the piece of parchment again. "Thank you."

We started to turn away, but Headmaster Bookbridger stopped us.

"One last thing," he said. "Some parting *advice*: Your instructor is one of the best in the world . . . but he is, ah, rather *eccentric* and may need some *convincing*."

"Convincing?" Eagan repeated.

"You'll see," Headmaster Bookbridger said with a grin like he was in on some cruel joke. "You wouldn't have been assigned to him if we didn't think you could handle it. *Best of luck to you.*"

CHAPTER 19

When Shattering a Park Bench with Your Face Fails to Impress Me

The state of Thufir Stonequarry Noblebeard's home was hardly comforting.

It was an especially shady-looking brick apartment complex near Humboldt Park on the West Side of Chicago. Our worries had nothing to do with status, though, but rather: training five Dwarves in the ways of ancient magic and warfare inside a tiny apartment simply seemed impossible. Complaints from neighbors seemed a near certainty at best.

Especially after the way Glam had regaled us all with tales of things she'd been able to smash apart with her head over the years. She'd definitely expected me to be impressed that she'd once cracked a city park bench in half with her face. *Cautiously impressed* would be a generous way to describe how I felt, but Lake and Eagan loved every word of every head-shattering story.

"Well, what choice do we have?" Ari said after a loaded silence at the front entrance of the huge yellow-brick apartment complex.

She pressed the buzzer for his apartment. There was no reply. She pressed it again. And again. We waited a few more minutes. Then Glam reached out and slammed her meaty finger onto the button and held it there for thirty long seconds. Several guys stared at us as they walked by.

Finally the door buzzed and the lock clicked open.

We worked our way up four flights of stairs and through a dirty hallway that smelled like a stagnant pond. We reached apartment 412 and Eagan knocked a few times. There was no response. Glam pushed him aside.

"Move," she said.

She pounded with a fist the size of a brick, rattling the cheap, flimsy door (clearly Human manufactured). There was no way anyone alive inside the apartment hadn't heard the knock. But nobody came to the door.

"Well, *somebody* buzzed us up," Eagan said.

"I'll just break it down," Glam said. "Step aside."

She enclosed one fist in the other, creating a miniature wrecking ball at the ends of her arms. She reared back and I was certain it would have blasted the door into pieces had Ari not stopped her.

"Wait," Ari said. "It might be unlocked." She grabbed the knob and opened the unlocked door. "See?"

"Smashing is more fun, though," Glam said dejectedly.

The five of us stood at the precipice of the creepy apartment, unsure of what to do. What if the address had been wrong? Should we really just step into some strange apartment uninvited? But Glam didn't hesitate for long. She barged inside the dark apartment, shouting as she disappeared into the black void.

"Instructor, teach me to crush monster skulls and Elven ribs! I demand it of you!"

Eagan, Ari, and Lake looked at me, then we all grinned and followed Glam inside.

The tiny apartment was in total disarray.

All the lights were off except for the glow of an ancient boxy TV. Old takeout containers were strewn everywhere, half-filled with nearly rotting food. Empty cans of Dr Pepper were stacked in impossible, intricately chaotic piles on the table and in the corners of the room like modern art pieces. The place reeked with a body odor that was unmistakably Dwarven (it had taken me just two days living in the Underground to recognize it). A slovenly man was on the couch, wearing only sweatpants. His torso was so hairy he might have been half bear. Or at the very least would have ended up on an episode of *Hunting Bigfoot* if he ever decided to wander around the woods alone and shirtless. He stared vacantly at the TV as his fingers danced across a video game remote control.

There was no way this was our new teacher.

"Um, hello?" Ari ventured.

The man didn't look up.

"Tis thee thyne instructor of ye Dwarven arts of yore?" Lake asked.

No reaction. We still couldn't even tell if he knew we were there at all. Eagan picked up a flyswatter in desperate need of a good rinsing and gave the man a few quick pokes on the shoulder. He sneered, but still didn't look at us and just continued playing his video game as if he were in a trance. Eagan poked him again, this time in the face.

"Ewww, that has dead flies all over it!" Ari said.

"I highly doubt he'll mind," Eagan said. "Look at this place."

But it didn't matter either way. The man kept playing right through a fly-gut-encrusted flap of rubber ramming repeatedly into his cheek and eyelids and nostrils.

"I guess maybe this is what Headmaster Bookbridger meant when he said he might need some *convincing*," Ari said.

Eagan continued to jab the old man's face with the fly-swatter. Then Glam shoved him aside so hard that he stumbled backward and fell into a perfect sitting position on a stained, torn recliner chair.

"I'll get the old codger's attention," she said.

We took an instinctive step back as Glam grabbed Thufir Stonequarry Noblebeard's shoulders and began shaking him so violently that I half expected the man's head to snap off and roll across the scuffed hardwood floors.

"Train us, old man!" Glam screamed into his flopping face. "I want to learn how to beat Elves to a pulp with their own body parts!"

Finally the man hit Pause and looked up. Glam released him.

"Why on earth would you want to do that, you ghastly beast?" he asked.

"It's what Elves deserve," Glam said, apparently taking no offense at his insult.

"I don't dispute that," the man said. "We *all* deserve such a fate. But why waste the energy?"

His bare hairy arms groped around the couch, eventually finding a mostly empty can of Dr Pepper. He finished it off with a loud guzzle and then tossed it aside where it crashed onto an impressive pile of empties. The pile shifted from its newest addition and the clinking of aluminum cans was the only noise in the living room for a few moments.

"How can you say that?" Eagan asked from the recliner. "Standing up to Elves is never a waste of energy."

"Because what does it matter?" Thufir Stonequarry Noblebeard said. "Let the world go to hell—just as long as I have my noodles, my video games, and my Dr Pepper!"

"Sir, you're supposed to train us," Ari said. "To be Dwarves again. To fight like Dwarves. To be ready to face the new world."

"Can you believe this nonsense?" Thufir said, gesturing at the TV, ignoring Ari. "Stereotype-ridden drivel, this game! I can't believe it was ever made!"

The paused game showed a frozen battle between Humans, Elves, Dwarves, and a massive dragon. He picked up the TV remote and threw it at the screen. It bounced off it harmlessly and shattered onto the floor, the batteries scattering in opposite directions. Apparently satisfied that he'd at least tried, Thufir looked at us again.

"It's not decent to break into people's homes," he said. "Get lost, will you?"

"Well, we thought you were our instructor, but maybe we've made a mistake," Eagan said hopefully. "You're not Thufir Stonequarry Noblebeard . . . are you?"

"No . . ." he said, rubbing his forehead as we all seemed to breathe a collective sigh of relief. "Nobody calls me that but my mother. Well, her and that foolish Dwarven Council. Everyone else calls me Buck."

Our sighs of relief came rushing bitterly back into our mouths as shocked gasps. So it was true: This *really was* our supposed instructor. Disappointment shone in all our faces, but perhaps for different reasons. For me, I just wanted to find my dad and this was only delaying that.

"Didn't they inform you that you were to begin training us today?" Eagan asked.

Buck shrugged and slumped back into the couch.

"They wouldn't have sent us here otherwise," Ari insisted.

"Perhaps they did," Buck said. "Feel free to check my mail."

He gestured over his shoulder toward a small table in the dark kitchen. A massive pile of unopened mail spilled onto the floor. The letters on the bottom were yellowing and crinkled and might not even have been from this decade.

"But we must start training!" Eagan said. "Galdervatn is coming back—they've already found some!"

Buck looked slightly interested for the first time.

"Did they now?" he said. "So Trevor was right all along, that infectious lunatic."

My heart skipped a beat at the mention of my dad's name.

"Yes!" Ari and Eagan both said excitedly.

"Thou lessons shant be-est postponed further!" Lake said. "Ye instruction musttofore commence henceforth!"

Buck sighed, shrugged a single shoulder, and picked up his game controller.

"It's not my problem anymore," he said. "Nothing will ever change, anyway."

"How can you say that?" Ari asked.

"You'll figure it out someday," Buck said lazily as he resumed his game. "It's better to be unhappy and know the worst, than to be happy in a fool's paradise."

None of us knew how to respond. We watched him fall into a catatonic state again, his unblinking eyes fixed to the TV screen, his fingers moving across the remote control buttons on their own.

"I'm going to smash his TV!" Glam said.

Her knuckles cracked loudly as she clenched them into fists.

"No, let him be," Eagan said. "Come on, I'll just go to my dad and get us a new teacher."

Glam nodded but rammed a fist into the wall anyway, easily punching a massive hole in the drywall and splintering one of the wooden studs behind it. Eagan and Lake rushed over to calm her before she broke anything else. Buck either didn't notice or didn't care about the hole in his wall.

He seemed like a lost cause. So we reluctantly left and headed back to the Underground, dejected and downtrodden.

Even for Dwarves.

CHAPTER 20

My First Dwarven Weapon

B ack in the Underground, Eagan, Lake, and Glam went to find Eagan's dad to tell him about Buck.

Which left Ari and me standing there uncertainly in the dark tunnels.

"Want to go hang out in the Arena?" Ari asked, when it was obvious I was just going to stand there in silence like an idiot.

"Um, sure," I said.

This was the first time a girl had ever asked me to do anything that wasn't *Please get out of my way* or *Leave us alone, Fatmont*. I would have been more nervous if Ari wasn't so easy to be around. But even as it was, my palms started getting clammy as we walked through the halls.

The Arena was nearly deserted since most other Dwarven kids were with their competent instructors, actually training. But there were still a few other kids scattered around the cavern, making potions or playing games.

We stood at the entrance and looked at each other awkwardly. To be honest, I wasn't sure what "hanging out" with a girl actually entailed since I'd never done it before.

"Do you play chess?" I asked.

"Um, no, but I've always wanted to learn," Ari said.

"Oh," I said. "Okay."

Looking back, I should have seen this for what it was: an invitation for me to offer to teach her. But I completely missed it and just kept staring at a kid brewing some sort of potion in the alchemy alcove.

"Um, well, want to see me make something?" Ari asked, nodding toward the blacksmith station.

"Yeah, of course!" I said. "I'd love to watch you . . . uh, make something, I mean. You know, only if you want to?"

I tried not to grimace as I totally lost whatever cool points I'd managed to amass in her head. But Ari only laughed, and not in a mean way.

"I wouldn't have asked if I didn't want to!" she said. "Come on."

I followed her over to the part of the cavern containing vats of molten metals, anvils, racks of tools, thick aprons, and several red-hot kilns among other equipment.

"I'm not quite as good as my brother, though," she said. "I spend too much time at shows, probably."

"Shows?"

"Yeah, you know, like music shows?" she said.

"Like a traditional Dwarven folk festival or something?"

Ari laughed as she strapped on a thick blacksmith apron.

"No, like a rock concert!" she said. "A band with guitars and drums on a stage in a club?"

"Oh, yeah, sorry," I said, blushing. "How did you end up liking modern music so much?"

"Just because I'm a Dwarf doesn't mean I've lived in a cave my whole life," she said.

"Umm, well . . ."

She froze, startled, and then laughed that loud, charming laugh of hers.

"Okay, bad expression," Ari said. "Anyway, I really do appreciate being a Dwarf, but it doesn't mean I have to hate *everything* about the modern Commoner world. In fact, in a lot of ways, it's probably the reason I've grown to love modern music so much. It's so different and interesting compared to what I was raised with down here. It feels exotic to me. Sort of like you."

"Me?"

"Yeah, you're really the first Commoner-raised kid I've ever been friends with," she said.

Hearing her call me her friend made my palms get clammy again. I guess I was already starting to consider her and the others my friends, but just sort of figured they viewed me as *that new kid with the missing dad who we should just be nice to.*

"Oh, uh, am I making a good impression?" I asked. "Am I representing Commoner kids well?"

Ari laughed again. I wished I were funny enough to just assault her with jokes so she wouldn't ever stop laughing.

"You're all right," she said with a grin, as she began working.

"Well, I've never been to a musical concert before," I said. "Don't the other Dwarves, like, not approve of that stuff?"

"Do you *only* do the things that your dad approves?" she challenged me, having to shout over the noises of steam and fire.

"Well, mostly . . ." I said.

I didn't add that I'd drunk some tea against my dad's wishes, which was what got me into this mess in the first place.

"You do?" She seemed surprised. "Well, maybe I'm too rebellious, but I sneak out of here to go to shows all the time. We can go together sometime. You know, before the modern world comes to an end and everything."

"Yeah, uh, that sounds nice," I said.

She smiled and I felt my face turn red in the heat from the nearby vats of molten metals.

Before the modern world comes to an end . . .

Ari seemed so at ease with it. And I supposed it made sense; she'd known since birth that the world wasn't what it seemed to Humans and kids like me.

I watched her in silence for a while. It was a marvel how she moved around the workshop with ease, fluid and graceful. Outside the workshop, I'd noticed she was a little clumsy, like she thought about every step before she moved. But here she was a totally different person. Every motion was automatic and intricately efficient. It wasn't long before she was hammering something glowing and hot. She struck and struck again rapidly, never seeming to get tired, and never missing. Eventually she moved the object over to a vat of water and plunged it in.

Steam flared up with a *hiss*, shrouding her behind a hazy cloud. When it faded, Ari held up a smooth, exquisitely curved dagger blade with a pair of iron tongs. I saw my distorted reflection in the surface.

"It needs to cool and then I'll polish and sharpen it," she said. "There's a lot more work left, but you'll eventually have yourself a pretty nice dagger."

"*Me?*" I said.

"Of course," Ari said. "I already have like twenty. All Dwarves need a dagger. It's like a right of passage. You know, like Commoner kids getting their first bike. I assume you don't have one yet?"

"A bike?"

"No, a dagger!" she said, laughing.

"No," I admitted. "That's really cool . . . I mean, thank you!"

"Sure," Ari said, like it was no big deal.

She grinned and then looked away briefly. For a second we both just sat there and looked at the stone floor of the cave. Then she began cleaning up her tools, filling the silence with clanking.

"Do Elves get, like, daggers as kids, too?" I asked, wondering how many cool weapons Edwin might have stashed in his huge room.

"I have no idea," Ari said. "They're pretty secretive. What's it like to actually be friends with an Elf?"

"Well," I said, pausing to think it over carefully. "I guess I don't really know. I mean, I didn't even know he was an Elf until a few days ago. But he's a great friend. I can't even imagine what the last three years would have been like without him."

Of all my new Dwarven friends, Ari was the one I expected to understand. Which was why it was shocking to see a skeptical look on her face.

"Really?"

"Yeah, really," I said. "He risked his life to save mine, you know. Saved me from a polar bear."

"Well, everyone knows Elves can control animals," she said. "Just like they can influence weak-willed Humans. So he wasn't really *risking* anything . . ."

At least now I knew how he had managed to get the bear to stand down just by staring. But even still, he'd stuck his neck out for me countless other times over the years, not that I would be able get her to understand just how close he and I were. The kind of friendship Edwin and I had was hard to put into words.

"I thought you wanted to work with the Elves to help the Humans?" I said, getting defensive. "To have lasting peace?"

"Well, just because I don't want any more conflict, and think working together will help avoid that, it doesn't mean I actually *like* Elves!" Ari said. "Or would ever completely trust one . . ."

We stood there and stared at each other. Suddenly the hot blacksmith workshop felt as icy as the Antarctic tundra. The bad blood between the two races clearly ran deeper than anything I could comprehend.

"Why, exactly, does everyone dislike Elves so much?" I finally asked. "None of you even *know* any Elves. What have they ever done to you? I mean *you*, specifically. I just don't get it, you all mistrust a whole group just because you've been *told* to."

Ari slowly shook her head and then actually scoffed, which seemed unnatural for her.

"You just don't understand the things they've done, Greg," she said.

"Well, then help me," I said. "Explain it."

"There's not even enough time to begin—"

"Sure there is," I insisted. "You have to start sometime or else I'll never truly get it, right?"

Ari nodded reluctantly, took off her apron, and hung it next to the rack of tools. She motioned for me to follow her. We went to another alcove near the back of the cavern. It was a cramped library filled with hundreds, maybe even thousands, of old books.

"These are newer editions of some Dwarven texts that survived the fall of Separate Earth," she said. "We're still looking for many of the originals, but even what has been lost in translation can't hide the injustices and cruelties the Elves have committed. There are more examples in this library than you can even imagine. Plus, there's countless more stories that have been passed down through the generations."

"Tell me some of them," I said.

And so she did.

What I heard that afternoon changed the way I considered the entire situation going forward. And it convinced me that the Council's suspicions might be right: The Elves very well could have been responsible for the Egohs attack. Based on the horrific stories Ari told me, it wouldn't even come close to the worst of the acts they'd committed.

CHAPTER 21

Being a Dwarf Is Not a Valid Excuse for Losing at Chess

D unmor and Fynric had forbidden me from seeing Edwin.

Which was why I had to sneak out of the Underground to meet up with him later that night. Though it had only been two days since I'd last spoken to him, it felt like a lifetime.

"I was told to never talk to you again," I said as Edwin sat down across from me. "And definitely not to trust you."

His smile faded as he settled into the couch in the corner of a small coffee shop.

"They still dislike us that much?" he asked.

"Yeah," I said. "They refused to believe that any Elf can be trusted. They definitely don't want your help investigating the attack."

Edwin nodded as if he'd suspected this would be the outcome. Then he frowned and sighed deeply.

"The Elven Magistrate told me the same thing," he said. "I'm defying a direct order from the Elf Lord, *my dad*, by being here with you right now. Which is something normally punished by death. Or at least back in the day. Now I think you just have to pay a fine or something . . ."

"So we've been banned from seeing or trusting each other," I said.

Edwin nodded, still frowning. He took a sip of his latte. It might seem weird for a thirteen-year-old to drink lattes like water, but not for kids at the PEE. I personally hated coffee, but that probably had more to do with being raised on my dad's teas.

"The good news," Edwin said slowly, carefully, "is that you won't need the Elves' help investigating the attack."

"What do you mean?" I asked, my stomach on fire.

"Well . . . I mean, before you freak out, please listen to the whole story . . ."

"Just tell me, Edwin," I said.

"It *was* the Elves," he said, barely able to get the words out. "We . . . or *they* took your dad."

His eyes were red and he bit his cheek. It was clear finding this out had hurt him almost as much as he was sure it would hurt me. Which was why I hesitated before yelling at Edwin, intending to call him names that'd make a pirate blush. But even beyond the anger boiling so furiously that I could feel my own pulse in my right eyeball was the blooming sense of betrayal in my gut. Like someone was setting off firecrackers in my belly.

But he cut me off before I started.

"It wasn't me or my parents though!" he said. "It was not an Elven-sanctioned action. It was a rogue Elven group who call themselves Verumque Genus. They're a faction of Elves who have been rebelling against the official, organized Elven establishment for decades. They've long believed that we've gotten too soft in regards to Dwarves and other remnants of Separate Earth, including Humans. *They* were responsible—not us."

"How do you know it was them?" I asked, my hands still shaking with fury.

"Because we've caught one of them, apparently," Edwin said. "And he confessed."

"Then how have you not found my dad yet?" I demanded. "Why would he not tell you where he is?"

"Look," Edwin said wearily. "I wish I knew. I'm trying as hard as I can to find out more, but it's not like my parents have time to debrief me every day. I'm as frantic as you are over this—especially now that I know Elves were probably involved. Even if they're not friends of ours."

I could see in his eyes that this was true. Not because they were a window to his soul or something cheesy like that, but more so because they were red and raw, surrounded by dark, puffy eyelids. It looked like Edwin hadn't slept properly in days.

"Okay," I said, nodding.

"Supposedly he's claiming he doesn't know where your dad is, otherwise he'd tell us," Edwin said. "He claims it wasn't supposed to go down like that. They sent the Troll with one of their spies as a precaution, since Elves don't exactly trust Dwarves either. They were merely trying to *investigate* your use of magic and your father's discovery. But then something angered the Troll and he transformed and . . . well, things got out of control."

Something had made the Troll mad. And I knew now that the something was *me*. I had insulted the Troll—even after being warned not to. *I* made him transform. Which only supported this version of the events.

But this new layer of guilt didn't completely wash away my frustration.

"There's got to be a way to find out where he is, now that we know who was responsible," I said.

"It's not so easy," Edwin said. "My parents have been trying to shut down the Verumque Genus for decades. But they're good at hiding their operations. If we knew where they were, they wouldn't exist anymore."

"Well, at least I finally know that *some* Elves really are just like the Dwarves say."

"What do you mean?" Edwin asked. "What have they told you about us?"

"I've just heard some stories," I said.

"What kind of stories?"

"Oh, you know, stuff like how almost all the terrible people throughout history, including most dictators, were Elves."

"That's not true," Edwin said. "There are an equal number of bad Dwarves, historically. Lee Harvey Oswald for one."

"He was probably framed by Elves," I said. "An *Elf* was the *second gunman*!"

"Oh come on!" Edwin said. "Get out of here with that conspiracy stuff. Besides, individual examples are meaningless. There were and are all sorts of good and bad Elves and Dwarves. But you're missing the point again, Greg. Elves and Dwarves are just as flawed as Humans, individually. Some are good, some are bad. And we all make mistakes. Pointing out who is who accomplishes nothing. It's kind of ignorant and racist. I mean, Miley Cyrus is a Dwarf and Justin Bieber is an Elf. What does that really tell us about anything?"

He made a good point. We could go back and forth all day, and small examples didn't mean much since everyone, Elf,

Dwarf, or Human, is an individual and not part of, like, an insect colony or something with a hive mentality.

"Okay, so maybe modern celebrities and historical figures are meaningless," I admitted. "But what about Separate Earth? What would you have to say about an Elf called Vulmer Chaemaris?"

Edwin froze mid-drink and then slowly put his coffee cup back down. He raised his eyebrows and then smirked.

"You've been doing some research," he said.

"Yeah, and how can you explain what he did?"

"I can't, but trust me, Greg, you don't want to go down this road," Edwin said.

"No? So should I not bring up Elyon Liaris and her brutal reign of terror in Ven Faldhir?" I said, remembering just a few of the horrible stories Ari had told me earlier that day. "They were kids, Edwin. All of them, just innocent Dwarven kids. It'd be bad enough if they were adults . . . but *kids?*"

Edwin kept shaking his head. He seemed sorry, not for what his ancestors had done to mine, but for something else entirely. And I was clearly about to find out what.

"You've only heard one side, Greg," Edwin said. "Separate Earth was a different time. The world back then was . . . brutal, less sophisticated in general. *Everyone* committed atrocities. I'm sure your Dwarven friends have conveniently left out the fact that Dwarves used to make their traditional wine from the blood of innocent Woodsprites? Or how they used to torture animals for sport? Yeah, there was an actual Dwarven game that was simply who could torture an animal the best. It was called BloodCost. The winner was determined based on how long they were able to keep the animal alive to suffer. Didn't hear about that, did you?"

I shook my head, unable to look him in his piercing blue eyes any longer. I desperately wanted to assume he was lying, but I knew that wasn't the case.

"I told you not to go down this road, Greg," Edwin said. "There's also the tale of Jog Coinfoot and Huk Forgebender, two Dwarven entrepreneurs, one a merchant and the other a blacksmith. Did you read about them? What they did?"

I shook my head again. "Forget it, I don't want to know," I said.

"Too late, Greg," Edwin said. "You need to know the context of our past. Jog and Huk were two scheming Dwarves, always on the hunt for rich Humans to dupe. They once made and sold—at an exorbitant price—two matching goblets of the finest craftsmanship to a greedy Human family of royalty. But they didn't tell the unsuspecting king and queen that they'd constructed the goblets using the skulls of their two sons, the princes. And so the royal parents unwittingly drank mead and wine from the hollowed-out brainpans of their deceased children—killed by Jog and Huk! They did this just for fun! As a joke!"

I sat there unable to say anything. It was too awful to wrap my head around.

"So I know you have more stories for me about Elves," Edwin continued. "But save them. Separate Earth was an awful place, full of violence. But our past doesn't make us who we are; we make ourselves who we are in the present. I *know* you're a good Dwarf, Greg, just like you *know* I'm a good Elf. Right?"

I looked up and nodded.

"Which is why we can't let this progress any further," he said. "Enough ugliness will come back on its own with the return of magic. We don't need to add another Elf-Dwarf war to the mix. We can get along; you and I are *proof* of that. We can foster a lasting peace. It's why we're doing everything we can to help you find out what happened to your dad—even beyond me caring because I'm your friend and I love your dad like an uncle. That's why *I'm* helping, but my parents are helping because they want to avoid more war at all costs. We're not the monsters Dwarves say we are."

I nodded slowly. He was right. Without the Elves, I'd still have no leads at all. And if Edwin was right about this rogue group's involvement, then his parents were truly the only ones who could help me find my dad. I doubted Dwarves even knew there was any infighting among various Elven groups at all, let alone knew how to find one.

"Try to check your email when you can," Edwin said. "I'll be in touch soon—hopefully with more news."

"Okay, I will," I said. Of course there was technically no email in the Underground (though some Dwarves had contraband cell phones), but there was free Internet at libraries all over the city.

Edwin sat there and looked at his empty coffee cup for a moment. Then he grinned and looked up.

"The Rock," he said.

"What?"

"Dwayne 'The Rock' Johnson," he repeated. "He's shockingly a Dwarf. Funny, right?"

I grinned in spite of how terrible I felt. Such was Edwin's way—he could get a dying man to laugh if he needed to.

"And check this, Kanye West—"

"Let me guess," I said. "Elf?"

"No, *Human*," Edwin said.

I laughed.

"Also, by the way," Edwin added as he stood up. "*Checkmate.*"

The finality in the word made me nervous. What had he meant by that? Had he just pulled some trick on me and I hadn't even been aware? Were Elven spies rushing in right now to apprehend me?

"Why do you look so startled?" he asked. "You knew this was coming."

"What—what do you mean?" I finally asked.

"In the game, dude," he said. "Checkmate. Your last move was abysmal. But I'll give you a pass since you're clearly distracted. Maybe the next one, right?"

"Yeah, next time I'll try not to be such a *pawn*."

Edwin smirked at my horrible pun before leaving.

He'd only been referring to our chess game. I should have felt relieved, but for some reason I was suddenly more anxious than ever. Might the other Dwarves actually be getting to me? Maybe I *didn't* completely trust my best friend anymore?

The thought made me sick—because if it were actually ever true, then my dad would probably be lost forever. But I *did* still trust him—I knew this because I'd already decided not to tell the Dwarves what I'd learned (that a rogue, radicalized group of Elves were behind the attack). At least, not yet. They already seemed on the brink of conflict with the Elves, and if I confirmed this suspicion (even if it wasn't the official Elven leadership responsible), then surely a new war would be inevitable.

Instead, I would just have to trust that Edwin and I could solve this on our own somehow.

CHAPTER 22

The Most Powerful Relic of the Ancient World Makes a Fantastic Back Scratcher

Y ou'll get no new assignment," Dunmor stated flatly.

Because his father ran the Board of Dwarven Education, Eagan had been able to get us a meeting the next morning with Dunmor and Borazz Redmantle—the educational director of the BODE.

"Thufir Stonequarry—er, *Buck*, is the best mentor we have, you must trust me on that," Borazz insisted over our groans of despair. "Just keep at it, he'll give in eventually . . . he always does."

"What do you mean *always*?" Eagan asked. "I thought this was the first time you've trained Dwarven kids in the ancient ways of combat."

Borazz looked to Dunmor for guidance with his answer. Dunmor considered his words carefully before speaking.

"It's the first time we've trained on this scale," he said. "But every decade or so, going back thousands of years, each regional

Dwarven sect selects a handful of candidates for training. They become a sort of Dwarven National Guard: warriors ready for battle in the case of an unforeseen catastrophe. We call them the Sentry. But anyway, this is how we know Buck's skill as a trainer. We're technically not allowed to tell you this since instructor assignment is supposed to be random, but he's the *best* trainer we have. You must stick with him. It will be worth it in the end. Now off with you."

And so we were stuck with Buck and he was stuck with us.

Later that morning, we once again found Buck on his couch playing video games—as if he hadn't moved from that spot the whole time.

The room was stuffy, partially from the wheezing, overheated video game system that perhaps never got switched off. If it could talk like a magical ax, I could only imagine it'd be begging me to put it out of its misery.

"Why are you back?" Buck said without looking up. "I thought I told you it would be pointless to train."

"Well, the BODE disagrees with you," Eagan said. "They *made* us come back. Frankly, we'd asked for a new instructor."

"And they were fools not to grant your request," Buck said before taking a swig from a can of Dr Pepper, still not peeling his eyes away from the screen.

He tossed the empty over his shoulder, reached around the side of the couch, and grabbed something leaning against it on the far side. It was a huge battle-ax with a shining black double-edged blade. The handle was inlaid with intricate carvings. It was the Bloodletter. The same ax my dad had used to save my life during the Troll attack.

And it called to me now, the same way it had several times before.

Greg.

Nice to see you again.

Please save me from this man.

I want to go destroy things.

I tried to ignore the strange voice in my head while we watched in horror as Buck used the ax to scratch his hairy back. Then he tossed it aside like a hunk of garbage rather than an ancient relic with supposedly unrivaled powers. It crashed onto the floor with an impressive THUNKAGONG.

"They gave the Bloodletter to *you*?" Eagan asked in a dismayed whisper.

If anything, that fact alone easily supported what Dunmor and Borazz had said about Buck being the best.

"The *what*?" Buck said, glancing at the ax. "Oh, that thing? Yeah, someone brought it over and said some nonsense about it being an important something or other in a prophecy or whatnot. I don't know anything about that, but it certainly makes a good back scratcher."

Eagan and Lake shuddered in disgust. Glam punched another hole in the wall, right next to the one from the day before. Buck looked at her and grinned.

"Let me tell you, girl," he said. "You should save your strength. Don't waste your abilities on walls; you only get so much energy in this life. Consider that some free parting advice."

"Wow, you're negative even for a Dwarf," Eagan said.

"A smart man once said: *The cleverest one of all is he who calls himself a fool at least once a month*," Buck said. "So if I do it once a day, what does that make me?"

He followed this with a chuckle and then found another Dr

Pepper that was stuffed into his couch somewhere. He cracked it open and chugged the whole thing in one massive swig, then let loose an imposing belch and tossed the can aside.

It clanked off the Bloodletter and rolled under the couch.

Do you see this madness?

Save me.

I made myself pretend that an ax was not telepathically speaking to me. I swallowed any reply and instead focused on Buck. My father was still missing, and this was a waste of time.

"What happened to make you like this?" Ari asked him. "You can't have always been such a curmudgeonly old gwint."

Everyone in the room (except Buck) gasped in shock. I only did because *gwint* was a word Edwin had made up for me in the moments I was being too negative. How had Ari known about it? And, for that matter, why had it upset everyone else so much?

"Don't use that word, Ari!" Eagan said.

"So uncivilized," Glam said disapprovingly.

"Father hast failed thee ye holy pursuits lest thee speaketh such atrocities," Lake said.

"I don't get it," I said. "What's a gwint?"

Everyone shuddered again.

"It's derogatory slang for *Dwarf*," Eagan said. "It's what Elves have always called us. Think, like, the worst word in the English language you could call someone. It's like ten times worse than that, it's so offensive."

"A *hundred* times," Glam said sternly, glaring at Ari.

I couldn't believe it. All this time Edwin had been calling me a racist slur for *Dwarf*. And he'd always done it so casually. Once again I found myself rethinking just how much I really knew about Edwin and Elves. If they were really so good at manipulating other beings, then it was entirely possible he'd completely hoodwinked me. It's not like I had a bunch of other past friendships to compare ours against.

"*Nothing* happened to me," Buck said. "I've always been this way. And I've never claimed to be any good at anything, or of any use to anybody. Now, if you'll excuse me, I have an online gaming appointment to keep with some kid in Omaha with the handle Booger Goblin."

He gestured at the screen. The kid's username was spelled thusly: BooG3RGoBLiN.

"We're not going anywhere until you start our training," Glam said, stepping in front of the TV.

"Well, then, you'd better get comfortable," Buck said.

Glam didn't move as Buck struggled to see around her thick frame. He sighed, but he didn't give in. Instead, he just kept playing as if he could see right through a Dwarven teen the size of an NFL linebacker.

Ask about the photo.

The Bloodletter was speaking to me in my head again. I looked around until I saw a photo of a woman and a young boy hanging on the wall.

"Is that your wife in the photo?" I asked.

"What is it with you and your nosy questions, kid?" Buck said, jabbing a meaty finger in my direction. "*To love is to suffer and there can be no love otherwise.*"

Ugh, I'm so tired of him quoting Dostoyevsky. It's insufferable. Sometimes he does it even when no one else is here.

I ignored the Bloodletter, mostly because I had no idea what it was talking about.

"So you loved her . . . *Them?*" I asked Buck.

"Of course I did, you hairless nitwit!" Buck said, finally turning away from his game so he could glare at me. "I wouldn't be suffering otherwise . . . *Don't you listen?*"

"What happened, did they die?" I asked.

Ari nudged me, likely thinking I was being too intrusive. But I ignored her and didn't look away from Buck. He grimaced and shook his head.

"No, but it almost would have been better if they had," he said. "She left me and took my son with her! He was just six years old—likely doesn't even remember me. Good-for-nothing Elves . . ."

"Elves?" Eagan asked.

"Yeah, Elves!" Buck yelled at him. "Can't you hear, you lanky inchworm?"

"What did Elves have to do with her leaving?" Ari asked, apparently on board with my plan now.

"Well, *everything!*" Buck said. "She was an Elf, after all."

The five of us stared at him in shock. Buck had been married to, and had a kid with an Elf? Personally, this wouldn't have been at all unusual or shocking to me if it weren't for my knowing how all the other Elves and Dwarves viewed each other.

"Yeah, she was a no-good, lying Elf," Buck continued. "She met another Elf, a rich and famous video game designer. He made some game about the Wild West that made a ton of money. She fell in love with the lousy Pointer jick and ran off with him and took my son. She enrolled him at some hoity-toity Elf school and I haven't seen him in almost ten years. I send letters, but I doubt he's gotten any of them. If I can just figure out how these games work, I can design my own someday . . . get them both back, maybe."

My eyes widened as a shocking revelation hit me like an old 1880s steam-powered freight train.

"I can get you your son back," I said.

Everyone in the room stared at me in shock.

"*How?*" Buck asked.

"Hard to explain," I said. "But if I can get you a meeting with your son, will you actually *train us* for real?"

"Greg, *what* are you doing?" Ari asked me desperately.

"Trust me," I told her.

"A meeting . . ." Buck said, actually sounding hopeful. "With my son?"

I nodded. I wasn't sure I could actually do it, but I had to try. Otherwise I'd never get the training I needed to get my dad back. Assuming he was being held captive in some hidden fortress meant I couldn't just stroll in without a clue how to fight Elves—especially since I already knew they had at least one Troll on their side. I needed this training more than all the other Dwarves realized.

"That's all I need," Buck said. "I just want him to know I didn't abandon him, and still love him. I don't care what he does after our meeting, but he needs to know how much I'm trying, how much I still care . . ."

"He will," I said.

No! Please don't leave me here with this guy! He eats his toenails! I can't watch that anymore.

I tried to shrug off the Bloodletter's pleas. Because what else could I do at this point?

"So we have a deal?" Eagan asked.

Buck looked at me, searching my eyes for something. I didn't know what he found there, but whatever it was apparently satisfied him.

"We have a deal," he said. "Get me a meeting with my son, and I will train you properly. Do you need his name?"

"No," I said. "I already know him."

CHAPTER 23

Glam Threatens to Smash My Pretty Face

W hat in the world was that?" Ari asked as we headed toward the bus stop down the street from Buck's apartment.

"Yeah, I certainly hope you know what you're doing, Greg," Eagan said.

"How hath thyne acquired ye knowledge of Buck's first-borne?" Lake asked.

"I went to school with him," I said. "At least I think I did."

"You *think* you did . . . ?" Ari asked.

I stopped and nodded.

"Well, yeah, I'm pretty sure," I said. "There was this kid at my old school whose backstory fits that one perfectly. I mean, what are the odds it's a coincidence?"

"Probably fairly high, Greg!" Eagan said. "This is a city of almost three million people—*ten* if you count the burbs!"

"If you're wrong, I will smash your pretty face," Glam threatened. "Okay, maybe not your face, it'd be too much of a shame. But definitely your arms and legs."

I took a step back, holding up my hands.

"At least give me a chance," I said. "We have to try *something*."

Lake and Ari nodded.

"Okay," Eagan agreed. "It's probably the best shot we've got to actually start training."

"So where does this kid live?" Ari asked.

"Well, um, I'm not really sure," I admitted. "But I know where to find him."

"Great, let's get going!" Eagan said. "Where is he?"

"The Isaacson Preparatory Empowerment Establishment," I said.

They all gave a collective sigh of exasperated defeat.

"You mean the biggest *Elf school* in the whole city?" Ari asked.

"Well, uh, yeah," I said. "But I have a plan. We have something they don't. Something that can help us get in and out and avoid any real danger."

"And what's that?" Eagan asked.

"How possible do you think it would be to steal some Galdervatn from the Grand Hall of Dwarven Artifacts?" I asked them.

One by one, their skepticism turned into mischievous grins.

The way home, on an empty bus, they chatted excitedly about seeing the Bloodletter in person at Buck's place:

"I can't believe these eyes actually saw the Bloodletter . . . it was like right there in front of me!"

"Just to be in its presence was incredible . . ."

"Lest be thy hand doth taketh holdeth of ye sacred handle for but ye rarest fleeting moment!"

"I'd smash stuff with it. Smash everything!"

"I can't believe they gave it to Buck! Is Dunmor insane?"

"He was using it as a back scratcher!"

"Does he even know what it is?"

"Clearly not . . ."

"Guys, wait a second!" I said loudly enough to drown out their excited chattering. "You want to fill me in on why this ax is so special?"

One by one, they looked at Eagan. He grinned and took a moment to clear his throat. Then he began the story:

"While there are many tales of uniquely powerful Dwarven weapons, none is perhaps more unsettling and important than the Bloodletter," Eagan said smoothly, with the same voice as that guy who does all the voiceovers for movie trailers. "It is a weapon that has brought every owner great power and then, eventually, even greater misery. It was forged for a mortal noble-man shortly before the fall of Separate Earth. He commissioned a young Dwarven smith named Lorcan Bunbrass for the creation of an ax that would strike fear into the hearts of his greatest enemies with a merciless edge and devastating presence. Lorcan created the ax with great care and fervor, spurned by greed for the nobleman's wealth. As a down payment, he'd received a diamond-encrusted key worth easily a small fortune in itself—and upon delivery of the ax, he'd be given the treasure chest that it opened along with all the riches within.

"The Bloodletter was a marvel of Dwarven skill. Its edge was blacker than an empty soul and sharper than anything made before or since. It also carried a powerful will of its own—a desire to draw the blood of its owner's enemies. Even the finest Dwarven blacksmiths are not able to control the powers their weapons possess. And so it was that the Bloodletter established

its own unique ability. The ax grants its chosen owner fulfillment of their ultimate personal vengeance. But with such bloody
vengeance comes only temporary respite, and then eventually
great suffering.

"Lorcan Bunbrass, upon delivering the ax to the Human
nobleman, anxiously awaited the rest of his promised payment.
The nobleman had the treasure chest, indeed large and itself
made of gold, platinum, and an array of precious gemstones,
set at Lorcan's feet. As the greedy Dwarf bent over to open it,
the nobleman struck him down with the Bloodletter's wicked,
fired-black blade. He then returned the treasure chest and key
to his own vault.

"The nobleman carried the Bloodletter for many years. It
aided him in restoring justice against all who wronged him.
But, as was foretold, the ax eventually brought great tragedy to
its first owner. After having taken his revenge on many enemies
over the years, the nobleman was increasingly wary against possible retribution from the family members of the Bloodletter's
many victims. And so he slept with the ax always by his bedside,
ready to be taken up in self-defense.

"One night, after having gotten drunk on the newest ship-
ment of wine from his vineyards, he passed out in his bed
without remembering to lock the chamber door. His young
daughter entered his room to wake her father and inform
him of a visitor at the front door of the castle. The nobleman,
paranoid, sleepy, and still drunk, groggily mistook her for an
intruder and hastily killed her with the Bloodletter before he
realized what was happening. In anguish, he stumbled down-
stairs and took his own life. The Bloodletter rested at the feet
of his corpse.

"His visitor that night, ironically enough, was indeed family of one of the nobleman's many enemies: Kynwyl Brunlead, cousin to the very Dwarf who had created the Bloodletter and was then murdered by the nobleman. He stumbled onto the nobleman's dead body, a bit disappointed that revenge was not achieved by his own hand, but nonetheless pleased that the man who'd slain his cousin was now dead himself. Kynwyl took the ax and it was passed down among various Dwarves within the same family, clan, and village for generations.

"As far as we know, the Bloodletter continued to have a powerful yet dark presence over all of its owners, granting them great victories and then eventually greater tragedy. Long ago, however, before the fall of Separate Earth, it vanished from recorded history and has been missing for thousands of years. It was written in the recovered texts of the *Dwarven Armament Histories, Volume II* that the Bloodletter would one day select a new owner, a Dwarf that would rise up and restore our great race to their rightful glory— to achieve ultimate vengeance for all Dwarves."

Eagan finished his story looking exhilarated.

"Wow," I said, and I meant it.

"Yeah, and now it's been given to Buck," Ari said drily.

This set them off again—excitedly discussing the possibilities and horrors of what the ax meant. Eventually that turned into even more breathless chatter about actually getting to try Galdervatn tomorrow when we attempted to infiltrate an Elf school. When I told them, before we got on the bus, that I'd actually tried Galdervatn and had performed magic they all went deathly still for nearly thirty seconds before exploding like a bomb. I'd let them grill me about what it was like while we waited at our stop. I tried my best to answer their questions, but they seemed mostly disappointed by what I described. I'd finally gotten them to settle down by reminding them that they'd all find out themselves what it was like soon enough.

But I barely listened to them chattering about Galdervatn this time. Instead, I couldn't stop thinking about a certain part of Eagan's story:

The ax grants its chosen owner fulfillment of their ultimate personal vengeance.

This was my answer! The Bloodletter could help me get my dad back. I was so overjoyed I had to concentrate to keep from smiling like a lunatic on the mostly empty city bus. The ax had already spoken to me, after all, a sure sign that it must have *some* powers. I now had an actual part of a plan to save my dad. I would break into the PEE, talk to Buck's son, and help him get Buck to train us. Then I'd go along with training just long enough to learn how to use the ax and get my hands on it.

Upon whence I would take the Bloodletter and use its powers to save my dad.

CHAPTER 24

— ❖ —

It's Proven That Nobody Wants the Death of a Turtle on Their Conscience

"Are you okay, Greg?" Ari asked as we sat on the Red Line train en route to the PEE. "You look a little *Orc-ish*."

It was a Dwarven saying that essentially meant I looked like I was about to barf. They'd been trying to teach me all the well-known Dwarfisms I'd missed out on living as a Commoner.

And I *was* nervous—so nervous I'd only eaten half of my lunch: four ham sandwiches (light on the bread . . . okay, actually no bread at all, it was really just four small piles of ham), along with a plate of beef jerky, four hard-boiled eggs, mustard, French fries, and a strawberry.

"I'm fine," I said. "Just a little anxious . . ."

"I thought you said this would be easy," Eagan said.

"It should be," I said. "You know, I just haven't seen any of these kids since I found out they were Elves and everything."

This seemed to satisfy them and they went back to their conversation about whether Wraiths would return once Galdervatn came back and the New Magical Age officially began. Eagan had read in one of the recovered scrolls of Azac Duskgranite's *War Logs* that scores of different magical creatures and races had either disappeared or gone into hiding at the fall of Separate Earth.

After stepping off the train, we huddled in an alley around the corner from the PEE. Eagan pulled out the small vial of Galdervatn.

Stealing it had been shockingly easy.

We'd made some Snabbsomn smoke bombs using something called Snabbsomn Potion, naturally, which Ari's friend Alfy Silverbrew had traded her in exchange for a sword and a few other items she'd smithed last summer. Then we'd tossed a few smoke bombs into the Grand Hall of Dwarven Artifacts and let the purple gas do its thing. We'd stepped around the guards' unconscious bodies, broken into the Galdervatn case using Ari and Lake's superior metallurgy prowess, taken a vial of Galdervatn, and replaced it with a vial of something called Ragnbage Myst—which looked remarkably similar.

The guards wouldn't even realize anything had been taken. We figured they'd be too embarrassed, upon waking, to report the incident at all. And, as of that morning, no incidents had been reported.

We looked at the vial of swirling Galdervatn with wonder. The fog inside twisted and changed colors like a living rainbow.

"So . . . we just drink it?" Eagan asked.

"How much?" Ari asked.

"I really don't know," I said, shaking my head. "Maybe we should each just drink a drop or two until it's gone? And then, uh, you know, the magic will just sort of happen if you need it to. And if you have the Ability . . . I—I guess."

Eagan looked at each of us, still holding the small vial in

his shaking hand. Lake gave him an excited nod. Ari seemed a bit more apprehensive. Glam scowled and took the vial from Eagan's hands. She promptly drank nearly half of it.

"Glam, don't drink it all!" Ari said, reaching for the vial.

"It's not like you'll have the Ability anyway," Glam said.

Ari rolled her eyes and then took a tiny sip before passing it to Lake. He grinned, his eyes nearly glowing with excitement. He took a tiny drink and passed it to Eagan.

"Maybe one of us should hold off," Eagan suggested, looking at the Galdervatn uncertainly. "You know, just in case. So one of us will have, like, a clear head?"

"I already told you it's a really subtle feeling," I said. "It's not like you'll—"

I stopped myself, suddenly remembering that it was the Galdervatn that had likely nudged me into picking a fight with Perry, thus exposing my dad's discovery to the Elves, thus prompting the rogue faction to go to our store, thus prompting me to piss off a Troll, thus leading to my dad's still unresolved abduction.

"Maybe you have a point," I said, taking the vial from him.

Eagan seemed disappointed for a mere moment, but then nodded, clearly relieved.

I finished the last few drops of Galdervatn. The swirling, foggy "liquid" was so light it felt like I was drinking vapor. It was mostly flavorless, but sent a cold sensation shooting down my esophagus—like I'd just guzzled tiny ice particles. The feeling passed quickly.

"That's it?" Glam asked, seeming disappointed.

"Well, like I said, it's more subtle . . . and gradual. Plus, you might not even have—"

I stopped when I saw her eyes turn into sledgehammers that

threatened to bash in my head. I wasn't sure if I should hope (for our sakes) that Glam ended up having the Ability, or if I should hope (for the sake of the rest of the world) that she didn't.

"Okay, well, let's go," I said.

We walked straight into the school through the front door. I'd timed our arrival to correspond with the end of fifth period—when all the kids would still be in class. But also right before lunch, the one time when I'd know exactly where to find Buck's son.

———✠———

Mrs. Enlen, the school attendance secretary, greeted us with a frown.

"What are you doing here, Greg?" she asked coldly.

"What do you mean?" I asked. "I go to school here."

"No, you've been expelled, Greg," Mrs. Enlen said smugly. "Your locker will be emptied and the contents mailed to you in two to six weeks."

"Oh, well, um, that's the thing," I said, trying to hide my shock at my sudden expulsion. Was it because of the incident in the stairwell or simply because I was a Dwarf? "One of the things I left in my locker was alive and needs to get fed! It doesn't have two weeks to live. Do you really want to be responsible for the loss of a life, Mrs. Enlen?"

"Alive!" She gasped with full notes of disapproval. "Good heavens, Greg!"

"I know," I admitted. "But anyway, can't I just go grab my stuff really quick and then we can avoid the school killing a little kid's pet turtle? Plus there'd be the dead animal smell and all of that . . ."

She scowled at me.

"Who are these . . . *kids* with you?"

"Just some cousins to help me carry stuff," I said. "I left a *lot* here."

"You all need to sign the visitor list." She tapped a pen onto a clipboard.

"Thank you so much, Mrs. Enlen," I said, writing my name and the time on the sheet. "Sorry for all the trouble."

She frowned and shook her head slowly.

Lake, Ari, Eagan, and Glam also filled out the visitor log. Mrs. Enlen couldn't suppress her fascination with the muscular and mustachioed preteen girl scrawling *Glamenhilda* onto the page with big, crooked strokes of the pen (which she held like someone would hold a tennis racket).

"Good, now please wait here for Mr. Phiro," Mrs. Enlen said with a smile. "He'll be down shortly to escort you to your locker."

"Escort . . ." I repeated weakly.

"Yes, well, we can't just have five nonstudents roaming the halls freely, can we?" Mrs. Enlen said with obvious satisfaction. "As you well know, Greg, not even *enrolled students* walk the halls during class without a pass."

Suddenly I wanted to kick myself in the teeth for being so stupid. Why had I ever thought they'd just let us waltz in and go to my locker unsupervised? How could a Dwarf ever have been so optimistic? Maybe all the time I spent with Edwin had rubbed some of his Elven overconfidence onto my psyche?

I forced a laugh—it sounded terribly fake.

"Yeah, of course," I said, nodding. "Mr. Phiro."

"Please wait for him out in the hall," Mrs. Enlen instructed, struggling to politely cover her nose from Glam's body odor.

We stepped outside and huddled together casually, trying not to look like we were formulating a plan.

"What now?" Eagan asked. "Who's Mr. Phiro?"

"That's an Elven name, you know," Glam said. "Can I bash his knees?"

"Just relax," I said, checking my watch. "And *no* knee bashing. Let him take us to my locker. Once there, we'll find a way to ditch him."

"We'll just . . . *find a way?*" Ari asked skeptically.

"Well, yeah, I think that's kind of how the Galdervatn works," I said. "It, like, helps you when you need it most . . . I guess."

They looked at me skeptically.

"Thenceforth perhaps ye brutal bashing suggested by Glamenhilda aye doth ye suitable resolution," Lake said.

I didn't get a chance to reinforce that we *should not* bash *anything.* Because Mr. Phiro, the head of school security, was suddenly there, standing right behind us.

"Okay, Greg, let's go," he said.

Surely my Dwarven companions now recognized why it was so imperative to not try to take Mr. Phiro by force. The PEE's head of security towered over us like a monument. He was well over six feet tall and had arms like a professional football player. A walkie-talkie and Taser were strapped to his belt.

"Come on, I don't have all day," he boomed.

I nodded and the five of us followed him down the hall toward my locker. Mr. Phiro's heels clacked loudly on the polished floor. Once at my locker, he pivoted and pointed at it with his walkie-talkie, which looked like a plastic toy inside his huge mitt.

"Go on, get your stuff," he instructed.

I put in the combination and opened my locker door. It was mostly empty, exposing the ruse.

Mr. Phiro scowled and raised the walkie-talkie toward his mouth.

But Ari's hand shot out like lightning and grabbed it before it got past his waist. Even Ari seemed shocked at her own speed and dexterity and I knew instantly it was the Galdervatn kicking in.

What happened next confirmed it.

Water began pouring out of the walkie-talkie's seams like it was connected to a hose. Ari let go and took a step back in surprise. Mr. Phiro, still startled, held on to the short-circuiting electrical device as sparks flew.

A sizzling *crack* snapped in the air.

Mr. Phiro collapsed onto the floor in a heap.

"Is he . . . is he dead?" Ari asked in a horrified whisper. "I didn't mean to . . . I just . . ."

Eagan quickly bent down and put his hand on the security guard's heaving chest.

"He's still breathing," he said, then stood up and nudged the smoking walkie-talkie, lying in a puddle of water, with his foot. "I don't think this carries enough voltage to kill a dude that big. Which means he'll probably wake up before long."

"Does this mean she has the Ability?" Glam asked, clearly jealous.

"Looks like it," I said, smirking at Ari.

The normally unflappable Ari blushed, the red in her cheeks making her silvery-purple hair look even shinier.

"We need to go," I said. "Class will be getting out soon and the halls will be full of Elves."

"We still can't just leave him here," Eagan said, pointing down at Mr. Phiro, who was already beginning to stir. "Once he wakes, he'll put the place on lockdown."

We looked at Mr. Phiro in a panic. We'd have a hard enough time even lifting this guy, let alone finding a place to stash him. But before we knew what was happening, a dozen thick green vines came slithering out of my open locker and wrapped themselves around Mr. Phiro's legs.

We watched, stunned, as the vines dragged him easily, feet first, into my narrow locker. But even as the vines pulled him in past the knees, we knew an Elf this size would never fit. I stepped closer and then finally saw that the back of the locker was gone. Behind it was a small cave the size of a large closet. It had dripping granite stones and little stalactites and everything.

"How?" Eagan whispered in awe. "How is this possible?"

"Galdervatn," Ari said quietly.

The vines dragged Mr. Phiro the rest of the way into the small cave behind my locker. One last vine shot out, grabbed the locker door, and slammed it closed. We stood in a semicircle gaping.

"So which one of you did that, then?" Eagan asked.

"I have no idea," I said slowly.

"It was me!" Glam said, though the shock and confusion in her large eyes betrayed her words. "*Obviously* I did it!"

"Where did the cave come from?" Ari asked. "Is he okay? What will happen to him?"

"I don't know," I said. "But we don't have time to worry about it right now. Class is out in one minute, and we need to get to the cafeteria!"

They followed me down the hall, leaving behind my locker, and the strange cave, and the sentient vines that were holding an Elf hostage and that one of us had apparently generated with Dwarven magic.

CHAPTER 25

I Do Declare a Forthcoming Pun: Perry Makes Multiple Trips to the Cafeteria Salad Barf

We made it to my old lunch spot without being noticed.

As we hid behind the couch, I was disappointed to see that someone had apparently pulled and disposed of my arugula plant. The first lunch bell rang seconds later. Ari, Lake, Eagan, and Glam looked dazed as we heard the first few kids stream into the cafeteria around the corner.

"It's real," Eagan whispered. "Galdervatn is *real*. Dwarven Magic really *is* coming back . . ."

"Ye Magical Age indeed draws nigh," Lake agreed with an awed grin. "Tales ye elders foretold fortnights past doth come to pass."

We let his heavy words linger. It was really happening. Dwarves everywhere with the Ability would eventually regain their full magical powers. And so would the Elves. Amid the awed silence, we heard soft footsteps approaching on the marble floors. The steps stopped just across from the couch. A soft *creak* marked the owner sitting down on the chair opposite us. Right where he always sat.

Then came the low murmuring of Froggy's voice.

"Hey, remember when we could save kittens from trees," he said in that bizarre, nonsensical way that he always talked to himself in. "Or lunch on skyscrapers, bring the villains to their knees . . ."

I motioned for my friends to stay put as Froggy rambled on about time machines or something, then slowly scooted around to the other side of the couch and climbed into my usual spot.

Froggy stopped talking and looked at me.

He remained expressionless as he continued to unwrap the sandwich he'd brought from home. Then he finally gave me a single nod of recognition.

"Froggy . . ." I started. "Um, I'm not sure how exactly to tell you this . . . or even if you're the right kid . . . uh . . ."

He waited patiently for me to sort it out.

"Your dad . . ." I said. "I mean, not your stepdad, but your real dad. I don't know how much you remember him, or if you know what happened to him, but he misses you. I've . . . well, a series of strange events has led me to him. It's too much to explain right now, but he misses you and wants to see you. I can take you to him."

Froggy's face remained expressionless. I wasn't sure if he was busy processing everything or had no idea what I was talking about or simply didn't care either way.

But then he finally grinned and nodded.

"Really?" I said.

Froggy nodded again.

"Yes," Froggy said. "I'd like to see him now. My mother will never tell me where he is."

"Great, let's go," I said, standing up. "I happen to know exactly where he's at!"

For a second, I thought he wouldn't actually follow me. But then he set aside his lunch and stood up.

"Froggy, I'm here with some friends," I said, as they emerged from behind the couch.

"Are they Dwarves, too?" he asked.

For some reason I was surprised he knew the truth. But then again, he had a Dwarf for a dad and an Elf for a mom, and attended an Elf school. So I supposed I shouldn't have been too shocked.

"They are," I confirmed. "But I'll introduce you later. We need to get out of here now."

Froggy nodded and we headed toward an exit door just across the room.

"That's it?" Glam asked.

"That's it," I said, surprised myself. "This door will take us down a back stairwell and directly outside."

"So I never got to use magic?" Glam asked angrily, her fists balled up. "I never got to fight an Elf?"

We stopped just a few feet from the exit door. On the other side of the large room, kids were emptying their lunch trays in the cafeteria. They wouldn't notice us as long as we didn't make some sort of scene in the next ten seconds.

"Glam, you can get upset later," Ari said, recognizing the same thing. "We need to get out of here . . . *quietly*."

"You got to do cool magic," Glam said loudly, raising a hand as if to point accusingly.

We stared in shock as her hand came up. It was no longer a hand at all. Instead, both of Glam's hands had been transformed into granite boulders the size of basketballs.

Her eyes went wide.

Then she smiled.

"For smashing!" she said.

"Glam, no!" Eagan, Lake, and I all said in unison.

But it was too late.

The prospect of getting to use magical boulder fists to smash something was more than Glam could possibly resist. She was a Shadowpike after all, so it was hard to blame her entirely. She reared back one boulder and slammed it into the brick wall by the exit door. A huge crater appeared as chunks of mortar and red brick sprayed everywhere.

She struck the wall again. Kids across the room looked our way. There were two massive dents in the brick wall and chunks of it everywhere. Her fists shrank back down into hands just as suddenly as they'd turned to rock. Glam seemed disappointed she couldn't smash more, but there was still a grin on her face, mustache stretched thin.

Then I heard a voice I'd hoped to never hear again.

"Is that *Greg Fatmont*?"

I looked up. Perry and six of his cronies were stalking angrily toward us.

"It *is* Roly-McBowly!" Perry shouted. "I knew I smelled gwint in here today."

Before I even knew what was happening, they had surrounded us. Perry stepped forward and grabbed my shirt, easily hoisting me up off the ground.

"Came back to let me finish what I started," he sneered in my face. "Your freakish *Dwarfy* tricks won't save you this time."

But of course he was wrong. We'd apparently each consumed way more Galdervatn than I had last Friday and still had plenty of magic left in us. He was right about one thing, though: it wasn't *my* magic trick that saved me this time.

It was Glam's.

She shoved me from Perry's grip and stepped between us. Glam opened her mouth to scream something at him, but no words came out. Instead, her eyes widened and she promptly began projectile vomiting thick, black soil all over Perry's face.

It was dark and damp and smelled fertile as it spewed from Glam's mouth into his face. He let out a startled cry and took several steps back, attempting to spit out chunks of dirt and mud as soil kept pouring all over him.

At first, Perry's buddies weren't sure what to do. They just stood there in shock and stared at the girl vomiting up dirt. But then they finally rushed into action. Two of them tackled Glam to the ground. Dirt sprayed toward the ceiling like a soil fountain.

Two more of Perry's friends wrapped their arms around Ari and Lake, easily restraining them. Another shoved Eagan halfway across the floor. He hit the marble hard, then gasped, the wind knocked from his lungs. Froggy cowered against the wall.

Glam angrily wrestled with two of Perry's cronies. The two large teens struggled to corral the muscular, flailing Dwarf. For all her strength, though, it didn't look like she could hold them off for much longer.

Perry wiped the remaining dirt from his eyes and grinned at me, his teeth black with muck.

"Nice trick, but you won't get away this time," he said. "Boys, just hold them here. We'll wait for school security. I'm sure the Elf Lord will want to interrogate these gwints to see what they're really up to."

I could have grabbed Froggy and made a run for it—we would have gotten away. But Lake, Ari, Eagan, and Glam would not have. As much as I was doing this for my dad, there was still no way I'd leave my friends behind. If I had only known how to do different kinds of magic on purpose, I maybe could have done something to get us out of this. But turning into stone or growing an arugula plant didn't seem like they would be particularly helpful at the moment.

I tried to shoot rocks from my eyes. I tried to breathe fire. I stood there and desperately tried to do something, *anything* magic. But nothing happened.

Suddenly, out of nowhere, someone collided with Perry and sent him sprawling. With uncanny grace and speed, the assailant lurched over to the two kids holding Ari and Lake hostage. He dropped them both easily with lightning-fast strikes to the sides of their heads.

I finally recognized who it was.

"Greg, get your friends and run," Edwin said, already rushing over to help Glam get free. "I can't hold them off forever and security is on the way. Get out of here!"

I grabbed Froggy and ran over to help Eagan to his feet. He was still catching his breath. Ari, Lake, and Glam joined us as Perry and his buddies converged on Edwin. It was six on one. We had to help him.

"I've been waiting for this for years, Edwin Aldaron," Perry sneered. "Your dad won't protect you now that you're aiding and abetting trespassing gwints."

"Greg, go!" Edwin yelled from behind the mass of Elven bullies as they began throwing punches.

I had every intention of staying and helping—I couldn't

abandon my best friend either. But something in his voice told me we *had* to leave. Now.

We bolted for the nearest hallway, since the exit door was now blocked by seven fighting Elves. Sixth period had technically just started, so the halls were empty as we sprinted through them. At least until we rounded a corner and found ourselves face-to-face with Mr. Phiro, Hot Sauce, and four school security guards.

"There you are," Mr. Phiro said, grinning.

Chunks of yellow dead vines were still wrapped loosely around his legs.

"These *Dwarves* have broken the peace treaty," Hot Sauce sneered. "They've violated ancient law and must be apprehended forthwith."

The guards rushed forward.

We ran.

But they weren't far behind and would easily catch us before we got to the exit at the end of the long hallway. I panicked as their footsteps thundered closer behind us. And then I heard cries of surprise. Grass was sprouting underneath my feet, right through the tiled floors.

I glanced back.

Behind us, a lot more than grass was growing. A whole jungle of plants and vines spontaneously sprouted in the hallway. Massive trees crashed up through the floor, ripping apart the marble tiles into small shards. Plants spread from lockers and cracks in the walls and tangled in the guards' feet, tripping at least two of them.

Mr. Phiro's fading anguished cry confirmed that the jungle hallway was so thick it was impassable. We kept running until we got to the door and rushed outside. I took one last look back. The entire hallway was a wall of brown and green. Of crisscrossing tree trunks and flowering leaves and plants. A blanket of shrubs and grasses. All that was visible of Mr. Phiro, Hot Sauce, and the guards, still trapped halfway down the hall, were a few desperately flailing, straggling arms and legs sticking out of the thick foliage.

I didn't know who'd made the magic cave behind my locker, but I knew for certain this was my handiwork. And for the first time I was excited about my training for reasons other than saving my dad.

If a couple Dwarven kids could "accidentally" do stuff like this, then *imagine* what we could do with proper instruction.

———✦———

The six of us barely spoke on the way to Buck's.

What had happened to my instinct to stay out of things? Stealing Galdervatn from the Grand Hall of Dwarven Artifacts? Using it to break into the PEE, thereby starting a war with Elves? These were things I never would have considered doing just a week ago. Then again, a week ago, my dad was perfectly safe. I'd had no reason then to act boldly, to break rules and risk my life even though a lifetime of bad luck would have ordinarily told me not to.

"So, that guy who saved us," Ari said from the seat behind me. "Was that your Elven friend?"

"Yeah," I said, turning around in my seat. "See why I'm so adamant we can trust him? He's nothing at all like the Elves you've described to me."

"It's just a trick," Glam said. "I think they let us escape. It was too easy."

"*Too easy?*" Eagan said. "One of you turned the hallway into a rain forest! Otherwise we'd have been caught for sure."

"Don't forget we would have gotten away much more easily if you hadn't smashed apart that wall!" Ari said.

"Glam smash," Glam said with a sheepish grin. "I couldn't help it . . ."

"Yeah, give her a break," Eagan said. "We all make mistakes."

"Glamenhilda hath interceded ye assault on Greg's personage," Lake added.

I could tell Ari was frustrated that the two of them continued to defend Glam, almost certainly just because they thought she was attractive and liked her mustache. But at the same time, Ari couldn't deny that Glam *had* stepped in right away to help me fend off Perry.

"Thank you for getting me out of there," Froggy said a few minutes later. "I never wanted to go to that school. My stepdad made me."

It was perhaps more words than he'd said to me in three years combined.

"Is that why you never wanted to interact with anyone?" I asked.

"Mostly, yeah," he said. "Also, a lot them . . . well, I'm half Dwarf. That doesn't really fly around there. You know?"

I nodded, suspecting I did.

"So can you finally tell me what's up with all that weird rambling you do?"

Froggy smirked.

"They're just song lyrics," he said. "I listen to a lot of music. You know, helps with the isolation. I really dig fun lyrics."

"Why didn't you tell me that all the times I asked?" I said. "Instead of giving me those weird answers."

"I did," Froggy said. "I always told you the names of the bands."

I grinned and shook my head as Froggy pulled out a pair of wireless headphones and put them into his ears. And I thought back to all the times I'd talked to him: it was partially me. I hadn't actually spoken to him nearly as much as I'd always thought I had.

—◆I◆—

Thirty minutes later, watching Froggy meet with his dad was both touching and a little awkward. Something we probably shouldn't have witnessed at all. It didn't help that he was already a strange kid, and his dad a grouchy, verbally abusive video game addict. But they both obviously missed each other.

It went something like this:

Froggy: [Stared at his dad with red eyes and said nothing.]
Buck: [Stared at his son with red eyes and said nothing.]
Froggy: . . .
Buck: Did you get my letters?
Froggy: [Shook his head no.]
Buck: I knew it! Never trust an Elf.
Froggy: . . .
Buck: Well, you're half-Elf, so I guess I mean never trust your mom, anyway. I sent lots of letters. I missed you. She took you from me.
Froggy: [Offered a weak smile.]
Buck: Do you want to stay with me and train with the other Dwarves? It's all pointless and useless and a waste of time, but they're on some mission to do something or

other. Do you want to move in here with me? It's messy, but it's the best I've got.

Froggy: [Nodded.]

Buck: [Nodded.]

[A long silence ensued—the rest of us stared at our feet awkwardly.]

Buck: Do you need to get any stuff from your mom's?

Froggy: No, I have everything I need right here. [Held up an iPod and headphones.]

Buck: Okay, good. We can go get you some new clothes and stuff tonight. I just need to find my car keys.

[He began digging through his piles of empty Dr Pepper cans and takeout containers—eventually noticing the rest of us standing there.]

Buck: What are you all still doing here? Come back tomorrow and we'll begin training.

[We shuffled toward the door, not wanting to challenge him or do anything to make him change his mind—especially after all we had done to get to that point.]

Buck: Greg, one last thing—*thank you.*

CHAPTER 26

Edwin Gets Banned from the Qitris Festival

I made up some excuse to leave the group on the way back to the Underground, and then went to the nearby public library.

There was an email from Edwin sent shortly after the incident at the PEE—which meant he was okay. Okay enough to type a very short message anyway:

Greg, we need to meet up. That was not cool today.

As I typed a reply, my email instant messenger box popped up:

Edwin Aldaron: Greg?
Me: Yeah . . . I'm at the public library on Fullerton in Logan.
Edwin Aldaron: Don't go anywhere. I'll be there soon.

Fifteen minutes later, we were sitting across from each other at a table in the back of the library. Edwin glared at me with one eye—the other was black and purple and swollen shut.

"Thank you—" I started.

He just shook his head.

"I know," I said. "I'm sorry. But I had to, it's . . . well, it's *complicated*. But you saved us, Edwin."

"I know," he finally said. "And it got me in big trouble. Huge trouble."

I started nodding, but he stopped me.

"No," he said. "You really have no idea. I could lose my birthright for this. My dad won't even speak to me. My mom actually slapped me, not hard, but still . . . she's never done anything like that before. I risked everything for you today. And it all but killed my chances of finding out what happened to your dad. You realize that, right? I think I have a right to know why."

"That's okay," I said. "I think I have a new plan to get him back. But I'll tell you about that later. Because, first, you're right . . . you deserve to know why we were there."

I explained the whole situation to him. Well, *almost* the whole situation. I didn't actually tell him about Dwarves training. I wasn't sure why I held that part out. Maybe deep down I thought if he knew the Dwarves were training it would mean we were planning some sort of war—which wasn't really the case. It was more disaster preparedness, for the return of monsters or in case the Elves attacked us. But Edwin might not see it that way. Either way, I told him Buck was a Dwarf helping me find my dad (which wasn't technically a lie), but the rest I laid out exactly as it happened. Buck's depression impeding his ability to help me,

Froggy being his estranged son, and my arrangement with Buck to reunite them.

Edwin listened, nodding thoughtfully. When I was finished, he sighed.

"Greg," he said, leaning forward. "Why didn't you just come to me? I could have passed Froggy a message. Why go to all that trouble and danger?"

"I . . ."

The truth was, a lot of it had to do with the revelation of what gwint meant. Could I really fully trust a friend who would use a derogatory name for his unsuspecting best friend? But at the same time, he had risked his butt yet again to save us at the PEE earlier. So it was clearly still more complicated than it seemed.

"Do you not trust me?" Edwin asked as if reading thoughts were among his Elf powers. "Even after today?"

"No, it's not that. I trust you," I said, which was true—I wouldn't even be there otherwise.

"Well, I guess it doesn't matter," Edwin said. "You guys did what you did, and now we have a problem even bigger than your dad's whereabouts. The Elves are *really* upset. They saw this as an act of aggression, Greg. At least, as best I can surmise, since, you know, my parents won't actually tell me *anything* anymore."

"I know we messed up," I said. "It's what we do. We're gwints, after all, right?"

Edwin grinned.

"You finally found out what that means, huh?"

"Yeah, and how can you be smiling?"

"What do you mean?" he asked innocently.

"Ed, it's like the most offensive word for Dwarves imaginable! Honestly, that's a big part of why I suddenly wasn't too keen on contacting you."

"What? No way," he said. "It's just, like, good-natured trash talk. All Elves call all Dwarves gwints. It's no big deal."

"Well, it clearly is to the other Dwarves," I said. "You should have seen the way they reacted when someone said that word. You can't possibly tell me you had no idea it was so offensive."

Edwin's mouth opened but he said nothing. The smile was gone and I saw true concern in his eyes.

"I mean, I guess I figured it wasn't like a pet name, but I had no idea it was *that* bad," he said.

"Well, now you do," I said. "And you'll stop using it?"

"Uh, well, I still don't think it's—"

"Promise me you'll stop calling me or any other Dwarf by that name," I said. "You owe me that much as a friend."

Edwin finally nodded, breathing out what felt almost like a sigh of relief.

"So what's this new *plan* all about?" he asked.

"Well . . . it's . . ."

Once again, I found myself hesitating to share details with Edwin. Maybe a true sign that the Dwarves were getting to me. That I truly didn't fully trust Edwin anymore. Or maybe not so much him specifically, but Elves in general. And if I told him something I shouldn't, then maybe he'd let it slip accidentally to other Elves?

"It's hard to explain," I finally said.

Edwin frowned. He was clearly getting annoyed. And looking at his black eye, the one he'd gotten saving me, I was feeling pretty guilty.

"Look, I don't even really know yet how the plan will work myself," I said, which was true. I still had no idea how, specifically, the Bloodletter could help me find my dad. I just had this feeling, an intuition that it could. "It involves magic. And an old

Dwarven relic that I'm trying to find a way to get my hands on. Once that happens I'll know more."

Edwin finally relaxed and nodded.

"Maybe it's better I don't know too much anyway," he said. "The Elven Magistrate suddenly thinks I'm a Dwarven spy or something because of today. I'll be lucky to even get invited to the next Qitris Festival. So the less I know, the better. Plausible deniability."

"Qitris Festival?"

"Yeah, it's a dumb Elven holiday," Edwin said. "Like the Elven version of the Fourth of July or something. I guess it used to be really traditional, with archery and magic contests and other cool stuff like that. But now it's basically just a bunch of self-important, rich Elves having catered parties all week, drinking expensive whiskey, pretending they're not trying to one-up each other when they clearly are. But now I'm likely banned anyway . . ."

"Sorry," I said.

Edwin shrugged.

"It was my choice to intervene," he said. "But I still wish you'd told me. You could have avoided all of that."

I nodded. He was right. I felt like an idiot.

"Well, I really am sorry," I said. "Let's meet again in four days, same time and place. Maybe a few days apart can help both our causes—it can get the Elves off your back and allow me to figure out how to get my new plan into action."

"Yeah, sure," Edwin agreed. "See you in four days."

He got up and left.

There'd been no lame puns, no talk of chess, and very few smiles.

CHAPTER 27

We Are Celebrated like Heroes for Starting a War

Dunmor needs to see you to discuss what you and your friends did today."

This is how Fynric greeted me the moment I walked into our small Underground apartment that evening. The truth was, though we both slept there, we rarely saw each other. He was always up early, off to work on something important or the other.

"Umm . . ."

"He's waiting for us now," he said. "Come on, let's go."

Lake, Ari, Glam, and Eagan were already waiting in Dunmor's office with their parents, seated at a table in the corner of the room. Fynric and I sat at the end, next to the Shadowpikes.

Glam's parents looked just like her: thick and hulking and hairy. And although I still hadn't quite gotten used to what Dwarves considered attractive qualities, there was something almost regal about them. They were *impressive* in a striking sort of way. It's hard to explain.

"I've received an official communiqué from the Elf Ambassador to Dwarven Affairs, Ailas Presceran," Dunmor said as soon I at down. "He claims that five Dwarven youths, earlier today, violated the Thrynmoor Pact by utilizing magic against Elves—which is strictly forbidden by section 3, article 14, sub-section 4a, clause 3 in our long-standing peace agreement."

He paused, then, shockingly, smiled at us.

"Of course, the good Ambassador Presceran failed to also mention that Elves may have violated the treaty first, just five nights ago, if in fact they hired a Troll to apprehend one of our Council Elders," Dunmor said, the bitter smile turning into a scowl. "Needless to say, we cannot substantiate this. But that is of no importance. Who broke the treaty first is irrelevant. What *is* relevant is that tensions are now higher than they've been in hundreds of years."

I sat there and stared at the floor. The very thing I'd tried to avoid by keeping the fact that I knew it was (sort of) Elves that had taken my dad was now happening because of it. In trying to solve the case on my own, I'd broken into an Elf school and now had tensions on the rise to the brink of actual conflict.

"There is but one course of action from here," Dunmor continued. "Training must be accelerated. Galdervatn shall be introduced very soon. We're awaiting the arrival of more from mining operations in Norway and Bulgaria. Galdervatn is also being shipped to other Separatist sects across the globe so they, too, can begin training. We must condense our schedule. Make no mistake: some form of conflict is coming. Whether the Council accepts such with an official vote at the upcoming Global Session is immaterial. But what matters is that all of you shall *complete* battle training in no less than one month's time."

I felt sick to my stomach. This was why I'd always avoided

drastic actions in the past. Stormbellys have terrible luck. We only make things worse. I was living proof of that. I had almost singe-handedly brought us to war. Was there anything I could even do now to get us out?

"Sooooo . . . we're not being punished?" Glam asked.

"No. Your bold actions have shown me, all of us, what Dwarves are capable of," Dunmor said. "You should be an example, something to aspire toward. You took initiative, and then fought in the face of your own certain failure. You rejected the pessimism, the acceptance of miserable luck that usually holds us back. You are the sort of Dwarves who will help us regain our former glory. Or die trying."

———❖———

The next day, we finally began training with Buck.

The others speculated excitedly on the bus ride there about what we'd learn first: Ax fighting or magic? Archery or defensive combat techniques? Dagger throwing or something much cooler that we couldn't even imagine?

Which was why we were all brutally disappointed to be spending the day outside in Humboldt Park literally hugging trees. Green ash trees to be exact.

"A Dwarf's power comes from their link with the earth," Buck reminded us for the ninety-eighth time. "Power in battle is not about speed, or skill, or dexterity; it's about connecting with your environment. With the earth itself. It gave us life, and it can take it away whenever it pleases."

I was lying on the grass face-first, trying to breathe in "first blade oxygen," as Buck had instructed. But really I was trying not to think about all the dogs that had probably pooped there, in that very spot, before this.

Ari was hugging a nearby tree, trying to "learn its life story."

Lake was rolling in the dirt on a small baseball field several hundred feet away, "discovering the difference between native and transient earthly materials."

Eagan was high up in a big tree behind the field, dangling in the branches, "learning about variances in the natural forces of our surroundings" (but also mostly just trying not to fall).

Froggy was near the huge pond in the center of Humboldt Park, collecting stones and then rubbing them onto his face, "conditioning his exterior to the powers of the interior."

Glam was picking wild weed flowers, being as careful as she could not to crush the petals or pollen, "learning the origins of what makes us move."

These were Buck's instructions. To me it seemed like total foolishness. A complete waste of time when I could have been out trying to track down the Elves that took my dad.

"I thought we were going to learn how to squash Elves?" Glam complained for at least the tenth time.

"You will understand, eventually," Buck said, taking another sip from one of the cans from the twelve-pack of Dr Pepper he'd carried over with him. "Until then, you must continue to speak with the earth. You will not become a true warrior without this connection. Now, rotate!"

We all traded places. It was my turn to hug the green ash tree again. This was at least our third time through this rotation of earthly exercises.

A few homeless guys staggered by, staring at us in wonder. One of them asked Buck for his last can of soda. Buck picked up a long stick and chased the man away, shouting obscenities. Then he limped back toward us, tossing the stick aside.

It was probably a good thing he'd left the Bloodletter at his place, as much as I'd hoped he would bring it with us. It had spoken to me again that morning when we'd arrived for training.

Finally, you begin, it had said.

It had been leaning against the wall, next to Buck's couch.

I'm tired of being wasted here.

You will use me soon to avenge yourself.

In time, we will achieve glory.

Or at the very least, we will destroy a bunch of stuff.

I'd stared at it, once again wondering if I was going crazy. Why was nobody else hearing it speak? Or was it saying these things to the others as well, and we were all just pretending it wasn't? Maybe the Bloodletter called out to everyone? Maybe I wasn't special at all.

We spent the rest of that day hugging trees, climbing them, lying in the grass, finding rocks, rolling in dirt, picking flowers, speaking to the elements, whispering to the wind (no, I'm not kidding), dodging several random vicious attacks from squirrels and birds, and just generally making fools of ourselves while Buck verbally assaulted every sort of person that came to his mind:

Wood Sprites were lazy.

Goblins were smelly.

Dwarves were failures.

Elves were greedy.

Orcs were morons.

Rock Trolls were even dumber.

Wraiths were soulless wenches (like his ex-wife).

Policemen were crooks.

As were politicians and teachers and chefs and bus drivers.

Forest Nymphs had bad breath.

Etc. Etc. Etc.

It seemed as though he had nothing nice to say about anyone. But I hoped for my father's sake that all this dippy earth stuff would eventually pay off and turn me into at least a passable warrior.

—•I•—

The next few days of training were a lot more exciting.

There was a flurry of activities and exercises much closer to what we'd all expected going in. Well, we spent one more half day frolicking around in Humboldt Park like a bunch of psychopathic hippies. But after that, once we seemed to fully understand why we were out there, Buck finally stopped us and said: "You're all ready now."

And then things got a bit more focused and visceral . . . and violent.

We learned about battle stances. The way to shift your weight, the way to stand for easy, fluid movement. We learned some basic sword-fighting techniques using real Dwarven swords. We learned about Dwarven shield types and sizes and tensile strengths. We learned how to throw small axes (Froggy and Ari were especially good at this). We learned about many different types of Dwarven weaponry (there were a lot). The whole thing frightened me but the others seemed excited. Maybe not at the prospect of real battle, but at least at getting to use cool weapons in practice.

But I was growing increasingly frustrated. After all, I was only doing this to get my hands on the Bloodletter to enlist its help finding my dad. But the one time I asked Buck about it, he told me brusquely that I wasn't close to ready yet.

Of course, we did not learn all these things outside in

Humboldt Park for the whole West Side of Chicago to see. Imagine a bunch of kids and one soda-guzzling adult throwing small axes at things in the middle of a city park.

Our training actually occurred right above Buck's apartment.

The second day, after leaving the park, we went back to his apartment. The Bloodletter was still there, lying on the floor halfway under the couch. It spoke to me again.

Are you done picking flowers yet? Pick me up. Let's cleave stuff.

I made a move toward it, but Buck scooped it up first. Then we went into the hallway and up the final flight of stairs. At the top was a single door covered in graffiti and seven locks that were obviously Dwarven-made, based on the intricate carvings etched into them.

The entire fifth floor of the apartment building spread out behind the door—one massive room, broken up only by a few support columns. It was a veritable warehouse of Dwarven armaments and training stations. There was a small archery range, plastic target molds lined up for ax and knife throwing, racks of dull practice swords and training armor, practice battle-axes, maces, and crossbows among other weapons and armor I could not identify.

It was a real Dwarven training facility.

It was there where Buck brought us for the next three days from sunup to sundown, leaving us so exhausted that all we wanted to do at the end of each session was go home and pass out. It was there that we first started becoming warriors. Some of us nervously (Ari, Eagan, and myself). And some of us with great zeal (Glam, Froggy, and Lake). And it soon became clear that all of us were *good* at the things Buck taught us—even as crude and mean as he was about our failures.

And he *was* mean about them, especially to me for some reason I didn't understand.

When Ari threw an ax and it clipped the target on the edge and bounced away, clattering to the floor, Buck said things like, *Nice throw, you just need to snap your wrist more. Like this.*

When I threw an ax and it buried itself into the target just a few inches from the center, Buck said things like, *You missed. Your opponent survives this wound and now likely kills you with one easy stroke. You're dead, Greg. Not good enough. You throw like a Human. Your hands are too small for this, don't you eat enough pork? Everyone knows that's what makes your hands big. What are you trying to do, tickle it? Put some mustard on that ax, noodle-arm!*

Of course, he didn't say those things all at once, but it's a selection of the things he said after every one of my throws.

Or when Glam went berserk on a training dummy with her battle-ax, smashing it into tons of pieces while screaming furiously, Buck said, "I like your passion. Nice enthusiasm, girl."

But when I accidentally hit one too hard and clipped off its fake arm, Buck said, "Nice going, Greg, you just ruined the darn thing! Those aren't free, you know."

When Lake fired an arrow and missed the target completely, Buck gave him helpful pointers to correct the mistake.

But when I lined up for a shot, Buck frequently walked by and clipped my heels with a stick, causing my shots to miss badly. In one case, my arrow even lodged in the ceiling. Then he'd get in my face and scream things like, *Concentrate, Tubby!*

Plus, the more time I spent around the Bloodletter, the more intensely it spoke to me. The more it made me want to just grab it and finally get down to the business of saving my dad. This felt like a waste of time, even though I knew it wasn't. I knew that this was training I would need for my rescue mission. After all, I couldn't expect to free my dad from captivity using politely worded, stern threats.

But the Bloodletter taunted me to stop being so patient.

He's not looking, take me now.

I'm wasted on a Dwarf like Buck. I belong to you.

If you had me, you wouldn't be getting yelled at so much.

Do you really want to save your dad? Then stop wasting time and come over here and liberate me!

Come on, let's go get some tacos. I know this great stand just down the street. After that, we'll destroy the place just for fun.

It was distracting enough having a teacher who seemingly hated you, but having to constantly shut out the increasingly louder voice in my head (a voice an inanimate object was telepathically beaming into my brain) made it a wonder I'd managed to go three days of training without accidentally chopping off my own foot or something.

But I put up with it because I knew it was the key to saving my dad. The problem was, Buck was always holding the ax and he never let anyone else touch it. The second time I asked him about it, he tripped me and I smashed my face onto the hardwood floor.

"That's for asking dumb questions," he'd said.

So I knew I had to bide my time, keep up with training, and then eventually I'd get my chance. Besides, it'd likely be better to know how to actually use it before picking it up.

Training was hard, but in the evenings when we had any energy left at all, we went to the Arena. There, my friends taught me about the old Dwarven trades. I learned the basics of glassblowing, and cave diving, and potions, and alchemy, and metallurgy. Even though I basically stank at all of them, it was still fun to learn.

The fourth day of training, as we were leaving, the Bloodletter called out to me again from underneath a pile of trash in the kitchen.

The next time we meet, you will pick me up for the first time.

And everything will change.

You will avenge your father.

Chills ran down my spine. It was not a question. Not a request. Not a suggestion.

It was a command.

CHAPTER 28

My Dagger Has a First Name, It's B-L-A-C-K-O-U-T

"It's finally ready," Ari said, pulling me aside later that evening in the Arena.

"What is?"

"Your dagger," she said. "Remember, the one I started making for you?"

She handed me something wrapped in cloth. I was surprised by how light it was. Ari watched anxiously as I unwrapped the small piece of fabric folded around the weapon.

It was breathtaking.

The blade was ten inches long, sharpened on both sides and so shiny that I nearly blinded myself when the glare from a wall torch caught my eye in the reflection. The knife almost sparkled like a gemstone. It was perfectly symmetrical and carved with an intricate design that I eventually realized spelled out my last name: *Stormbelly*.

The hilt was wrapped tightly with soft leather that fit my hand so perfectly I sort of wondered if she'd snuck in and taken measurements one night while I was sleeping. The bottom of the hilt bore no fancy gems or gold, but was fused with a rounded, polished, bright purple stone.

"Do you like it?" Ari asked.

"Yeah, I mean . . . it's . . . holy crap, it's *amazing*," I said.

Ari smiled, looking relieved. As if she had somehow thought there'd be a chance I would think this knife was anything short of spectacular.

"You really made it for *me*?"

"Of course!" she said. "We all got our first daggers when we were like eight years old. We haven't really ever used them, but the tradition is still fun."

"So it's more like a decorative piece . . ."

"Well, they always have been in the past," Ari said. "But now . . . with everything that's going on, you may very well need to use it someday."

I looked at the blade, letting her foreboding words sink in. At first I couldn't imagine wielding this sharp blade against anyone or anything. But then I thought about my dad and the Troll that attacked us. Anger rose in my throat and suddenly it wasn't so hard to envision using the dagger.

"Every Dwarven weapon crafted specifically for somebody has a name, too," Ari said. "Yours is called Blackout."

"Blackout," I repeated. "Cool name. What made you decide on that?"

"I *didn't*," Ari said with a laugh. "Dwarven weapons name themselves. Every night, after I finish a worthy weapon, I dream about it—and in that dream the name is revealed. Yours took the name Blackout. They also say that when magic returns, some of our weapons will develop special powers. But who knows . . ."

"Thank you," I said. "I mean . . . I don't even know what else to say . . ."

"Don't worry about it," Ari said.

Then I told her something I probably shouldn't have. I'm not sure why. Maybe I felt I owed her something in exchange for the knife. And since I had nothing to give, I figured a secret was as good as anything else. Or maybe I was just tired of keeping things from my friends.

"I'm still meeting up with Edwin," I blurted out. "Dunmor forbade me, but we're still talking every few days."

Ari didn't react the way I expected. I thought she'd understand. I thought she'd be sad for me and my doomed friendship. After all, she had been there when Edwin saved us at the PEE. Boy, was I wrong (proving that I understood Dwarven girls maybe even less than Human and Elven ones).

"Greg, did you tell him about our training?" Ari asked in a panic. "I know he's your friend, but you can't tell him these things. It could compromise us all!"

"But he's my best friend," I said. "He saved us the other day—"

"That doesn't matter."

"It does," I said.

"No, you need to be more careful, Greg," she insisted. "As much as I want peace, Elves cannot be fully trusted. It's something Dwarves have painfully discovered over thousands and thousands of years. You can't let one perceived exception undo all of what history has taught us."

What if she was right? What if Edwin really couldn't be trusted? *I trusted him*; nothing could change that. But what if I was wrong? Who was I to believe that my judgment alone was better than that of millions of Dwarves before me? Just the same, I knew Edwin better than that. History didn't have a face (but if it did, it'd almost certainly have a beard). Or emotions. It was just a collection of events, each separate and with their own context. History wasn't the same thing as a connection between two living things.

"Imagine if someone told you to never again trust Lake. Or Eagan," I said. "How would you react? Because that's what you're telling me to do."

Ari studied my face and her expression softened. It was as if she truly understood for the first time that I'd never had any other friends before her and the Dwarves. That Edwin had been my first and only friend for a very long time.

"I'm sorry," she said. "I shouldn't have gotten so mad. I'm being a hypocrite, after all. I'm on the side of the Riven that believes we need to work *with the Elves*. That we need to work together, all races, all creatures, to ensure the safety of everybody when magic returns. And here I am getting angry that you're talking to an Elf—"

"Well, there *is* more . . ." I said.

She arched an eyebrow nervously.

"Edwin is pretty sure that Elves were behind the attack on my dad," I said. "Not sanctioned Elves, though, but some rogue group trying to start a rebellion against his dad and the Elven Magistrate or something. I never told anyone because I didn't want it to lead to war . . ."

Ari's face dropped as if her heart had just shattered. But it wasn't for me or my dad. She believed what I did: that once this was discovered by the Council, a new war was all but assured regardless of which exact Elves were responsible.

"I'm not going to tell anyone else about this," Ari said. "For the same reasons you didn't. But be careful, Greg. We can't risk doing anything to push us any closer to war. Keeping the peace is . . . well, it's bigger than your dad."

I took a deep breath, knowing she was right. At the same time, I still didn't even know where my dad was. So I wouldn't have to grapple with that just yet.

But once I found out where he was being held, could I (would I) really risk causing an all-out war trying to rescue him?

⸻✠⸻

Edwin was already at the library that night when I arrived, a chessboard set up in front of him.

"Thought it'd be fun to dominate you at chess again," he said with a grin. "Like old times."

"Yeah, well, think again," I said, sitting down. "I can do magic now, remember? If I lose, I'll just turn you into a wombat with my sick magic skills."

"Yeah, like a Dwarf would," he said.

He meant it as a joke, but it still felt dark somehow. And so our smiles faded and Edwin motioned for me to begin. He let me be white, knowing he was better, and that I'd need the 1 percent advantage that getting to go first provided. It gave me some control of the direction of the game. The opening I chose would have a domino effect.

I made my opening move.

Edwin made his counter automatically—he didn't even need to think it over.

"Are your parents talking to you again?" I asked.

"Yeah, sort of," he said, frowning at the chessboard. "They've banned me from most family functions and all their office buildings in town. But they forgave me once I told them the truth:

that I had only protected my best friend from the immediate danger of a jerk named Perry. I hadn't been thinking about the sociopolitical consequences or anything like that. They seemed to understand, despite being disgusted that I called you my best friend. It helped that my parents have never really liked *Periwinkle's* family."

"That's good," I said, making my next move. "I guess he *parried* with the wrong Elf, eh?"

Edwin smirked at my awful pun.

"Yeah, I put a real *winkle* into his plans," he replied drily.

We both laughed, but it sounded emptier than usual. Edwin hesitated at the chessboard, and I thought perhaps he was actually thinking over his next move. But then I realized it wasn't that at all—he was trying to decide how best to tell me something I wouldn't want to hear.

"Things are getting complicated, though," Edwin said. "I mean, it's . . . I just wish I could stop all of this."

He paused to move a pawn, but I could barely focus on the game anymore. I waited for him to elaborate.

"My parents are planning something," he said. "I'm pretty sure it's not about your dad, but I can't figure out what it is. I know it can't be a good thing. Especially because of what else is happening."

I let out a long sigh and looked at the board, not wanting to hear whatever came next. I made my next move, a bold, aggressive play that would force his next few moves in a way I could hopefully predict. He was good at making surprising moves, and so my strategy this time was to try to force his hand as much as possible.

"The Elves are preparing for a major conflict," Edwin finally revealed. "Nobody is actually *calling* it a war, but . . . well, we start training tomorrow. Everybody. And I don't think it's just related to fending off monsters when magic returns . . ."

We both sat there silently and stared at the chessboard. Neither of us was thinking about the game, knowing full well what Edwin's last statement actually meant. We were natural-born enemies, and we could not escape it, even if we tried our best to ignore it. If at one time we thought we could help both sides avoid conflict, now it all felt hopeless. Some sort of war seemed inevitable. I just hoped it would remain a cold war for as long as possible.

But I was also wrenched apart over the fact that I'd hid our own training from him. He'd trusted me enough to reveal the Elf training as soon as he found out. We'd been training for four days now and I still hadn't mentioned it.

"There's nothing we can do to stop this?" I asked.

Edwin made his next move in the game. It was not the move I thought I'd forced him into, but was something I'd never even considered.

"I don't think so," Edwin finally said, shaking his head slowly.

"We're training, too," I finally revealed.

I expected him to be surprised. But he just nodded calmly.

"I figured as much," he said. "Elven spies are everywhere, Greg. So of course we already knew."

It felt more like a warning than a threat. But it was heavy and menacing either way.

We sat there in silence and finished the game. Edwin beat me. But it hardly mattered. He didn't even fake gloat at the end. He took no satisfaction in it. Edwin had set up the game, knowing what he knew, but it seemed as though he hadn't truly considered the weight of what it meant until the words had left his mouth.

If both sides were now preparing for a war, then our destiny to be mortal enemies was becoming a reality. But we made plans to meet again in four days. Because we were still best friends. And maybe that could remain, regardless of a possible war.

It seemed like a silly hope to hold on to, but the alternative was just too depressing to consider.

CHAPTER 29

Lomdul Hardsword Breathes Fire

We discovered the next day that there was just *one* Dwarven magic expert in the entire world.

Since nobody (aside from my dad and a few other conspiracy theorists) ever believed magic would come back, barely anyone had bothered to learn much about how it worked. And so we began magic training that day pooled collectively into a larger group inside an abandoned warehouse near the edge of a particularly desolate industrial section of Garfield Park.

We filed into an auditorium among hundreds of other Dwarven kids. A man stood on a stage in the middle of the otherwise empty room. He was short and round and had bizarrely misshapen red eyebrows. White hair billowed around him like he was wearing a cheap wizard Halloween costume. All that was missing was the pointy hat. But then the man reached into his robes and pulled one out and placed it on his head.

I rolled my eyes.

"I've heard about this guy," Eagan whispered to us. "Fenmir Mystmossman. The greatest Dwarven magic scholar alive today. My dad said he doesn't have the Ability himself."

"So you mean Mr. Wizard up there isn't actually a wizard at all?" I asked.

Eagan grinned and shrugged helplessly as Fenmir Mystmossman quieted the crowd with a few cheap firecrackers that were meant to look like magic. Some kids oohed and aahed, but most snickered.

"Welcome! I am Fenmir Mystmossman!" he yelled. "I am your magic instructor. Ancient Dwarven magic is our most powerful ally. It involves using the elements of the earth to assert your will. Any questions so far."

Several hands shot up into the air. Fenmir ignored them and kept talking.

"Dwarves are master manipulators of raw materials. Dwarven magicians are no different. Their magic operates on winds, rains, mists, earth, fire, and other such natural elements. Any questions."

At least twenty hands rose, maybe more. Once again, Fenmir continued with barely a pause.

"Dwarven magic is a manipulation of what already exists!" he screeched. "It is *not* a creation of new energies, as many erroneously believe, and which, of course, is an utterly ridiculous idea."

He stopped briefly to laugh smugly at such a thought.

"Questions so far."

This time nobody even bothered to raise their hands.

"Good," Fenmir said. "As you know, very few original Dwarven texts regarding magic have been found. But this will not be a problem! I am an *expert* in Dwarven magic. Questions so far. Right then, we will begin by performing the Ability test, one child at a time, to see who has the right to stay and train. And which of you are unworthy of magic instruction."

We were herded into a massive line in front of the stage. There was complete silence as the first kid to be tested, an eleven-year-old girl named Rabo Mudview, climbed the steps up onto the stage. Fenmir held out an eyedropper filled with Galdervatn. He squeezed a single drop of the swirling, colorful, ghostlike liquid onto Rabo's tongue, and then beckoned her to take a step to the side, where an assistant held a knife and fork. She sliced a small sliver off a brick of something brown and gelatinous.

"This substance that Rabo is about to consume," Fenmir Mystmossman yelled out to the crowd, "is of a most abominable, disgusting nature. It is called seitan, something Humans frequently use as a meat *substitute*."

Cries of horror and disapproval rang out from the crowd. Fenmir nodded vigorously with regret.

"I know, I know," he said. "A tragedy, to be sure. However, it becomes very useful when testing for the Ability. Performing Dwarven magic is not an entirely conscious act. It needs to come instinctually. And seitan, which is nothing more than pure wheat gluten, is quite disagreeable to Dwarven tongues and digestive systems. And, therefore, violent reactions upon tasting it are unequivocally unavoidable. Let us proceed."

His assistant fed the small sliver of seitan to Rabo Mudview.

She chewed it and gagged. Suddenly, leaves began shooting out of her ears. Leaves from all sorts of trees—at least ten different kinds by my count. They fired out, unfurling and floating down toward a crowd of excited, screaming kids, most of whom were witnessing real Dwarven magic for the first time in their lives. It stopped after fifteen seconds or so, with hundreds of leaves now drifting toward the warehouse floor.

Rabo looked startled.

"Congratulations!" Fenmir said. "You *most certainly* have the Ability."

A huge smile spread across Rabo's face as she celebrated with a bunch of her friends from the crowd. The next kid was led up the stairs.

"Oh no," Ari whispered.

"What's wrong?" I asked.

"This won't work on me, I've eaten seitan a bunch of times," she said. "It was gross at first, and hard to get used to, but I don't mind it anymore."

"See, this is why we always told you it was a bad idea for a Dwarf to be vegan," Eagan said.

"And unnatural!" Glam added.

"What am I going to do?" Ari asked.

"Well, we *know* you have the Ability already," I said. "So we'll figure something out."

She nodded, but seemed unconvinced.

The next Dwarf was Umi Magmahead. After the test, nothing happened. Fenmir shook his head slowly and Umi looked close to tears. A disappointed gasp rose from the crowd.

One by one, Dwarven children were tested. True to what Dunmor had told me that first night, only about one in ten kids tested positive for the Ability. Those who did had a wide variety of reactions to the seitan:

- Lomdul Hardsword actually breathed fire for a few seconds.

232

- Kasus Underdigger's arms transformed into tree branches.
- Mamreginn Leadbasher made it rain on the stage, right there in the warehouse.
- Gorol Darkbrewer levitated a few feet off the ground, but then lost control and tumbled back down onto his head with a solid THUMP (but he was okay thanks to his thick Dwarven skull).
- Thikk Alecloak instantaneously grew a huge beard for several seconds before it fell off and drifted to the ground around her feet (the crowd really loved that one).
- Orir Koboldgrip vomited up some sand and then a cactus plant grew out of the top of his head.

After nearly an hour, we finally reached the stage.

Glam went first (she'd insisted, rather violently, by shoving her way past the rest of us). Her eyes bulged with disgust as she chewed the seitan. Then daisies sprouted all over her face and arms—covering her in pretty flowers. She looked disgusted and started tearing them off as the crowd giggled.

Lake looked nervous as he ate the seitan. And despite a whole lot of gagging and shuddering, nothing magical happened. He was clearly devastated as he shuffled off the stage with his shoulders drooping.

Froggy also tested negative. But he didn't seem to care. In fact he was probably happy since it meant more time training with his dad instead.

Ari bit her lip nervously as she walked up onto the stage. I held my breath as she drank the Galdervatn and then received

◆

her small slice of seitan. She chewed and pretended to hate it—she even made a big show of coughing and choking. But nothing else happened.

"Negative!" Fenmir declared.

"But, *no*, I actually have the Ability," she said. "I swear."

"That's what they all say, kid," Fenmir said. "Next!"

Ari shot me a desperate look. I didn't know how to help her. But I didn't need to. Her face lit up with an idea.

"Beef jerky!" she called out. "Who has some beef jerky?"

I almost laughed at the thought that anyone would just randomly have beef jerky on them. But nearly all of the fifty or so kids left in line raised their hands. I'd forgotten that I was in the company of Dwarves. Someone handed a piece of beef jerky up to the stage.

Fenmir seemed dubious but allowed it.

Ari had vowed at age five to never eat an animal ever again. She struggled to chew the tough meat. Her fists balled up and her face reddened with disgusted anger. Thunder boomed outside and the whole warehouse shook as if it might collapse. Lighting arced across the ceiling, frying one of the huge industrial lights with a CRACK. Sparks and glass sprayed onto the floor behind the stage.

Everybody gasped. Then one kid cheered, and the rest of the kids joined in.

"Well, I guess we all make mistakes . . ." Fenmir said. "From time to time."

Ari left the stage looking startled, relieved, and a little embarrassed.

"You go next," Eagan said. "I'm too nervous. *Scared*, actually."

"Don't worry, I bet you'll have the Ability," I said.

Eagan shook his head emphatically.

"No, I'm not afraid I won't have the Ability," he said. "I'm terrified that I *will*. I don't want to do magic. I never have. I prefer to take up arms with things I understand, like language and reasoning."

He was probably the only Dwarf there praying he wouldn't have the Ability.

"Let's go, we have limited time!" Fenmir shouted at us from the stage.

Eagan nervously walked up onto the stage, drank some Galdervatn, and then chewed the seitan with great difficulty. But nothing happened. Eagan was the first Dwarven kid with a negative test to leave the stage beaming, arms raised in celebration.

Then it was my turn.

The seitan was mushy and tasted like poison. I nearly gagged as I tried to chew it but then just swallowed it whole. As I did, I realized all the kids were laughing madly.

I looked around.

Even Fenmir and his assistant were struggling to hold back laughter. I finally looked down and noticed that my legs had turned into two stumpy logs. Amber sap oozed out of my tree trunk legs and dripped to the floor. A woodpecker poked his head out of a small hole near where my knee should have been. He flew out an open warehouse window behind me.

When I looked back down, my legs had returned to normal, but my shorts were stained with gooey, yellow tree sap. A few kids were still snickering as I went down the steps and joined my friends.

"Well, I guess this is where we part," Eagan said. "But we'll see you guys at Buck's again tomorrow."

"Oh, lest thyne assessment hath but yielded results ye contrary," Lake mused with only half-kidding despair.

I felt bad for him. Of the six of us, he was the only one who seemed disappointed with his results. Ari gave him a pat on the shoulder and he grinned at her, his long, messy hair flying about as he added an exaggerated shrug.

And with that, it was finally time to learn real Dwarven magic.

CHAPTER 30

Ari Hits Me Repeatedly with a Huge Club

Only thirty-six Dwarven kids remained at the warehouse for the first session of magic training.

"We will start with a brief general lecture on the nature of magic," Fenmir announced. "And then you will be separated into smaller groups to work with my assistants. We *will* be performing magic today. Time is of the essence and so there is no point in Elf-stepping this."

The crowd laughed. I didn't get the joke.

"Now then," Fenmir said, clasping his hands together. "You will not learn any *abracadabra* here. Dwarven spells are *not* based on words—which of course is a totally ridiculous and stupid concept. Cannot the speechless perform magic? *Of course* they can. Merely saying a made-up word to cast a spell is a completely silly, illogical notion, one that books and movies have perpetuated, and that you can all forget right now.

"Real Dwarven magic is rooted in *intent* and *thought* and *feeling.* It is spiritual in nature, not cerebral. You have to *feel* what you need to happen or else it will not. But of course this makes our spells quite nuanced, for a feeling is hard to define, as is individual intent. Which is why three Dwarves may all attempt the same spell, and yet end up with three drastically different results. Feelings are unique to the individual and our intentions are innate and cannot be easily rebuilt. We desire what we desire, and we cannot lie to ourselves effectively . . . the Galdervatn will not let you. Which also makes Dwarven magic particularly dangerous for the untrained. Questions so far."

My mind suddenly wandered back to when Glam had smashed the walls at the PEE seemingly against her will. Was that what he meant? Was that why she hadn't been able to help herself? I didn't raise my hand, but instead just shouted out my question during his brief pause.

"So we can't fully control what magic we do?" I asked. "If my innermost desire is to eat, then magic will create food regardless of what I'm actually trying to do?"

Fenmir looked at me, startled, as if he'd never before been asked a question.

"To the untrained Dwarf, yes," he finally said. "This is accurate. Which is why our training here will be more focused on learning to address your innermost thoughts, to control them and harness them in a way that allows you to perform the magic intended. Furthermore, Dwarven magic is not for wanton uses. It is too pure; it is not for making life easier, but only for vital tasks. It can, say, help protect you, help feed you, help find you shelter . . . basic needs. But there is no Dwarven magic to help you do the dishes, or win at a game of basketball, or clean your room. These spells do not exist. If you attempt them, nothing will happen, or perhaps if anything, the opposite of what you desired will occur. Dwarven magic is *true* above all else."

This seemed fitting of Dwarves. They were practical, hard-working, brutally honest, and mostly incapable of being disingenuous or frivolous. Why should their magic be any different?

After Fenmir's brief lecture on how hard and dangerous it was to perform Dwarven magic, we were split into smaller groups of six to actually try it ourselves.

My group was Glam, Ari, myself, and three other Dwarves I hadn't met. Our Magical Instruction Assistant (or MIA, as Fenmir had called them) introduced herself as Tuss Pebblebow. She was young, still in her twenties from the look of it, and quite pretty in spite of (or maybe because of) a soft and feathery layer of hair resting on her upper lip. Maybe my Dwarven genes were kicking in and I was starting to find female facial hair attractive? I couldn't tell anymore, and I supposed it didn't really matter either way. People liked what they liked, who should care if others approved or disapproved, or whether or not it fit what was "supposed to be" or "normal"?

Fenmir stayed up onstage in the center of the warehouse. We were all given thimble-size cups of Galdervatn, which we promptly drank. Even the MIAs drank some. The only person who had yet to consume any Galdervatn was Fenmir himself.

"We will first try one of our most basic defensive spells," Fenmir said. "It could save your life in almost any conceivable deadly situation. MIAs, please demonstrate for the kids."

The six MIAs gathered in front of the stage. Three of them held massive, knobby wooden clubs. They looked hand-carved and very heavy. Glam stirred next to me, itching to get her hands on one of them.

"Proceed," Fenmir said.

The three MIAs with clubs reared back in unison as if taking synchronized batting practice. The room of kids collectively gasped as they swung them at the three unarmed MIAs. But just before impact, the MIAs turned into stone (of a variety of colors and types) and the clubs bounced harmlessly off their bodies with a series of loud THWACKS!

Or that's at least what happened for two of the three pairs.

The MIA on the far right did not turn into stone and the wooden club nailed him on the right shoulder. He flew backward and landed on the floor with a solid THUD. He rolled around in pain for a few seconds, then slowly climbed to his feet. The MIA who had hit him looked horrified and rushed over to offer her apologies.

He would be fine, though, since Dwarven bones were nearly unbreakable. But it had still clearly hurt—that sort of blow on a Human would have definitely broken bones.

Fenmir shook his head.

"You lied to yourself, Uruik," he said. "You didn't actually *feel threatened*, and the Galdervatn knew this." He turned to face the rest of us. "Now you will all try. The key is to imagine the pain, imagine the damage to be done, focus on protection, call back to the earth, think of stone, of hard rock, of the protection it offers. *Feel* threatened, *feel* the safety of hard stone, and you *will* turn. There is no magic word to help you, it is all about feeling."

The MIAs began passing out large wooden clubs to the Dwarven students. They were so heavy that some of the kids could barely lift them.

"Um, is it really necessary to use such dangerous weapons?" Ari called out.

Fenmir eyed her suspiciously.

"Were you not listening, child?" he demanded.

"Of course, but—" Ari started, but he did not let her finish.

240

"You must actually *feel threatened* to perform such Dwarven magic," he said. "A defensive spell will never work if there is no real danger. But I would still encourage you all to please aim for your partner's torso. We'll have no brain injuries today, please."

Tuss came back to our group with an armload of wooden clubs. She handed out three of them and paired us up. I was with Ari. She held the club tentatively, looking horrified, nervous, and perhaps just a little excited.

Glam got paired up with a little kid half her size. Her eyes glowed as she admired the huge club gripped in her massive hands. The little kid regarded her glee warily. He swallowed and took a step back.

"Do not worry," Fenmir reassured us. "Some spells are unique to certain Dwarves. Some, in all of recorded history, have only been performed by a single Dwarf. Everyone's magical abilities are unique and different. However, basic spells such as this are universal. You are *all* capable of achieving this. Proceed when ready."

All the kids in the room stood uneasily across from their partners. Only Glam seemed excited to bash her partner with a massive wooden club. Everyone else shuffled nervously and raised the lumpy weapons tentatively.

"Greg . . . I, uh, I don't really want to do this," Ari said, the club resting on her shoulder across from me.

"It's fine," I assured her. "You won't hurt me. I've already done this spell before, so take your best shot."

I really wasn't concerned—I'd already done this before I'd even known magic existed at all.

"Ready?" Ari asked, lifting the club from her shoulder.

"Pfft," I said jokingly. "Let's see what you got. I bet you can't even swing that thing with those dainty arms."

Ari grinned, taking the joke in stride.

"You asked for it," she said, swinging the club forward.

I braced myself, even though I already knew it wouldn't hurt. In fact, I'd feel nothing, just like when Perry had hit me in the face. I watched the club hurtle toward me, fearless, and waited for it to bounce off me like it was filled with air instead of being made of hard oak.

Then it crashed into my shoulder and everything went black in a jolt of pain.

I came to on the floor, looking up at Ari's concerned face.

"Omigods, Greg," she said. "Are you okay?"

My left shoulder throbbed and my arm felt like it might never move again. I sat up using my right arm. The left hung uselessly at my side. I realized I was nearly ten feet away from where I'd been standing. How hard had she swung?

"Greg," Ari said. "Say something!"

I was sure everyone was staring at me, the one kid who'd failed to turn to stone. But nobody was looking. Instead, half of us were crumpled on the floor. Nearly eighteen Dwarven kids rolled around in pain. Their partners hunched over them, apologizing profusely.

It appeared as if Glam's partner had been the only one to successfully turn into stone. He was still standing, dazed but unharmed. Glam looked in shock at her club—now cracked in half, the thick end dangling by just a few splinters.

"Do you have a concussion, Greg? Why won't you say anything?" Ari pleaded desperately, looking around the room. "Help, I think I gave my partner brain damage!"

"I'm fine," I finally said.

Ari looked relieved and helped me to my feet.

Feeling was coming back to my shoulder, but that only made it hurt worse. Our bones may have been nearly unbreakable, but our flesh still bruised like an old banana. There was a purple lump already swelling on my left biceps.

"You may be wondering why nearly all of you failed," Fenmir said smugly from the stage, not the least bit sympathetic. "You didn't *listen* to me! I told you: Dwarven magic is about feeling, reaction, *belief.* So why then did you fail? *Why?*"

When nobody offered an answer, he continued, still smiling.

"Because none of you actually believed you were in real danger," he said. "You cannot lie to yourselves and expect it to work. Galdervatn *always* knows what you really feel. If you do not feel threatened, or desperate, or whatever instinctual feeling correlates to the spell you want to use: then magic will not happen. Try again."

Everyone looked around uneasily, unsure we could endure more crushing blows from massive clubs constructed solely for smashing objects into oblivion.

Tuss brought Glam a new club and instructed her to switch places. Glam's eyes went wide with fear for a moment, but then she saw me watching and her face flooded with forced confidence. She handed her little partner the club and put her hands on her hips like she was indestructible. Her partner could barely lift the club, but finally managed to heave it up onto his shoulder.

We took our places again. Ari did not lift her weapon. She shook her head.

"I'm not going to hit you again," she said.

Fenmir must have been watching us, because he hopped down off the stage and walked over.

"You *must*," he said to her.

"But . . . does it have to be so *violent*?"

"Do you think Elves and Werewolves and Goblins will come at us with harsh insults and lawsuits?" Fenmir asked sternly. "No, those things will no longer matter in the new world. We must learn to defend ourselves, and this is the only way. Dwarven magic is about real necessity. We will not learn if we do not practice at full speed. Now hit your friend, or else someday watch his head get cleaved in two by an Elven blade!"

He stalked back to his post on the stage. Everyone looked at him, not moving.

"Now!" Fenmir screamed. "Let's go again!"

Collectively, Dwarven kids raised their clubs and assaulted their partners. Ari reluctantly lifted hers and took a step toward me.

"I'm so sorry, Greg," she said.

I braced for impact, this time panic rising in my chest as my sore shoulder throbbed, remembering the pain slammed into it just minutes ago. I cowered and almost dove out of the way. At the last second, I remembered that feeling of being stone, of Perry's hand slamming into my face like nothing.

Once again, everything went dark.

"Greg!" Ari said a second later. "You did it!"

I realized that everything had gone dark because I'd closed my eyes. I slowly opened them.

"I did it?"

Ari nodded excitedly.

"The club just bounced off you!" she said. "You turned into sparkly black granite. It was really cool."

It appeared that about half of us had managed to turn this time. The other half were again sprawled on the ground, writhing in pain (likely *double* the pain now that it was the second time around). Glam was on one knee, wincing and rubbing her right thigh. She was probably lucky her scrawny partner couldn't get much mustard on his swing.

Ari and I switched for the next round. I certainly had no desire to swing a giant wooden club at my friend. But I knew the trick was to sell it, otherwise she'd fail as nearly everyone else had on the first try.

So I scowled at her as I reared back the huge club, and said: "This is going to hurt! A lot."

I didn't hesitate or give Ari time to brace herself. I even let out a savage scream as I swung for added effect. Pure panic spread across her face.

And it worked!

Ari turned into an amazingly pretty shade of green-gray marble. A hunk of Dwarven-shaped, unrefined stone so striking that I almost dropped the club midair. But it was too heavy to stop either way. It slammed into Ari's marble ribs with a CRACK and bounced away harmlessly, sending painful vibrations down the handle and into my hands.

Ari came back to life a second later, still wincing from a blow that for her had never happened.

"I did it?" she asked, realizing she'd felt nothing.

I nodded, grinning.

She laughed.

We spent the next hour on the spell, since not everyone was getting the hang of it so easily. One kid managed to turn only his leg into a dull orange stone, and so the club still hit him pretty hard on the lower back. Another Dwarf turned into a ropy tangle of wood and vines instead of stone. He immediately turned back to flesh-and-blood Dwarf and cried out in pain. One Dwarf, instead of turning to stone, made a shocked, embarrassed face and then put his hands on the seat of his pants as several stones of various sizes tumbled from his pants cuff.

This got a howling reaction out of everyone who saw it. Except Fenmir Mystmossman. He shook his head in frustration and demanded that they try again. Fenmir insisted that we would not move on until every single one of us had mastered it. It was that important.

"That's all for today," Fenmir eventually relented, seeming dejected and tired. "Come back in three days, we will try again, and hopefully learn more spells. There is so much more to go over, Dwarven magic is nearly limitless in possibility. It will get better. It has to, or else we're all doomed."

CHAPTER 31

I Discover How Much I Miss Having Conversations with Inanimate Objects

Training at Buck's again the next day was a relief since my left arm was so sore I could barely even eat breakfast let alone get hit in the arm repeatedly with a huge club.

Throughout the day, Lake and Eagan asked about our magic training, but it was hard to give many definite answers. There was so much about Dwarven magic we still didn't understand.

"What do you mean there are no words?" Eagan asked as we practiced ax throwing.

"You don't speak at all to do magic," Ari said. "You just have to feel and think what you want to happen."

"Weird," Eagan said. "Sounds . . . easy."

Ari, Glam, and myself looked at one another and then laughed. Lake looked annoyed to not be in on the joke, and Eagan just looked confused. Froggy ignored all of us and threw another ax at the target with deadly accuracy. It turned out Froggy was an excellent ax thrower. Better than his dad, even.

Training that day, I was once again left frustrated. We'd been training for five days now and I was no closer to finding my dad. No closer to getting the Bloodletter. In fact, I hadn't seen or heard it all day. And I was surprised to discover I missed it. Especially after what it'd said to me the last time I saw it:

The next time we meet, you will pick me up for the first time.

And everything will change.

You will avenge your father.

When class was wrapping up that day, Eagan asked Buck to retell another ancient war story. It turned out Buck was a pretty good storyteller. And Eagan, Lake, and Glam frequently requested stories about ancient battles that weren't in any old texts, but instead had been passed down verbally through Buck's family for thousands of years. So after training, Buck settled into his living room to start the story. The six of us gathered around. But my focus wasn't on Buck at all. It was on figuring out where to find the Bloodletter.

Today was the day.

I was tired of waiting. My dad wasn't getting any less abducted.

"This one is called 'The Battle for Gnynt Fjord,'" Buck began. "It was a particularly brutal skirmish between a battalion of Dwarves and several companies of Orcs and Minotaurs, who had recently sided with the Elves Alliance. They guarded an especially important Fjord in the Eastlands of S'marth, just below the Mountains of Rijjvenfeld, and due west . . ."

I excused myself to use the bathroom. Nobody noticed my departure as Buck continued his story and I headed down the hallway, bypassing the bathroom and instead stopping at the next door. But it was locked. I was about to walk away to try the next door down when a familiar voice in my head stopped me.

Where are you going?

I'm in here.

"But it's locked," I whispered.

You're going to let a simple locked door get in the way of saving your father?

I was about to get defensive and start arguing with the Bloodletter, but it didn't even let me.

I'm just kidding—I can take care of that.

There was a sudden *click.*

I reached for the door, but stopped myself. There I was, in a grouchy old man's hallway, talking to an ax that had just magically unlocked a door for me as if it was an everyday occurrence, like grabbing a snack from the fridge.

Was I going crazy?

No, you're not. Proceed.

"Stop telling me what to do," I whispered at the door.

I'm only encouraging you to do what you know you must.

"I am not talking to an ax," I said slowly.

Well, technically you are, even if it is just in your head.

I took a deep breath and finally pushed the door open. The room was clearly Buck's personal armory. It had, at one time, merely been another small bedroom in an old apartment building. But now it was lined with racks of ancient weapons and armor of all kinds. Some weapons were rustic and plain, possibly bloodstained; others were encrusted with precious gems or inlaid with shining gold and intricate designs.

The Bloodletter rested on a rack, nestled in the middle of five other battle-axes of various shapes and sizes. The others faded into the background next to the Bloodletter, as if this was a documentary and they'd been pixelated like anonymous witnesses.

Pick me up.

Save your dad.

"How could you know what no one else does?" I whispered.

I don't know where he is. But TOGETHER we can find him. My power lies within you. Only you can unlock it. If you pick me up, if you let me choose you as my next owner, we will put right what was wronged.

I promise.

I took another step toward the weapon rack. The Bloodletter's silver handle, intricately carved with a swirling design, shone like it was charged with electricity. The blade was polished black like obsidian, even though it was metal and not rock. It gleamed and I knew that it was telling me the truth.

I reached out and wrapped my hand around the Bloodletter's surprisingly cold metal handle.

And the world disappeared.

CHAPTER 32

A Magical Ax and I Take a Psychedelic Day Trip to the Forest Moon of Endor

To say I was merely transported to another place would be an understatement.

When my hand touched the ax, my fingers went numb. Blue sparks arced into my palm and I could see right through my skin. I saw my own bones and veins and tendons glowing for a few brief moments.

Then my whole arm was on fire. The burning spread to the rest of my body. Everything else but the ax faded away, as if we were in a vacuum of dark fire. I was no longer aware that I could feel anything at all. Instead we were floating, nonexistent, *nowhere*. But we weren't even floating—there was no wind, no ground, no up, no down.

And then I saw my dad.

All I could see at first was his face, surrounded by the flickering edges of reality. He looked dirty, much thinner than I remembered. He was clearly exhausted, eyes sagging. I worried

I might be going crazy, but at the sight of my dad, I didn't even care.

Slowly, I saw more. His tangled, matted hair and his neck, and his dirty, ripped shirt (which was a My Little Pony T-shirt—showing that his captors either had a very low budget or at least some semblance of a sense of humor). His beard had been roughly shaved, leaving behind a dozen or more small scabs from little cuts. There were stones behind him, neatly assembled into a wall. A slab of wood was his bed, no padding, no mattress, no pillow. On top of it was a single, ragged book: *The Dark Elf Trilogy* by R. A. Salvatore. Whether this was meant as a form of torture, propaganda, or merely an earnest attempt to provide something humane was unclear. My dad was chained to the steel posts of the bed frame by both ankles. A small, filthy bucket sat in the corner of the cell.

That's what it was: a cell.

And I realized it was no dream. It was a vision. And I'd never seen my dad look so exhausted. And his captors had shaved his beard! For Dwarves, beards weren't a show of vanity, but rather a representation of the core of a Dwarf's character—like a measure of what lies within you. They knew this and had done that to him anyway.

My dad was speaking with someone just outside the cell. I could only see the back of the captor's head, but he had long, greasy hair slicked against his skull. He was tall and slight and had unmistakably pointed ears. I got the vague sense that he looked familiar—but that was absurd since I didn't really know any Elves aside from Edwin, and this guy was definitely older and taller than my best friend. Plus, I couldn't see the man's face, so how could he seem familiar? It had something to do with his gestures, his posture, the way he moved. It was almost as if

I knew his body language better than my own dad's—like I had spent more time with the guy holding my dad captive than with anybody else on the planet.

But that was obviously impossible.

Unless I didn't actually know the guy at all, but there was a different, perfectly rational reason he seemed so familiar . . . Like, maybe I knew someone who had spent his or her whole life trying to emulate this man? But I refused to believe that could be true. What it would mean was too devastating. I focused instead on my dad's determined face as he glared at the Elf through the bars of the cell.

Then, just as suddenly as it had all appeared before me, it was gone.

I was back in an empty, black space. The Bloodletter's handle burned hot in my hand, the only sensation I felt aside from the pain ripping into me from the inside—the pain of seeing my dad in such a state.

Then I was looking at myself. Playing chess with Edwin. Laughing with other Dwarven kids. Training with Buck and the others. Eating a silent, massive dinner with Fynric in our new makeshift apartment. Some of the scenes seemed real— like memories from the outside. But others felt hypothetical. Like eating dinner with Fynric—had he and I ever eaten a whole roasted boar for dinner? I didn't think so. But then again, so much of the past week had been a blur . . .

More than the question of reality, though was this: *Why?*

Why was the Bloodletter showing me these things?

What did it mean?

You still don't know? Maybe your friend Glam is right and you are cute but dumb? Fine, I'll show you more.

Next, I saw Luke Skywalker talking to Leia on a tree bridge

in an Ewok village from *Return of the Jedi*—a movie I'd only seen once and didn't even like. An elephant lumbered across a weedy desert. A depressed guy sat at a computer, scrolling listlessly through unknown content. A man chatted with another dude in a generic hallway, they both wore security keycards displaying a strange eagle logo I didn't recognize.

I had no clue why the Bloodletter would show me so many random things. For now I was the ax's prisoner, forced to watch this visual puzzle, helpless to even begin deciphering what it all meant.

And then, just like that, it was over. I was back in Buck's armory. The Bloodletter was lying on the floor at my feet. And despite knowing my dad was still alive, I felt no closer to finding him.

Do you know now what you need to do?

I shook my head.

But you saw your father?

I nodded.

You can trust what you see through me, Greg. You should know what to do.

"But I don't," I whispered. "None of it made sense. Can't you tell me—"

No. I know not what you saw, Greg. You can draw from my power, but what you find there is for you alone to decipher. Now, go, do what you need to before it's too late. I sense that deep down you already know the answer.

I backed out of the room, leaving the Bloodletter behind. It's not that I didn't *want* to take it with me. Part of me never wanted to be away from it again. But I knew there was no way I could smuggle it out of there.

I promptly left Buck's, ignoring my friends' questions as I rushed past them in the living room—I would explain later.

Because I *did* know what it all meant.

The Bloodletter was right. The first part of the vision was all I'd needed. The second part was just to get me to accept it—to convince me that my initial instincts had been right. Even as horrible as accepting that truth would be. The Bloodletter's words echoed in my brain:

Now, go, do what you need to before it's too late.

I needed to speak to Edwin—he was the last piece of this puzzle.

———◆I◆———

I went straight to the PEE.

Even though it was already close to 5:00 p.m., kids were still trickling out from various after-school activities. Edwin's black town car was parked on the corner, so I crossed the street and crouched behind a garbage can a few feet away.

An old lady walking by shot me a dirty look. Her little dog with a pink bow tie snarled at me ferociously. Determined to let nothing get in my way anymore, I growled right back at the little dog. It whimpered and the lady pulled on the leash, equal parts confused and offended.

A few minutes later, Edwin came bounding down the front steps, followed by his usual entourage of friends and pretty girls. He made some joke and they all laughed before parting ways.

He headed toward his waiting car as his driver, Benny, opened the back passenger door.

I stood and waved.

"What are you doing here?" Edwin hissed, shoving me into the backseat before any of his classmates saw me.

"Is everything okay?" Benny asked, eyeing me suspiciously.

"Yeah, it's fine," Edwin said. "Let's get going."

Benny closed the door and got into the driver's seat. Edwin immediately hit a switch and raised a soundproof partition between the front and back seats.

"What are you doing here?" Edwin repeated.

"I needed to see you," I said.

"Look, it's dangerous for you to be here—"

"No, it's more than that," I said.

Edwin searched my eyes and his expression changed.

"What's wrong?" he asked, sounding like he expected me to say my dad had been found dead.

"I know where my dad is," I said. "He's alive."

A relieved smile flashed briefly across Edwin's face, then he furrowed his brow.

"How in the heck did you find that out?" he asked. "And where is he?"

"It's a weird story," I said. "I've been wasting all my time pretending like I was coming up with a plan. Waiting for someone to tell me what I needed. But the truth is: I've had it all along. It's *you*. You know where my dad is at, and I can't ignore it any longer. This whole time, I've been a typical Dwarf, paralyzed into inaction by fear, or thoughts of bad luck, or whatever. But not anymore. Now I'm going to *do*. Nothing will stop me—"

"Dude," Edwin said softly. "Slow down. What are you talking about?"

"It wasn't some rogue faction of Elves that took my dad,

Edwin," I said, struggling to keep my intensity under control. "It was *your parents*."

Edwin shook his head, his mouth opening and closing like his jaw was broken.

"It's true," I said firmly. "Your parents lied to you all along, they did take my dad. I know you couldn't have known the truth. At least I hope not. If I thought you did I wouldn't even be here. And if I'm wrong . . . well, then you have me right where you want me and you can finish me off here and now."

"It can't be true," Edwin said, his face turning red. "Even if it were, how could you possibly know something like that?"

"I saw him talking to my dad in a prison cell," I said. "Don't ask how I saw this, it doesn't matter. But I saw it. It was him . . . he has your same mannerisms, or you have his, just like you said you always strived for as a little kid. It's almost uncanny. It was *him* and it was real. You have to trust me."

Edwin looked close to tears now. He *believed* me. He knew I was right, and maybe deep down had suspected it all along. But like me, he just hadn't wanted to consider the possibility it might be real. Edwin was clearly taking the news almost as hard as I had when I first realized the truth.

"The problem is that I still don't know *where* he's being held," I said slowly. "But *you* do. Maybe this means our friendship is over now. Or maybe it can still be saved. But either way, you can definitely still help me find my dad."

"I—I don't, I can't," Edwin said, shaking his head. "I swear I didn't even know my parents would *ever* do something like that to me . . . to *us*. I have no idea. I mean, even if my parents are holding him it could be *anywhere*. They own a whole fleet of private jets. They easily might have sent him to New York or

Europe or Antarctica! Even if he is still in Chicago, how would I know where, they own dozens of properties here."

"He's here in Chicago," I said. "In a secret dungeon. I know he is. The Bloodletter's vision wouldn't make sense otherwise."

"Greg, *you're* not making any sense!" Edwin insisted. "What's the Bloodletter? What vision?"

"I can explain that later," I said. "Just tell me this: Do any of your parents' buildings or houses have a secret section? A basement? A dungeon? A secret prison of some sort? Secret passages maybe . . ."

"I don't know—"

"Yes you do," I insisted. "Now think, Edwin! What about security keycards with a red eagle logo on them?"

"Well, I mean, yeah, that's the logo of one of my parents' companies," Edwin said, putting his hand to his chin. "They operate in an office building downtown, but . . ."

He suddenly froze and his eyes widened as if he'd just swallowed his own tongue.

"Oh my gods," Edwin said quietly. "The Hancock building. There's an entire floor that nobody knows about. A secret level between the eighty-second and eighty-third floors. Everyone thinks the building is one hundred stories, but it's actually one hundred and one. I never knew what the hidden floor was for, but this would make sense. Why else would my parents always be so clandestine about it? I shouldn't even know about it at all, but my grandpa always trusted me more than my own dad does. He told me about it in secret."

"That's it," I said, my hands shaking. "My dad is there."

Now you're getting somewhere, Greg. Let's go rescue him.

It was the Bloodletter. Calling out to me from across the city somehow. Maybe finally touching the powerful ax had established some sort of weird link between us like in that old movie *E.T.*?

"Can you be so sure that's where he is?" Edwin asked. "How do you know he's still alive?"

Saying *Because a magical ax told me so during a psychedelic dream vision* didn't seem like it'd be very convincing.

"It doesn't matter," I said. "But everything you just told me confirms it. It all makes sense now—it fits what the Bloodletter showed me. And now I need to go get him back."

"No, *don't*, Greg," Edwin said. "I need to check it out first. It'll be way too dangerous for you to try to go in alone. Promise me you'll wait."

"I can't do that, I'm done waiting."

"Greg, I can't protect you there," Edwin said. "You'll start a war!"

"It's likely too late to avoid that now, anyway, Edwin," I said. "You know that. Your parents, whatever their motivations were, have already started it."

"No," Edwin said, shaking his head again. "No, they wouldn't risk everything they worked so hard for . . ."

"They did, though," I said. "You know I'm right. Just like you know *I have to* do this."

"Greg, don't. Please trust me as your friend. It's too dangerous. There's too much at stake here, just be patient."

"I've been too patient already," I said. "That was the whole point of the vision. And I do trust you, Ed. I know you're right. It is too dangerous and may very well escalate a war that your parents renewed. But my dad can't wait any longer."

But perhaps Edwin was right? Maybe saving my dad wasn't worth possibly pushing the Elves and Dwarves further into war? Some things are bigger than one person.

The new war is inevitable. It's already under way and you know it. Letting your dad die will only double the pain when the real fighting resumes.

"Leave me alone already," I said to the Bloodletter.

Edwin looked at me, confused and concerned.

"Hey, you came to me—" Edwin said.

"Sorry, I wasn't talking to you," I said. "It's . . . hard to explain. Anyway, what does this mean for us? I mean, your parents, the Elves, took my dad—they even shaved his beard."

Edwin winced.

"Exactly!" I said.

"I know," Edwin said, voice shaking. "It's unimaginable. But that doesn't change what I said. Let me find another way, Greg."

He's just trying to stall you so he can warn his parents.

I ignored the Bloodletter. I didn't believe it this time. Edwin couldn't have known. And even if he were somehow in on it, why would he have just helped me figure out the exact location?

Because he's setting a trap, that's why!

"Greg, promise me you won't go there," Edwin said.

"I can't make that promise," I said.

"Why not!" Edwin almost shouted, genuinely worried about my safety.

The car stopped at a red light in heavy traffic on Milwaukee Avenue. I opened the door.

"Because I don't want to lie to you," I said as I stepped out of the car and walked away, toward the nearby Blue Line station.

Edwin did not follow me. The light turned green and his town car continued traveling northwest. All I could hope now was that he wouldn't actually tell his parents about this conversation like the Bloodletter had claimed he would. That it wasn't a trap.

Or else they'd be ready for us, and it would likely mean certain death for me, my dad, and whomever else came with me on the rescue mission.

CHAPTER 33

I Am Rudely Assaulted by a Leprechaun

The Dosgrud Silverhood Assembly Hall was a massive chamber hidden among the complex maze of tunnels in the Dwarven Underground.

It was named after an ancient Dwarf, Dosgrud Silverhood: the very first Council Alderman. (Which was basically like the president of Dwarves, but with less power and responsibility than most countries' presidents. Because, you know, Dwarves.) Dunmor Beardbreaker was the current standing Council Alderman.

The Assembly Hall was easily the size of one whole end of Soldier Field, the massive stadium where the Chicago Bears played. The stone room was rounded, with several sets of intricate stone tables and chairs in the center. Dozens of rows of seats were built into the outer walls, encircling the room like an amphitheater. They would hold the 125 Council members, plus there were plenty of extra seats for visiting Foreign Councils and the public (some Council Sessions were open to all, and others were by invite only). Today, the place was packed with Dwarven dignitaries and local leaders from all over the world for the first Global Council Session in decades.

Seated side by side at a long table at the center of the Assembly Hall were eight of the nine Elders, the elected leaders of the Council. Each of their votes counted for ten times that of an ordinary Council member.

I sat alone at a much smaller stone table facing the Dwarven Council Elders. The only empty seat among them belonged to my father.

Dunmor Beardbreaker sat in the middle.

He did not smile, but nodded at me politely.

"It's good to see you again, Greg," he said. "I'm glad you're well."

"Thank you," I said, though I wasn't sure he heard me above the roar of the 125 whispering Council members (and the hundreds of visiting dignitaries) surrounding us on all sides.

Fynric sat at another table behind me. He was not allowed to sit with me, since only I would be speaking to the Council. Fynric had explained earlier that Dwarves valued highly the ability to speak for oneself. It was one of several reasons lawyers did not exist in Dwarven culture.

My dad's vacant Elder seat glared at me. It was still marked with his name—engraved on a large rock sitting in front of his chair at the end of the table.

I choked back tears. I had yet to cry over what had happened, and I wasn't about to now. Not when I was so close to getting him back.

"Order!" Dunmor said loudly once all of the Council had taken their seats.

His voice boomed throughout the well-crafted stone

chamber. The shape of the walls and ceiling amplified his voice perfectly and the room fell immediately silent.

"We're gathered for our first Global Session in almost thirty years," Dunmor said, the acoustics making his voice sound like that of a god rather than a stout Dwarf who ate chunks of old turkey from his beard. "So welcome to all those who have traveled from various Local Councils across the globe. The agenda for today will be brief, but surely the consequences of the decisions made will carry significant weight in our future. On the docket for today are the following issues: One: We will hear young Stormbelly's new evidence of Elven hostile transgressions and vote on a course of action. Two: We will debate and discuss the Riven and then conduct a final vote on the matter once and for all."

This was followed by a series of rumblings and mutterings from the Council members and audience. Dunmor ignored it and continued.

"But first let me introduce our young guest to the Elders," Dunmor said, turning to face me.

He went down the line from left to right:

- *Wera Flatpike*: A stout little woman with a wispy red beard. When introduced, she rubbed her whiskers lightly and I swore nearly every Dwarf there stared at her longingly.
- *Dhon Dragonbelly*: A scrawny man with graying black hair. For some reason Dunmor felt it pertinent to include that Dhon was a champion eater and had won the Chicago WingFest eating competition fourteen years running.
- *Forgie Onyxgut*: A round old man with wild white

hair. His teeth, when he smiled, were pure black.

- *Ara Cavehide:* A short, thin woman with a fluffy mass of curly white hair on her head. She wore a billowing fur coat and a lot of sparkling jewelry like she considered herself royalty.
- *Heb Blazingsword:* A tall (for a Dwarf—he was still probably only five foot ten), muscular guy with gray hair and a massive black beard. Dunmor said that Heb was the finest Dwarven swordsman alive today.
- *Foggy Bloodbrew:* A middle-aged woman who smiled warmly when introduced. Her eyes welled and I realized she must have been a close friend of my father. Dunmor said she was the Dwarven Underground's on-site physician and health-potion brewer.
- *O'Shaunnessy O'Hagen Jameson:* He was by far the smallest man in the room at just over four feet tall. He had a smear of wavy black hair on his head and smoldering, beady black eyes. His face seemed per-manently fixed into a sneer.

"O'Shaunnessy, who we all refer to as Ooj," Dunmor said, "is actually a Leprechaun, which is a very rare breed of Dwarf. He's one of just two hundred and seventeen known remaining Leprechauns."

My mouth dropped open.

"Leprechauns are real?" I said.

Ooj immediately leaped up onto his chair. Even standing on his chair, his head barely rose higher than the other Council Elders seated next to him. He scowled at me.

"Of course we're real, you pear-snacking animal lover!" he shouted.

I admit I sort of expected him to have an Irish accent, but his accent was so classically Midwestern Chicago that he should have had a thick mustache and a beer and hot dog in his hands. He must have noticed me fighting back a smirk, because he jumped up and down a few times in exasperated anger. Then he shook his little fist at me.

"Stop grinning at me, boy, or I'll come down there and wipe it off your bloated face with my knuckles!" Ooj screamed.

The other Council Elders rolled their eyes as if this was a common occurrence.

"Are all Leprechauns so angry?" I asked Dunmor.

"Oooh!!!" Ooj screamed, pointing a shaking finger at me. "That's racist!"

I shook my head, dumbfounded. The other Council Elders finally stepped in and tried to calm Ooj down. Foggy put a hand on his shoulder and said something I couldn't hear and it seemed to work a little. He at least stopped hopping angrily up and down on his chair.

"I'm sure Greg meant no offense," Dunmor said. "You have to remember, all of you, that Greg isn't yet familiar with the nuances of our culture. Now, please, sit down, Ooj, so we can begin."

Ooj finally sat down, but he didn't stop glaring at me.

"Okay, then," Dunmor said. "I officially call this Global Council Session to order."

—✦—

"What do you mean, *no rescue mission will occur*?" I demanded, openly shouting at the Council Elders shortly after I explained that I knew exactly where my dad was being held captive.

266

"We are not convinced of the veracity of your statements," Council Elder Forgie Onyxgut said.

"Why would I make this up?" I said.

"Because you can't trust a word your friend said," Dhon Dragonbelly yelled. "Elves are Elves, they're all the same!"

"Lying Pointers, all of them!" shouted a Council member behind me.

"He's spying for the Elves!" a conspiracy theorist screamed.

One of the few voices of dissent that I heard was that of Foggy Bloodbrew, the Underground's physician, and the Elder I suspected was my dad's friend.

"Let's hear him out!" she was saying. "He might actually know where Trevor is! Surely it's worth investigating—"

But it was to no avail. Either they weren't hearing her, or didn't want to listen.

"Greg, you must understand our point of view," Dunmor explained compassionately. "Even beyond believing what your Elven friend said, the *visions* you described are . . . well, entirely unprecedented. Furthermore, the Bloodletter would only tell you what you *want* to hear; it is not an all-knowing being. It thrives on your own weaknesses and desires, Greg."

"Pfft!" Ooj shouted loudly. "That's assuming it revealed anything to him at all! I highly doubt an artifact of such significance would select *this Dwarven impostor* as its next owner. It's preposterous!"

Cries of approval rose up from a large number of council members.

"If I may speak on behalf of the boy!" a voice called out behind me.

I turned around and saw Buck standing near the door, my five classmates in tow.

The audience gasped. Buck Noblebeard was apparently a legendary figure among Dwarves, one who rarely made public appearances.

"You may," Dunmor said.

Buck took a few steps forward until he was near the center of the room, almost directly behind me.

"The Bloodletter has given me *nothing*," he said. "It was placed in my care since I have distant blood ties to the last known owner. But that matters not! I am not who it chooses. Furthermore, the age and status of a Dwarf are *meaningless* to ancient Dwarven weapons. Assuming such things is Elven thinking!"

There were cries of outrage from the Council, most likely due to the offensiveness of his insinuation.

I was stunned that Buck was actually on my side. After all, he'd spent most of our training time deriding me for my miserable performance at basically every facet of Dwarven battle.

"Nobody knows how or why a weapon with powers chooses an owner," Buck continued. "Not even back in Separate Earth—it has always been a mystery. Even the best Dwarven blacksmiths did not select the means by which their finest enchanted weapons exhibited their true powers. It is the will of the earth and of the gods, *not of us*. It is dangerous to assume we know otherwise."

There was a rabbling of debate among the Council after he finished. Eventually they were called to order. Fenmir Mystmossman was summoned next to weigh in—being the preeminent expert on Dwarven magic. I fully expected him to take my side—after all, at one point he'd told those of us with the Ability that *we* were the special ones.

"I saw no special prowess whatsoever from the boy in our

training," Fenmir began, crushing my hopes. "He has the Ability, of course, which is admirable. But he is otherwise totally unremarkable."

Someone behind me (who sounded a lot like Glam) shouted:

"How would *you* know? It's not like you even *have* the Ability!"

This elicited a surprising amount of laughter among the Council members. Fenmir's face grew red with fury.

"Which is precisely my next point!" he screamed. "It's why I am such a good instructor, I understand it from the outside. Not having the Ability clears my judgment, it allows me to focus purely on the facts, the evidence, the knowledge of magic. And it brings me to a point nobody has mentioned, yet which should have dashed this boy's story as hogwash instantly: *How*, may I ask, is it possible that the Bloodletter produced any magical visions at all, true or otherwise, without the presence of Galdervatn?"

There was a hushed gasp of agreement from the Council. And I had to admit, I wasn't sure I had an answer for him either. How had the Bloodletter shown me things without magic?

I saw a lot of nodding among the Council and the Elders.

"More Galdervatn must be resurfacing than you suspect!" I finally said. "It has to be."

"Hardly possible . . ." Fenmir said dismissively.

"What about the animals?" I shouted back.

"What's this nonsense about animals?" Ooj shouted.

"Explain, please," Dunmor said.

I reminded them that animals were regaining their long-lost sixth sense: an instinctual hatred of Dwarves. Leading to all of us being attacked by random animals on a near daily basis. Dunmor himself had told me this was possibly a sign of

269

the impending return of magic. Why couldn't ancient relics be experiencing the same sort of thing?

"It is certainly an intriguing point," Dunmor agreed.

"It's a load of Elf spit is what it is!" Ooj yelled, sparking another round of heated shouting and debate among the Council.

Dunmor quickly called the room to order again.

"Let us vote on the matter," he said. "All in favor of investigating allegations that Elder Stormbelly is being held captive by the alleged Elf Lord, Locien Aldaron, inside a secret floor of the Hancock building, say *aye*."

There was a surprising number of ayes, but still no more than 20 of the 125 Council members present. Foggy was the only Council Elder to vote yes.

"All opposed?" Dunmor said.

The *nays* sounded like thunder in the acoustic chamber.

"What's the official count, Rungren?" Dunmor asked.

A frail Dwarf easily in his eighties or nineties, seated at a desk behind the Elders, glanced up at hearing his name. His hand continued scrawling madly on several scrolls loosely strewn about his table.

"That was seventeen ayes, including one Elder vote," Rungren said. "And one hundred eleven nays, including seven Elder votes. Five abstained. Final vote is twenty-six for, and one hundred seventy-four opposed."

I was astonished that the old Dwarf had been able to count based solely on the sound alone. To me it had all sounded like total chaos.

"Proposal rejected," Dunmor said unceremoniously.

A low sigh of defeat escaped my lips.

"The Council has spoken, Greg, I'm sorry," Dunmor said

sincerely. "But so be it: No action shall be taken by *any* Dwarf in relation to what Greg shared with us here today. There is still no proof that Elves have committed any wrongdoing. And until we have such evidence, we will not test their limits further by violating the Thrynmoor Pact again."

"Hear, hear!" Ooj shouted needlessly.

"Now," Dunmor said. "On to the second agenda item for today's Global Council—"

His words were cut off by the sudden sound of screaming in the hallway outside the Dosgrud Silverhood Assembly Hall.

It was followed by more shouts and screams—much closer this time. Then several loud crashes rocked the Underground so violently that chunks of concrete from the ceiling fell onto my shoulder.

"What in the name of Landrick the Wanderer is going on?" Dunmor said.

He was answered seconds later when the grand doors to the Assembly Hall exploded open, showering the crowd near the back in chunks of warped iron crossbeams and splinters that fell in twisting spirals.

Dust from the concrete door frame blanketed the entryway like a blizzard. A hushed moment of silence enveloped us as it cleared. And then it became evident rather quickly what we were dealing with:

Trolls.

CHAPTER 34

I Get Crumpled Up like an Empty Hamburger Wrapper

If there was any doubt as to what we were dealing with, Council Elder Heb Blazingsword erased it when he stood up and screamed, *"Mountain Trolls!"*

There were five in all, ranging in color from light gray to sickly green to dirty brown, and in size from large pickup truck to small semitruck. They had mostly bald, knobby heads, sickly complexions, yellowing teeth, and enough muscle between them to feed a small village of cannibals for a decade.

And they all had deafening screams of rage.

And bad breath.

At least Greeny did (the green Troll who was the leanest and tallest of the bunch). I knew this because he was in my face, roaring at me, his hot breath soaking me like rotting soup.

He swung his fist at me, and for a moment I almost stayed there and tried to initiate my stone spell. But then I realized I didn't have any Galdervatn. So I quickly dove to the side at the last second.

His huge green fist smashed the stone table into hundreds of crumbling pieces.

Screaming and crashing and destruction erupted everywhere. I tried to locate my friends, but I didn't have time, because Greeny was on my tail, already bringing his other fist down toward me like he was playing a carnival game called Whack-a-Dwarf.

I dove out of the way again. His fist pounded a small crater into the stone floor.

Dunmor's thunderous voice echoed loudly from the front of the room—even over all the madness: "Call for the Sentry!"

But I didn't have time to worry about that. Greeny was still on me as if he'd been sent there specifically for me. And I supposed that was possible, especially if Edwin had told his parents about my plans after all.

Which now seemed entirely feasible.

The devastation of this realization made me a tad late dodging Greeny's next blow. He backhanded me. It was more like getting hit by a wrecking ball than a gentlemanly slap. Had it not been a glancing blow, it surely would have killed me, strong Dwarven bones or not.

As it was, I flew across the room and up into the Council member seating. I landed half on empty stone bleachers and half on an older Council member who'd been sitting there with a hand over her mouth in shock. I'd forgotten that my dad and I had been the only living Dwarves to see a real-life Troll before this.

"Sorry," I mumbled as pain coursed through my bruised body.

She didn't even seem to notice that I'd landed in her lap. She just sat there shaking her head in disbelief, even as Greeny charged right at us, easily leaping up into the layers of stadium seating.

I rolled to my feet and quickly shoved her out of the way, ignoring my aching joints and the crippling back pain from where I'd landed on the stone benches. Greeny roared and dove at me face-first—as if he wanted to eat my head. And perhaps that was what he intended to do. I really didn't know if Trolls ate Dwarves or not. Maybe they were just really angry vegetarians?

Instead of dodging right or left this time, I decided to surprise the beast by charging right back at him head-on. As he approached, his yellow teeth just feet away from my face, I jumped forward as high as I could.

And landed right on his nose.

My hands, flailing for something to hold on to, grabbed his fleshy eyelids. They were surprisingly soft, and I made a mental note to pitch Troll-eyelid pillowcases and sheets to the next rich entrepreneur I happened to meet.

Greeny cried out in surprise as I clung to his face by his eyelids. My feet rested on his upper lip and my legs were squeezed around his pointy nose.

I began tugging mercilessly at his eyelids, trying to make as much contact with his gelatinous eyeballs as possible. He screamed and grabbed me around my midsection, trying to pull me off his face. But I tightened my grip and his eyelids stretched as he tried to get me off him. He roared with pure rage.

That's when he started simply squeezing.

My chest compressed and I couldn't breathe. It felt like my rib cage would crack any moment. Strong as stone and iron they may have been, but compared to Greeny, my bones were just strands of brittle crackling. But I held on and hoped his hand would tire out before I either suffocated or simply folded into myself like an empty hamburger wrapper.

After another ten seconds, moments before I lapsed into a coma, Greeny suddenly let go and I tumbled back onto the stone seats with a breathless THUD.

I rolled over, gasping for air.

Greeny flailed wildly in pain, trying to reach something on his back. As he spun and grasped desperately, I finally saw a Dwarven battle-ax buried in his lower back.

Ari was under his feet, dodging the wild, staggering steps. She rolled to the side and then ran toward me, bounding up the seats two at a time.

"Greg, are you okay?" She crouched over me.

I nodded, still gasping and unable to speak.

Lake, with several hatchets in his belt, clambered up Greeny's back, using the Troll's many warts as hand- and foot-holds. He was aiming to level the final blow as I leaned back and tried to catch my breath.

When I finally sat up again, Greeny was teetering wildly, then stumbled and finally crashed to the floor in a heap. Lake stood on the beast's chest proudly, holding one of his axes above his head in triumph, like a kid posing with a rifle next to his first deer.

That's when I finally saw the full chaos and destruction inside the Assembly Hall. Three of the Trolls were already dead: Greeny, Blue, and MudBrown. Knobby (the one with a particularly misshapen head) was currently backed into a corner by four or five Dwarven soldiers fully equipped with weapons and metal armor. He would be felled shortly.

Only Beefy (the thickest of the Trolls) still raged mostly unchecked. He gripped two hapless Dwarves, one in each hand,

and swung them around—using their bodies to batter more Dwarves on the ground. A few Dwarves were trying to wrap a chain around his Troll cankles.

I prayed to the Dwarven gods (who Buck had been teaching us about) that none of the lifeless Dwarves I spotted were friends or family. Not that it would have made the scene much less gut-wrenching.

"Come on, we need to go help them," I said as I started to get up.

But a sharp pain in my lower back brought me right back down again.

"Just stay here," Ari said, standing up. "You might be seriously hurt."

"Stay here, too," I insisted. "I don't want—"

"Greg." Ari grinned at me humorlessly. "I can take care of myself. Trust me."

She rushed away, toward the skirmish with Beefy.

He'd tossed aside the two Dwarves and now held the Council Elders' massive, curved table. He swung it from side to side like a stone saber, easily knocking away a whole squad of Dwarven Sentry warriors.

But Ari's help wasn't needed. One of the Dwarven Sentry guards had apparently taken some Galdervatn. Dozens of long vines snaked their way down through a few cracks in the stone ceiling. They descended on Beefy and wrapped themselves around the huge table in his hands.

He cried out in confusion.

The vines easily wrenched the table from his grasp and then began battering him on the sides of the head with it. Beefy covered his head with his arms and tried to flee. But the enchanted vines followed him easily, still swatting at the monster with the huge stone table like an old lady swatting at a dog with a rolled-up newspaper.

Beefy's muscles bulged beneath his folds of fat as he struggled to fend off the enchanted table. He flailed wildly, spinning to get away. Then he finally tripped over one of his fallen brethren and began stumbling.

The Dwarves around him cleared away as he cried out and came crashing to the floor. His face landed squarely on Greeny's heels with a sick PLOP.

And then it was finally over.

But the damage had been done.

It was a sight I'd never forget.

And even if I somehow eventually did, I knew that the Bloodletter would remind me again and again and again until vengeance was had.

———✦———

"This Troll is still alive!" someone shouted.

Ari was helping me limp down to the main floor of the Dosgrud Silverhood Assembly Hall. We watched several dozen Dwarves rush over and surround MudBrown, whose massive Troll chest heaved slowly as he struggled to breathe.

"Who sent you?" Dunmor demanded of the dying Troll.

MudBrown shook his ugly head. He either didn't understand or wasn't going to talk.

"Mooncharm!" Dunmor called out. "Where is he?"

"He's dead, sir," someone said.

My heart dropped into my feet. Eagan was dead? It couldn't be. I staggered, not able to walk, and Ari somehow held me up. Hadn't she heard? Wasn't she crushed? But then I heard Eagan's voice.

"I'm here," he said, stepping forward. "My father didn't make it, but I'm here, ready to help."

I was devastated for him—after all, I sort of knew how he felt. But Eagan seemed resolved to not let it break him. He held his head high, refusing to cry. I'd since learned of course that the old phrase *Belmonts never cry*, didn't apply just to Belmonts/ Stormbellys (like most things), but to all Dwarves.

Dwarves never cry. Ever.

Dunmor hesitated for a moment and then nodded, waving the boy over.

"I'm so sorry, son," Dunmor said, patting Eagan's shoulder. "But we need your help so we can avenge this tragedy. Use your Mooncharm ability and find out who sent them. Torture is not effective on Trolls—or so the ancient texts attest."

Eagan nodded bravely and approached the Troll. I wondered darkly if this might have been the very Troll that had killed his father. I shook away the thought before I could imagine it further. I had never gotten to meet Eagan's father, Kiggean Mooncharm, but by all accounts he was a great and kind Dwarf.

Eagan knelt next to MudBrown's massive ear, which was nearly as big as he was. He spoke into it but I couldn't make out what he was saying. Eagan spoke for a good minute or two, gesturing at some points for emphasis, though the Troll couldn't see him. At times, Eagan even rested his hand gently on the Troll's stringy, thin hair.

Eventually he stopped talking and stood, looking at the Troll's one good eye as it rolled over to see him. Then it searched past Eagan and found me. The eye widened and the Troll raised his massive arm and pointed at me.

"Him," MudBrown growled.

Everyone turned and stared at me in shock.

What was this Troll implying? I shook my head slowly. I hadn't done *anything*. Certainly there was no way I was responsible for *this* Troll attack as well.

"We *follow him* here," MudBrown said with his last breath and then fell silent.

Everyone stared at me, some accusingly, some angrily, some in shock. But most of the faces, Dunmor's included, merely looked sad. They had to have known I'd had no idea I was being followed. They had to know I would never willingly lead anyone else down here but a fellow Dwarf. Not even Edwin.

The very thought of my best friend seized my breath in my throat.

Even as Eagan's eyes flickered, fighting back tears, and he turned and angrily stalked away, my biggest concern was grappling with what I'd just realized: I had come straight to the Underground after meeting up with Edwin. That was surely where the Trolls had started following me. Was it possible *he* had sent them?

As heartbroken as I was, a new hope bloomed. With this attack, any last doubt over whether to mount a rescue mission for my dad had vanished. I was going to go get him back with or without the Council's approval, even if it would mean the end of my friendship with Edwin forever.

With or without any help.

I will help you.

I nodded to a magical ax that wasn't even there. That was all I needed. The Bloodletter and I were going to rescue my dad. And hopefully find a way to put an end to this war before it resumed.

CHAPTER 35

I Make an Inspirational Emotionally Charged Cry to Action That Would Bring Anyone Else but a Dwarf to Tears

Immediately following the attack, everyone carried the wounded to the medical wing of the Underground city.

I helped as much as I could with my aching back and joints, knowing that I couldn't run off to rescue my dad just yet. At least a third of the Dwarves were already angry with me: I was the boy who'd haplessly led five Trolls to a secret city that had never before been breached in over two hundred years of existence. Running off on some vigilante mission, leaving the wounded to suffer under debris would not help anything.

After most of the mess had been cleared and cleaned with remarkable efficiency, an emergency Council Session was called. The damaged Assembly Hall was still the best place to host it.

Dunmor began with a tribute to the fallen Dwarves:

One Sentry soldier had been lost. As had two Dwarves in the hallways of the Underground, who'd merely been in the wrong place at the wrong time. Five Council members had perished, including one visiting dignitary and Eagan's father, along with Elder Ara Cavehide.

Despite this, nearly every seat was filled, the departing members having already been replaced by the candidates next in line for Council consideration. Hundreds of others crowded into the room as observers, trying to find some resolution. I stood among them in the back with Ari, Lake, Buck, Eagan, Froggy, and Glam.

Even for Dwarves, the mood was abysmal. The impending vote on the Riven was entirely forgotten for the moment.

"We should just surrender," Elder Wera Flatpike said, not able to look up. "We simply can't afford another devastating attack of this nature."

There were a lot of nodding heads throughout the room.

"We cannot win," another Council member added. "We barely had a chance before . . . but now that we know Trolls are on the Elves' side? Pfft."

"Agreed," Dunmor said. "We're simply not ready for this type of combat."

More agreements from the room.

I couldn't believe what I was hearing.

After getting sucker-punched, they were just going to give up? Relinquish everything to the Elves? Even if it were typical for Dwarves to assume defeat, I simply wouldn't let them this time. In my mind, this wasn't even an option. The old Greg definitely would have been agreeing right along with them. Might have stood up and said, *This is our lot in life, we'd better just accept it with good humor rather than try to change anything.*

But I didn't feel that way anymore.

Even after all the disasters my actions had recently caused

(including this one), I was more certain than ever that injustices needed to be fixed. Wrongs righted. Fathers saved. We could not sit back and let the Elves win. More than anything, I knew it was how my dad would have felt—he'd never have sat back and let the fear of defeat, the specter of bad luck, push him into a tepid surrender.

"So we should begin drafting an unmitigated acquiescence treaty?" one of the new Elders asked.

"No!" I shouted, surprising even myself.

"Huh, the traitor speaks," someone said, but it drew little reaction from the weary crowd.

"We cannot give up like this!" I said, and my voiced boomed and echoed throughout the chamber, sounding more adult than it ever had. "We are *Dwarves*! We are strong, we are genuine, we are the original peoples of the earth! Dwarves do not back down from fights. Dwarves do not get bested by their enemies, even when outmatched. Dwarves are cunning, bold, hardworking; we are *survivors*, masters of the elements. And we *can* win this war! I know how to hit the Elves where it hurts most; I know where the Elf Lord's secret lair is located. We can sneak in when he least expects it! Without their leader, they will flounder, weak and afraid. Without magic, they will suffer under our new army of Dwarven Mages! I have seen them in action just yesterday; performing real Dwarven spells with vast skill and might!*

"We can and *will* win!" I continued. "We just need to believe in ourselves for once. We have the Galdervatn, they do not. We are Dwarves, they are not. Dwarves do not give up. Dwarves are mighty children of the earth, Separate and Now.

---

* Of course, that wasn't entirely what I'd witnessed the day before, but I was trying to give a rousing speech here, not be a typical Dwarf.

Dwarves alone will usher in the New Magical Age, and we alone will reign supreme. *We. Are. Dwarves!*"

I raised my fist into the air, waiting for the thunderous applause and shouts of approval. For the battle cries and tears of vengeful outrage. I waited, but none of that came. Instead, there was one lone voice from the back.

It said, "Meh."

"Dwarves lose, it's what we do," someone added.

"Yeah, we can't win. Not with our luck."

There were murmurs of agreement around the chamber and I slumped down in defeat. Embarrassed and crushed. But more determined than ever to do what I needed to do— with or without help.

After the meeting, everyone scattered. Either back to the infirmary to check on injured loved ones, or to begin making ceremonial death celebrations for those lost in battle. Or for some, likely just home to make a massive dinner to drown their defeated sorrows with heaps of meaty food.

I stayed behind in the Assembly Hall, looking down at my hands. What now?

You know the answer.

The Bloodletter was right. There'd be no waiting. I would leave immediately; I'd rescue my dad tonight, alone. Or die trying.

But then a hand passed in front of my face. I looked up and saw Ari smiling sadly at me. I grabbed her hand and she hoisted me up to my feet.

"I liked your speech, Greg," she said.

"Thanks," I said.

"Yeah, and we're in," Glam said. "We'll help you."

All of them were there. Lake, Froggy, Ari, Glam, and even

Eagan. I'd nearly gotten them all killed and yet here they were, willing to risk it all again to help me save my dad. I'd only ever had one friend like this before. My throat tightened and I couldn't speak or else I'd break the universal Dwarven rule.

"I don't blame you for my dad's death," Eagan said. "But I want to avenge him. I'll do whatever it takes."

I nodded.

"We know you're planning to go rescue your dad tonight," Ari said.

Froggy nodded at me with a solemn expression. I knew it was him saying: *You helped me so many times, and I won't back down when it's time to return the favor. Which is now.*

"Lest thee doth embark on ye endeavor in solitude," Lake said. "Whence failure doth don itself inevitable. Hold forth alongside thyne friend, thyne shalt commit."

I nodded again, still fighting tears and unable to speak. Part of me wanted to tell them: *No, stay here; don't endanger yourselves further on my behalf.* But the truth was if I really wanted to rescue my dad, I needed all the help I could get. Besides, it was nice knowing just how many friends I actually had.

Even if I'd maybe just lost one.

CHAPTER 36

Fynric Gives Me a Turkey Sandwich and a Bottle of Rum for My Mission

We didn't throw our hands into the center of the group and then raise them up and shout, "Dwarf Powers Activate!"

But it was essentially that in spirit. I told them I had no plan, no real idea of what to do once we infiltrated the surely well-guarded secret level of the Hancock building, but that we would simply improvise. They grinned and nodded and we broke away to gather what we needed from our rooms. We would rendezvous in the Arena in twenty minutes.

Before I even got halfway out the door, an arm grabbed me and pulled me aside. It was Buck. He had a bundle of blankets under an arm.

"I can't go with you, kid," he said. "I suspect I would find some way to sabotage the mission. Plus, Dunmor would notice my absence and then be cognizant of your plan and try to stop you. So my presence would not help. But this will."

He handed me the blankets. Something big and heavy was wrapped inside and I suspected I knew precisely what it was.

Finally I'm yours.

Which is a relief . . . I really can't handle living with this guy any-more. You should hear how loudly he eats cereal!

"Thank you," I said, trying not to smirk at the Bloodletter's comments. "And also for supporting me during the meeting. It surprised me since—well—"

"Since I'm so hard on you in training?" Buck asked,

"Well, yeah," I said.

"Greg, I'm hard on you because I expect *more* from you," he said. "You're a Stormbelly. And so you need to become the leader of your pack, the best warrior of your generation. It's in your blood, like it was with your father. He rejected his natural path. Of course he still became a special Dwarf in his own way. But you can be even better: you can become the best Dwarven hero to ever live. That means being the best student, the best leader in battle, being bold and strong and fearless like your father. That's why I'm so hard on you—it's to bring out the best in you."

I nodded, not sure what I could say to that. *Me* becoming the leader of a whole generation? It seemed like nonsense until I considered the fact that I was about to lead my five friends into a dangerous battle against an Elven fortress.

"Good luck," Buck said.

"Thank you," I said.

"And Greg?" Buck added. "Bring my son back in one piece, will you?"

I nodded, hoping it wasn't a lie, and then hurried along toward my apartment.

Fynric was there waiting for me. I put the wrapped bundle of blankets on my bed and faced his grim expression. He handed me a turkey sandwich—Dwarf style. Well, growing up we'd always called it a meatwich, but of course that was before my dad had wanted me to know I was a Dwarf. Now that I knew, it turned out that all Dwarves loved a meatwich (aka a Dwarf-style turkey sandwich): basically a mound of homemade deli turkey between two hamburger patties for buns.

I was hardly hungry in the face of what had just happened, but managed to get the huge sandwich down in a few reluctant bites. I guessed I probably did need the protein for, like, energy for facing an Elven army later that night.

"May the gods be with you," Fynric said after I finished the sandwich.

He knew what I was up to—this secret plan was the worst-kept secret plan ever imagined. But he made no move to stop me.

I nodded.

"And get Trevor back," he said. "I need to go, the Council is meeting to discuss a possible unconditional surrender. I can't be here when you leave."

He handed me a small box.

"In case you get thirsty on your mission," Fynric said with a sly grin, and then he left without another word.

I walked over to my bed, set the small box aside, and unwrapped the bundle of blankets Buck had given me.

It's nice to see you again.

"Yeah, you too, Bloodletter," I said.

Bloodletter!? Is that really what you've all been calling me?

"Uh, you didn't know?"

No! And it's horrible, so garish.

"Well, what did *you* think your name was?"

I've been referring to myself as Carl.

I nearly laughed. But I figured laughing at a magical ax that nobody could hear but me was that final step across the line into total lunacy. Actually talking to it was already standing on the line.

Well, either way, I'm excited to finally sample Elven blood again— it's been a long time. We are going to free your dad, Greg. It's why I exist, after all. Now let's get going, I'm thirsty!

I nodded and set the Bloodletter aside to change clothes. I grabbed Blackout, the dagger Ari had made me, and strapped it to my belt. Then I opened the box Fynric had given me.

It contained a small rum bottle. But it no longer carried rum. It was filled to the top with swirling, glowing, misty Galdervatn.

A grin spread across my face as I watched it change color.

The Bloodletter swore behind me in jubilant celebration (words I certainly never could have used without blushing).

This rescue mission suddenly seemed a lot more plausible than I'd previously thought.

———✦———

Instead of going to the official Underground Armory to gear up for battle, we went to the Arena.

Ari and Lake led us past a bunch of Dwarven kids making weapons in the blacksmith alcove. Of course, this was after they'd all made a big deal over seeing the Bloodletter in my hands. They saw it at Buck's all the time and had never stopped making celebrity-sighting googly eyes at it, but I think they were shocked Buck had given it to me.

Ari led us to a small indent in the natural rock wall of the cave behind the glassblowing workshop. She put her hands on the cold, wet stone and pushed. Slowly, a huge section of the cave wall slid to the side, revealing a secret chamber.

Lake and Ari climbed inside and motioned for us to join them.

Ari lit a torch on the wall. It instantly illuminated the small cave like an industrial fluorescent bulb. Not because the torch was special or anything, but because its light reflected gloriously off the cave's contents:

- Whole rows of shining breastplates and body armor
- Racks of swords and axes of all shapes and sizes
- Shelves of crossbows, wooden bows, bins full of arrows of various lengths and purposes
- Chain mail, helmets with horns and real fur padding, and an assortment of battle-ready footwear
- Shelving on one wall stacked with goblets, metal cups, dinnerware, and little metal animals

"That's just some of our early practice work," Ari said, seeing me looking at the shelves of non-weapons. "We couldn't bear to get rid of them. Sentimental value, you know."

"Wasteful thought yields nary sunder wasteful action," Lake said. "Or doeth sayeth ye manual of familial relevance artisanal trades."

I nodded, in spite of not quite picking up on what he meant.

"You guys . . ." Eagan said slowly, awed. "You made *all* of this yourselves?"

Ari's cheeks turned pink as she grinned and nodded.

It *was* impressive. Even Froggy's eyes were wide with amazement. The secret cave was the size of a living room. And it was stacked wall to wall with polished, beautiful, and striking Dwarven armor and weapons.

"What on earth for?" Eagan asked. "I mean, I thought you were opposed to violence in general—especially the brutal Separate Earth kind . . ."

"Well, I am," Ari said, embarrassed. "I didn't make all of this for any *real* war. We made all of this because we . . . *had* to."

"Someone forced you?" I asked.

"No, no, not like that at all," Ari said with a laugh. "We simply can't help ourselves. It's in our blood; it's like . . . *our calling*, I guess. When I'm not with friends, or at a show, I'm thinking about smithing. I dream about the forge every night. Lake and I used to spend every spare second of every day we could down here making stuff—back before so many other Dwarves moved their families to the Underground. I don't think I can ever stop—forging is like breathing to me, I guess."

Lake nodded.

The normally enigmatically stoic Froggy ran a finger along the metal hilt of a small shortsword. Glam had already managed to strap on a leather war belt containing three swords and a battle-ax. Plus, two more axes were strapped across her back. She was feverishly trying to find a place to store two crossbows she'd plucked from the shelves.

Glam stopped, realizing we were all staring at her.

"Overkill?" she asked.

"It's a bit much, yes," Eagan said politely.

"Plus, you're going to want to put on your armor *before* the weapons," Ari said with an amused grin.

Glam laughed and began unstrapping all the stuff she'd zealously laid claim to.

We spent the next twenty minutes gearing up for battle. Ari and Lake had to help the rest of us figure out how to put on most of the equipment. And in some cases, show us what was what—I'd mistakenly tried to wear a groin-plate as a helmet. Lake had giggled about that blunder for nearly two full minutes.

By the end, I was equipped thusly:

A metal breastplate that felt like it weighed forty pounds was strapped to my torso with leather cording. I wore a helmet with four small polished horns from some animal poking out from the top. There was no armor on my legs except for shin guards and thick leather boots tied with reinforced leather straps. I had metal protectors looped around my thumbs, covering the backs of my hands with chain mail, and two small shoulder guards hooked to my breastplate. For weapons, I carried only the Bloodletter across my back in a nifty leather-and-fur sheath and Blackout in its scabbard on my belt.

The rest of our band of warriors was suited up in a variety of ways. Ari had gone pretty light with the armor, but carried an array of small throwing axes and daggers. Lake had two small crossbows, a regular bow, and very little armor aside from some chain mail. Eagan had about the same amount of armor as me, plus a pretty wicked sword with a shiny gold handle on his belt and an ax on his back crisscrossed with a short broadsword. Froggy wore nearly a full suit of armor, and carried an array of small throwing axes and daggers, and a larger battle-ax.

And Glam . . . well, what *didn't* Glam have? She looked like a robot, there was so much metal. It was a marvel she could move any of her joints at all, let alone walk. Aside from full body armor with chain mail, Glam had two swords, a huge ax, two smaller ones, a dagger, and a crossbow. She clinked and clanked like the world's largest set of car keys.

The rest of us had a hard time keeping straight faces as we left and closed the secret entrance.

But knowing what we were about to face certainly helped.

CHAPTER 37

Paul Picks Up His
Weirdest Fare of the Night

The Uber driver who pulled up in a Nissan minivan looked about as stunned and confused as the people on the streets.

There were a lot of bizarre characters in Chicago (like the time I once saw three people dressed head to toe in amazing Ghostbusters costumes on a random night in February), but six kids dressed in full battle gear, carrying very realistic-looking medieval weapons, still drew a lot of interest.

"Um . . ." said Paul, our driver. "I *hope* one of you isn't Ari."

"That's me," Ari said, holding up her black-market iPhone.

"Right, uh, well . . ." Paul said as if he were about to tell us no weirdos were allowed in his van.

But it was too late—we were already piling inside, our weapons and armor clanking loudly. Paul looked back at us nervously.

"Try not to, uh, cut the upholstery," he said. "So is there, like, a *Game of Thrones* event downtown or something? Your costumes are pretty dope."

"Yeah, uh, there is," I said before my friends could say anything about the show either being racist or completely inaccurate. "There's, like, this huge fantasy event, uh, thingy, um, downtown."

It didn't seem like Paul believed me. But he shrugged anyway, and then pointed at a row of dark buildings we drove by.

"Can you believe this?" he said.

"What?" I asked.

"These power outages. This whole block is dark, lookit."

"Oh, wow," I said, finally noticing that aside from the streetlights, the entire block was dark. I'd never seen Chicago without lights before. It was eerie.

"Yeah," Paul said. "I guess they've been happening all night, all over the city. Internet even went down for like an hour earlier. The Uber app stopped working for a while, too. Crazy."

None of us really knew how to respond and so we nodded dumbly, our armor clinking and clanking as we did. I think had we not been on our way to engage in a real battle with Elves, we might have considered what it meant. We might have been able to predict what eventually would happen just after dawn.

Paul switched on the radio. There was a news story about a flurry of recent bird and squirrel attacks on people in Chicago's many public parks. The six of us smirked, knowing that all the victims were likely part-Dwarf and haplessly unaware.

As we approached downtown, I pulled out the bottle filled with Galdervatn and took a huge swig. I passed it to Ari. She swallowed several gulps and gave it to Glam, who drained the rest and grinned.

Paul's eyes went wide and he looked a few seconds away from a full-fledged heart attack.

"You kids can't drink that in my car!" he said.

"It's okay, it wasn't actually rum," I said.

"Well, what was it?" he asked, pulling up in front of the Hancock building.

"Magic potion," I said, grinning as I got out of his van.

"I guess this job wouldn't be interesting without nights like this," Paul said, shaking his head. "Have fun at your *Game of Thrones* thing."

Standing outside the Hancock building, pedestrians gawked at us. Several people snapped pictures and took videos with their phones. Some, though, looked at their devices in confusion, wondering why they'd suddenly stopped working.

"Come on," I said.

We stepped through the front doors into the Hancock building. Well, technically it wasn't officially called the Hancock building anymore, but typical Chicagoan stubbornness meant everyone still called it that anyway—the same way we all refused to stop referring to the Sears Tower as the Sears Tower. We entered the "Hancock building" opposite of the Signature Lounge, where the elevator bays were likely lined with tourists waiting to go up to the top floor bar and check out the great views. This side of the building was deserted aside from two security guards in blue suits.

Ari immediately incapacitated them with a Snabbsomn Potion smoke bomb. We grabbed one of their keycards and ran from the lobby to the small elevator bay behind it.

"Well, now what?" Eagan asked.

"Edwin said the secret level is between floors eighty-two and three," I said. "So I guess we start on eighty-two and try to go up somehow? There has to be a secret entrance of some sort."

They nodded. We climbed into the elevator and pressed 82. We watched in anxious silence as the elevator floor display flashed quickly from 1 to 25 to 47 to 69 to 82. There was a quiet chime and the doors slowly opened.

And we were face-to-face with three men wearing jackets with *City Safe Security* badges on them and earpieces in their ears like Secret Service agents.

"Got them," one said into his wrist mike.

They advanced, blocking any escape from the elevator.

CHAPTER 38

We Learn That Humans Live Miserable Lives

As my friends drew their weapons, I wondered if we were actually ready for this.

We'd only had one week of training. And though we'd learned some ax-throwing techniques, combat stances, and several basic sword parries, we really hadn't even scratched the surface of real combat. And magic training had just been one day of getting pummeled by oak clubs—hardly a tutorial in magical warfare.

The guards were too close to use Snabbsomn bombs, so the only option was to fight our way past them. But at the sight of our swords and axes, the unarmed security guards raised their hands and took several paces back.

We stepped out of the elevator.

One of them lunged at Glam's sword. Thankfully, her magical instincts took over before her warrior ones. Instead of swinging the sword at him, he was incapacitated by what surely must have been fifty gallons of loose gravel crashing through the cheap ceiling panels.

"What the—" he managed to say, before being blanketed in pebbles.

The other two guards stared in shock. Enough time for Lake and Ari to get close enough with their readied weapons to ensure they wouldn't attempt anything similar. A few minutes later, all three guards were bound with rolls of packing tape we found in an office storeroom. We left them there, taped to metal shelving housing hundreds of reams of printer paper.

The eighty-second floor was a giant office space. A massive ocean of cubicles and tiny offices separated by a labyrinth of gray hallways. The lights were dimmed, but not completely off.

"Humans really spend, like, all day here working in these little cubes?" Eagan asked.

"Yeah, lots of people have jobs like this," I said.

"Man, the Human world sucks," he said.

Let's destroy the place. You know, just for fun. And also it will be, like, compassionate of us, right? Saving the Humans from their dreary lives and whatnot and so forth?

I ignored the Bloodletter's attempt to talk me into destruction for the sake of destruction and pulled a hunk of beef jerky from my pocket. Because eating always helped calm my nerves.

Glam leaned toward me with a huge grin on her face.

"Got any more of that?" she whispered.

I handed her a piece.

"So your dad's really here somewhere?" Glam asked through a mouthful of jerky as she picked up a stapler from someone's desk and eyed it suspiciously.

I nodded.

"But the real question," I said, as we aimlessly wandered the hallways, "is how do we get up to the secret floor above us?"

"You're supposed to be the one with all the answers," Ari said. "This is your mission, we're just here to help!"

"I'm here to destroy Elves," Glam said. "Break their bones to dust like dried flower petals."

"Okay, well, the *rest of us* are just here to help you," Ari said.

"I want to avenge my dad," Eagan reminded her.

"Okay, forget why we're all here!" Ari snapped. "The point is, the Bloodletter guided us here, maybe it has answers . . ."

As she spoke, we rounded a corner and her words trailed off. Standing in front of us were six more guards. *Armed* guards who drew their weapons at the first sight of us.

Lake quickly pulled free a crossbow from his belt.

"Lake, no!" Eagan shouted.

But it was too late.

The guards pulled the triggers. But instead of a hail of bullets raining down on us, there were six miniature explosions as the pistols imploded in their hands. They winced and drew back their arms. Confused and in a lot of pain.

A pile of smoking guns lay at their feet, small stones lodged in the barrels of several of them. Others had warped to unrecognizable heaps of steaming metal. I wondered which of us had pulled off that spell.

The guards recovered quickly, less shocked than a Human security guard would have been.

"One of them has the Ability," one of the guards said. "And has obviously obtained some Yysterious."

"So the rumors are true," another of the Elven guards added.

The six of them drew small swords from somewhere within their billowing suit coats. Their elven swords were smaller and

298

thinner than ours, but the metal glowed nearly translucent. The blades looked sharp enough to shave a yeti bald without a single nick.

Lake fired his crossbow.

The lead Elf whipped his sword in a quick half circle, severing the tip of the speeding arrow and redirecting it over their heads. The blunted, wooden end bounced harmlessly off the wall behind them. The metal arrowhead clattered near the pile of broken guns.

Ari tossed her last two Snabbsomn Potion bombs at them. The capsules exploded, shrouding their end of the hallway in purple fog. But to our astonishment, the Elven guards were still standing as the haze began to clear.

"You think Snabbsomn potion works on Elves?" One of them laughed smugly.

"Well, then we get to do this the fun way!" Glam said with a grin, drawing a sword in each hand.

Ari, Lake, Eagan, and Froggy also readied their axes and swords. I reached for the Bloodletter, but it stopped me as soon as my hand made contact with the handle.

No, Greg. Let's go, this is the perfect distraction so you can complete your mission.

"But I can't just leave my friends," I said, watching as they steadily approached the Elves.

Forget about them. They'll be fine. Do you want to rescue your dad or not?

The ax was right. It was why we were here, after all. Besides, as my friends reached the Elves and swords and axes began clanging off one another, it actually looked like they could hold their own. Perhaps not in a totally fair fight, but it wasn't a fair fight. Glam and Ari had Dwarven magic, and the Elves apparently still had no Galdervatn (or Yysterious, as they had called it) of their own.

I slunk away and ran in the other direction, leaving them to distract the Elven guards.

"Where are we going?" I asked.

I don't know. Free me from this sheath and we will find out.

I drew the Bloodletter and held it in both hands. The glinting double blades reflected my face back from the black surface. My own expression startled me—it looked determined, but also furious. I'd never seen my face look like that.

Close your eyes.

I did.

Now, what do you want most?

Suddenly I was having another vision. This one was more focused than the first. I saw myself furiously chopping away at a wall with the Bloodletter. Through layers of plaster, drywall, even steel support beams and wooden studs.

And I knew what I needed to do.

CHAPTER 39

The Bloodletter and I Go Medieval on a Helpless Old Xerox Machine

A short time later I was hacking through a wall for real.

Although sweat dripped from my damp hair into my eyes, I couldn't believe the ease with which the powerful ax sliced through everything. The drywall cut like paper. The wood like Styrofoam. Even the steel studs carved away like a hunk of cheese.

After a few minutes, I was standing in another room, one disguised as an office supply closet. Two bewildered Elven guards dressed in leather armor with bows and swords flanked a door at the other end.

They scrambled to pull free their Elven blades. Although likely well trained, this was clearly the first time they'd ever been faced with real intruders. Nor had they ever expected to be from the look of it.

Move now! Cleave them in two before they regain their wits.

I almost listened to the Bloodletter, even taking a step forward. But the truth was, I didn't *want* to cleave anything living.

I'd never killed *anything* before, and had never wanted to, aside from probably a few ants and mosquitoes. Still, I must have felt real mercy then, in spite of the powerful, vengeful energy coursing through the Bloodletter. Because otherwise I'd never have been able to perform the magic I did next.

Lop off their heads, Greg! They're keeping you from your dad.

I ignored the Bloodletter and threw all my concentration at not allowing the Elves to draw their weapons. They struggled to pull their swords free, but it was no use. The blades were stuck in their sheaths—wedged in by thousands of grains of sand that had magically appeared in the narrow spaces of the inner lining of the scabbards. The Elven metal ground against the sand. The swords wouldn't budge.

Then the guards let go with yelps of pain and surprise as the hilts glowed red like they'd just been pulled from a searing fire. They looked at their burned hands and then back at me, now realizing I had used Dwarven magic. And also that they were outmatched because of it.

Then they did something I never expected: they fled, pushing past me nervously before taking off down the hallway.

It was foolish to let them live. Now they'll alert more capable reinforcements.

"It doesn't matter," I said. "We'll be gone before they get back."

Will we?

I ignored the Bloodletter and used it to smash open the door the Elves had been guarding. Beyond it was a small room containing only a massive Xerox copy machine. It was old and yellowing and had clearly been born way before me.

All that fuss over this contraption?

But the Bloodletter knew, as I did, that they were not merely

302

guarding an ordinary copy machine. It was too heavy to move, but I figured it might just need a secret passcode on the control pad. I hit the On button, but the screen remained dark and dead. The power cord dangled lifelessly on the floor next to the machine. I peeked behind the machine and saw pure darkness.

It was concealing a secret passage.

I tried to move it again, but it wouldn't budge.

You're wasting your time. The answer has been on your back all along.

I glanced at the Bloodletter's handle over my shoulder. Then back at the old Xerox machine. I shrugged and pulled the ax free.

Part of me expected the copy machine to put up some kind of fight. After all, the plastic shell and metallic inner components were solid and hard, and not made of drying rubber or crumbling wood.

But the Bloodletter cut right through it as if it were marshmallow. The black blade gashed the machine open, spilling wires and plastic guts everywhere on the first blow. The ax passed through the machine so easily that it lodged into the floor, just inches from my big toe.

I pulled it free and took another hack. Within minutes, the machine was cleaved into a thousand pieces, scattered around me like it had exploded. Behind it lay an opening to a secret hidden tunnel.

A tunnel I knew would lead to my father.

CHAPTER 40

It Turns Out That Goblins Are Every Bit as Ugly as Their Name Suggests

*W*hat are you doing, Greg? We need to go back and continue with your mission!

I ignored the Bloodletter again as I retraced my steps back to my friends. It made a strong case—being just minutes from finding my dad made it hard not to continue into the secret tunnel alone. But I also knew I couldn't just ditch my friends, leaving them to fight six Elven guards and untold numbers of reinforcements. Besides, surely there would be even more guards ahead. I was going to need their help to rescue my dad.

When I found them, the fight had pushed out of the narrow hallway and into the larger office space. There were broken cubicle walls and random boulders and tree trunks (probably debris from Dwarven magic) scattered about. It looked, despite the mess, as if it had been a rather easy victory.

My friends were presently restraining the six battered guards and taping their mouths shut. Eagan and Glam were in the middle of an argument.

"If we kill them, then what makes us better?" Eagan pleaded.

"Glam smash Elf!" she roared back, raising her magically transformed stone-wrecking-ball fists.

"Why?" Eagan said. "To what end? What will it bring you?"

Glam, coming down from some sort of frothy battle rage, finally looked doubtful as her hands retook their usual form.

"Okay, *whatever*," she relented.

She flashed me a flirtatious grin, trying to make what I assumed were doe eyes. In reality it looked more like she'd just swallowed a giant Rubik's Cube.

"Guys, I found it," I announced. "The secret entrance to the hidden floor."

—•I•—

"Geez, Greg, what did this thing ever do to you?" Ari asked, kicking at the shredded remains of the copy machine.

I shrugged, trying to hide an involuntary, half-embarrassed, half-proud grin.

"Thee doth volunteer ye commencement of ye forthwith invasion of yonder cave artifice," Lake declared heroically as he crawled into the secret tunnel. After a few tense seconds, he called out in a hollow, echoing voice: "Tallyho! Proceed post-haste on thyne heels!"

The tunnel was narrow and dark. As we crawled, every hand moved forward tentatively, uncertainly groping for spiders and rats. But after ten feet or so, the passage had expanded enough so we could stand and it was light enough for us to see. The walls were plaster and clean with surprisingly little sign of dust or cobwebs.

At the end of the tunnel was a metal ladder.

I climbed to the top and pushed on a trapdoor, which was

square and made of wood. It swung open quietly on greased hinges and slammed onto the floor above me. I climbed through the opening and stood quickly to assess any threats.

The hatch opened into a long hallway.

Any resemblance to the generic office setting of the floor below (and surely the floor above) was gone. This hallway was lit with soft green flames that danced on elaborate glass sconces along the walls, spaced every ten feet or so, leading to a T-junction several dozen yards ahead.

The walls themselves were no longer drywall and plaster, but carved from wood. Not *built* from wooden planks, but actually carved smoothly from a single, massive tree. Based on the wood-grain pattern, I surmised that the entire hallway was carved from the hollowed-out trunk of a giant sequoia (*Sequoiadendron giganteum*).

We were inside a tree trunk that had been turned into a hallway inside a massive Chicago skyscraper.

The smell of the wood was intoxicating. Soft music played somewhere, but the origin was hard to pinpoint. It sounded like enchanted flutes and small string instruments. The rounded hallway was like a giant acoustic funnel, the music bounced off the walls and echoed into the distance.

The others had crawled up through the hatch and stood next to me, staring at the secret floor in awe. It was like some kind of organic spa from a movie about people so exotic and rich it may as well have been a fantasy.

"Man, the Elves' version of the Underground is way better than ours," Eagan declared reluctantly.

"Heh, it's too soft," Glam said with a grin. "Too dainty, just like Elves."

"Come on, let's go," I said, pushing ahead.

306

My dad was so close now that I didn't have the patience to discuss a plan. Instead, I charged on and my friends followed me silently. At the end of the hallway, I took the right branch. A gut feeling.

Well, that, and also the Bloodletter telling me: *Go right.*

The deserted, ethereal hallways made the whole thing more eerie and tense than it already was. It felt too much like a trap. Glam even said as much.

But we were in too deep to back out now.

We pressed on, the Bloodletter not needing to give instructions anymore. I wasn't sure if it was the Galdervatn coursing through me, or some of the Bloodletter's own enchanted brand of magic, or some unspoken connection to my father, or just my own innate Dwarven sense of direction (or perhaps a combination of all of the above), but I suddenly knew exactly where I was going.

I knew how to find my dad.

I charged ahead through the empty wooden hallways, each one carved from a different chunk of pure ancient sequoia. Each one lit by the strange green flames. Each one echoing that bizarre, captivating music. We were close now—I could feel it.

But then we rounded a corner and found ourselves face-to-face with a small army of Elves blocking the only path to my dad.

It wasn't just any army. Standing at the front were the striking faces of Locien and Gwen Aldaron, Edwin's parents—the reigning Elf Lord and his queen. Behind them were ten Elven soldiers armed with glowing blades and elegant bows. And flanking them, from opposite hallways, essentially trapping us, were a dozen ghoulish green creatures with long, spindly legs and misshapen heads on lanky, grotesque torsos.

They were no larger than small men, but they had a savage, wiry appearance.

"Goblins," Lake whispered softly, looking at the awful creatures with shiny green skin.

"How is that possible?" Ari said, readying her weapons.

But we didn't get to speculate any further—Locien launched his attack without hesitation. Without ordering us to drop our arms and surrender. Without even so much as an acknowledgment to the boy (*me*) who had been to several of his houses many times for barbecues and his own son's birthday parties.

"Wait, Mr. Aldaron!" I yelled. "It's me, Greg. We can talk about this."

Locien Aldaron merely smiled. But calling it a smile wouldn't be accurate, it was more like a sadistic leer, like a small heartless snake wriggling its way across his face.

Wow, that's cold.

You're really friends with this psycho's son?

But I didn't have time to respond to the Bloodletter, because Locien was already mid-attack. The Elf Lord waved a long staff with a glowing blue orb at the top in a small arc and then thrust the end forward. A blue energy ball fired from the orb and zoomed right toward us.

We flinched instinctively; there wasn't time to do much else.

The blue light collided with Ari's shoulder and my heart leaped into my throat.

But she turned to stone right before the impact, and the energy ball dissipated harmlessly on her rock-shoulder with a sizzle. She returned to her own form, looking unharmed but stunned.

Locien Aldaron had just used Elven magic.

Now we were both severely outnumbered *and* no longer had a magic advantage. The six of us tensed as the Goblins approached from the sides and the small army of Elves advanced in front. Locien sneered at me again and waved his staff, preparing another Elven spell.

We readied ourselves for the fight of our lives.

CHAPTER 41

———— ✦✦✦ ————

Okay, So Sometimes Dwarves Do Cry

Greg, you cannot stay. You must get to your father.

Almost as if she'd heard the Bloodletter, Ari seconded the thought a moment later.

"Greg, run! Go find your dad," she said breathlessly. "We will hold them off."

I didn't want to leave them this time. Not facing such insurmountable odds. But I knew I had to. If I stayed, and we were all defeated together, then this whole mission (and our likely demise) would have been for nothing.

My friends engaged the oncoming Goblins and Elves. Chaos exploded around me. I spun and chopped at the wooden walls with the Bloodletter, not looking up to see what was happening, who was winning or losing.

The Bloodletter made short work of the wall. I squeezed through a small hole into an adjacent wooden hallway. I ran down it and cut my way through another wall to the back side of the hallway that led to the prison.

I hacked and cut and chopped my way to a wooden door in

an empty hallway. Strange that nobody guarded it—but then again, all hands on deck were presumably back there, engaged in a massive battle with my friends.

I sliced through the door quickly, not even bothering to see if it was unlocked. Behind it lay a dank stone hallway much more like the Underground than the pleasant hallways we'd traversed to get there.

It was lined with steel bars, rows of prison cells. Most were empty. A few contained a scowling Goblin or two, and one held an Elf who pleaded with me to break him out as I passed. I ignored his cries, but did wonder what he'd done to earn imprisonment by his own kind inside the Elven version of Guantánamo. Maybe he was in that radical group Verumque Genus, that Edwin's parents had blamed the Egohs attack on?

Finally, I reached the third-to-last cell and faced the iron bars. A hunched figure lay on the floor in the corner.

"Dad?" I said.

The man rolled over and sat up. The eyes were wild and the fresh beard thin and scraggly on his gaunt face. But it was my dad; there was no mistaking it.

He grinned.

"I knew you had it in you," he said proudly.

"I'm so sorry, Dad," I said. "I shouldn't have—"

"No, Greg," he interrupted. "You've done nothing wrong. Let's just get out of here."

I swallowed and nodded and told him to stand back. He huddled in the corner as I swung the Bloodletter at the iron bars, half expecting the ax to bounce away in a shower of sparks. But the black blade stayed true and sliced through three of the thick bars with a jolt. I hacked through the bottoms and then two more full bars.

My dad rushed into the hallway.

He wrapped his arms around me and though he smelled awful, even for a Dwarf, I hugged him back. Only then did I realize I hadn't really ever expected to see him alive again. I finally let the tears flow. He was crying, too. Neither of us cared that Dwarves didn't cry. I never wanted to let go. But eventually he pulled away. After all, we still had to get my friends and escape somehow.

Cue the sappy music.

I ignored my ax and sheepishly wiped at the last few tears. My dad rubbed his wet eyes, confused, as if he'd never cried before. And I supposed he maybe never had. I certainly hadn't—and now I understood why that rule existed. It was a really unpleasant feeling. My eyes burned and my face felt tacky with salt.

We both coughed uncomfortably, trying to pretend we hadn't just broken the universal Dwarven rule.

Wow, this is pretty awkward, Greg.

"Was there no resistance?" my dad finally asked, probably thinking the "too easy" escape was a trap.

"My friends are fighting the guards right now," I said.

"Friends?" he asked. "What about the Dwarven Sentry?"

"The Council didn't believe me that you were here," I said.

"Figures . . . Dwarves . . ." my dad muttered. "Well, come on, let's go help them."

I nodded and led the way. We rushed back through the regular hallways, and not the holes I had chopped, hoping to flank the Elves on the other side. I unsheathed the Bloodletter and tossed my dad the dagger Blackout.

Screaming, shouting, clanking metal, and all sorts of other

bizarre noises echoed down the hall ahead of us. Even if my friends were losing, they were still putting up a fight from the sound of it.

The Bloodletter screamed with excited rage.

We rounded the corner and joined the battle.

CHAPTER 42

It Turns Out That Rock Trolls Really Are as Stupid as Buck Claimed

The first thing I saw was a Goblin.

His back was to me as he flung stones down the hallway at some unseen target. I wasn't sure how he'd gotten from the Dwarves' right flank all the way back here, but then again, I had no idea how battles like this were supposed to play out.

I took a step and swung the broad side of my ax at the back of the Goblin's knobby head like a huge flyswatter. It connected with a THUMP and his gangly green body slumped to the smooth wooden floor in a heap.

The Goblin groaned in pain as I stepped over him and quickly parried a strike from a nearby Elven sword. I rolled as the guard counterattacked, moving faster than I would have thought possible. His sharp blade missed my shoulder by inches.

My dad was already engaged with two nearby Elves, barely able to hold them off with his clumsy movements and just one small dagger. The only thing keeping him alive was wily desperation and the natural warrior instincts of a Stormbelly.

The Elf and I exchanged several parries and strikes with my ax and his sword. Every time the blades met, green and blue sparks sprayed around us. He bested me several times, clearly far better trained at hand-to-hand combat.

Only Galdervatn and Ari's armor saved me. The elf's blade bounced harmlessly off stone body parts or metal plates each time it got past my slow blocks.

I finally managed to roll away from him into a small clearing in the cramped hallway. He pursued me, but a stone came flying out of nowhere and struck him square in the face, knocking him unconscious.

Behind me, Ari grinned, and then desperately avoided a Goblin's lunge for her neck. I didn't know who else was alive or what else was happening. It was pandemonium. Suddenly, the Bloodletter was wrenched from my grip and all I saw was the ugly face of another Goblin above mine—our noses inches apart.

Two more Goblins held my legs and arms and I had been rendered prone and helpless almost before I could even register what was happening.

Eagan screamed somewhere. Lake shouted desperately back. They both sounded so far away.

Over one of the Goblin's shoulders, I saw my dad, also being subdued, blood oozing from multiple gashes on his arm, shoulder, and ribs. Panic ripped through me, and suddenly all I wanted was to be out of there. Out of that cramped wooden hallway where the Goblins were about to tear me into pieces with their bare hands.

Blackout, still clutched in my dad's hand, began glowing bright red. It shone and hummed with energy and I knew right then it was developing a power—as Ari had said it someday might. The blade glowed brilliantly, brightly red, startling the nearby Elves and Goblins into brief inaction.

And then all the lights went out.

Not just the lights of the building, or the lights of the city outside, but seemingly all light everywhere suddenly ceased to exist. We were all cast in total darkness. I heard screaming and shouting as the surprise gave us a chance to free ourselves from danger.

The Goblins' grip weakened. I closed my eyes and imagined escape, disruption, and destruction. I heard a loud CRACK and the tumbling of rocks. The Goblins let go of my limbs among dull THUDs and I fell to the ground. And I knew, even though I couldn't see it, that I had just used magic to summon several large boulders that crashed through the ceiling and onto the Goblins.

I ran, even though I couldn't see, relying only on instinct and Galdervatn. I heard shouting and commotion around me. The light suddenly flooded back. Lake and Eagan were disarming a nearby Elven guard. Ari hit an Elf in the shoulder with an arrow. Glam smashed a Goblin in the face with a boulder fist. We were turning the tide of the battle.

But that's when the Rock Troll showed up.

Because, *of course* a Rock Troll would show up in the middle of a huge battle between Elves, Goblins, and Dwarves. If I hadn't been so busy fighting for my life, I'd have been rolling my eyes dramatically.

The Rock Troll came crashing through the walls, screaming out in rage, not making any coherent words—just savage roars of hostility.

It looked different from a Mountain Troll. Less Human. It had a humanoid-ish shape, more or less, but its skin was covered in scabby, pointy rocks. It had big hands and legs and was hunched over, though easily still nine or ten feet tall and as thick as a small house.

"Kurzol!" Locien Aldaron called out to the Troll. "Smash them to pieces!"

Kurzol roared again and then slammed his fists onto the floor. They broke right through, creating two massive holes. A nearby Goblin fell into one of them.

"Don't smash the building, you moron!" Locien shouted, struggling to free himself from magical vines wrapping around his arms. "Smash the *Dwarves!*"

Kurzol roared again.

"I'm not afraid of you," Glam shouted, widening her stance next to me as if she actually meant to wrestle the Troll one-on-one. "Bring it on, Fluffy."

I leaped toward her without thinking and tackled her to the ground just as Kurzol charged at us.

"Get off me!" she yelled. "I had him right where I wanted him!"

Kurzol landed a few feet away, both fists extended like a battering ram, promptly crashing all the way through the floor, splintering the entire cross-section of wooden hallways into oblivion.

I felt myself turn into stone as I fell down with them, to the floor below among a jumbled mess of Goblins, Elves, weapons, wood, and other structural materials.

We all landed in a loud, chaotic pile of dust and debris, and for several glorious moments there was only silence and darkness.

CHAPTER 43

Okay, So Rock Trolls Are at Least Smart Enough to Learn from Their Mistakes

When reality finally came back, we were one floor below.

That whole section of the hidden level had caved in, and we were now back among the ocean of office cubicles on the eighty-second floor. The huge Rock Troll, Kurzol, was lying face-down nearby.

It didn't take long for the fighting to resume, even among the rubble and madness of the whole battle being swiftly deposited thirteen feet below to a different level of the Hancock building.

Greg, find me. You need me.

I looked around desperately for the Bloodletter, dodging several swinging swords in the process. At one point, I would have been as good as dead from a blade right through my back had Froggy not hit the Elf at the last second with a small throwing ax from across the room.

Over here, Greg. Hurry.

Finally I saw it, glowing purple beneath a pile of rubble. I sprinted forward and dove, dodging an Elven arrow as my hand wrapped around the Bloodletter's handle. Its energy coursed through me as I pulled it from the debris pile.

Then we rejoined the battle.

The ensuing fight was relentless and mostly ineffective; the magic each side wielded was inelegant and offsetting. Arrows were deterred by spells, opposing spells canceled each other out, swords and axes were rendered nearly harmless by defensive magic and enchanted armor. It was obvious that both Elves and Dwarves had not engaged in such forms of combat for thousands and thousands of years.

Through it all, I realized two things:

1. Somewhere in the fracas, Locien and Gwen Aldaron had gone missing among the wreckage of the collapsed ceiling. Their foot soldiers screamed in panic, searching the rubble for their fallen leaders.

2. We were going to lose. Even though the collapsing floor had neutralized a good number of the Goblins and Elven soldiers, three times as many reinforcements had arrived. And Kurzol had regained consciousness. He'd learned from his mistake and was now carefully walking across the room to launch brutal, nearly unstoppable attacks.

Not long after the fall, we found ourselves surrounded, trapped in a generic middle manager's corner office. A smashed mahogany desk was all that separated us from an Elven army that included an angry Rock Troll. We could not fend them off much longer, even with magic. Behind us, walls of solid glass provided spectacular views of Lake Michigan and downtown Chicago.

But offered no escape routes.

The only good news was that we were all there. And though not entirely unharmed, we were all still alive (for now): Froggy, Ari, Lake, Eagan, Glam, and my dad. Lake was unconscious and draped over one of Glam's shoulders, and most of us were bleeding from at least one wound or another.

But we were cornered—even after everything we'd done, the mission was on the brink of failure.

"You have nowhere to go," one of the Elven officers said as they encircled us. "Throw down your arms and surrender."

Behind him, Elves screamed in panic at their continued efforts to find the Elf Lord and his wife among the debris.

"What do we do?" Ari asked.

Her hair was matted with blood and she looked exhausted. We all did. My dad was barely standing, having suffered a number of wounds. I looked behind us—out the window, where the Great Lake stretched into the darkness of night beyond the city. I glanced down at the busy streets lined with headlights, over eighty stories below.

We really had only one choice.

"Jump," I said.

"What!" Eagan shouted.

I spun around and smashed open the massive window behind us with the Bloodletter.

"Jump," I repeated.

CHAPTER 44

─────◆─❈─◆─────

Just Seven Dwarves Flying Through the Chicago Skyline

W e may very well have all jumped to our grisly deaths.

But deep down, I knew that wouldn't be the case. And not because our strong bones would prevail—part of me suspected that even Dwarven bones couldn't withstand a fall from this high. Rather, it was Dwarven magic that would save us. It came from the elements of the earth. It used and manipulated the environment around us.

And the wind had told me to jump—as lame as that sounds.

Which is pretty lame, Greg.

After I smashed open the window, the Elves surrounding us stared in stunned shock. My companions looked at me like I was crazy, and for a moment I thought I'd be the only one jumping. But then they nodded in solidarity and we all grasped one another and leaped through the shattered office window, one mass of seven Dwarves flying out into the breezy Chicago night sky.

The Elves barely had time to react, and what would they have done anyway? Followed us out the window?

At first, we plummeted, as a group of seven people would after jumping out an eighty-second-story window. But then, as I focused and threw all the conviction I had into the wind, the gusts picked up. We were suddenly caught in a violent, swirling wind tunnel so powerful it not only stopped our descent but also blasted us east, out toward Lake Michigan.

Cars on Lake Shore Drive rocked unsteadily with the gusts as we soared past them overhead.

The seven of us flew over a concrete pier.

Over a dark, empty beach.

Several hundred yards from shore, the wind died out and we plunged into the cold lake. The armor we wore sank us like rocks. I struggled to free myself from the dented and dinged breastplate strapped across my chest. Whether it was more magic or just getting the straps untied that finally freed me, I'll never know. But once the heavy metal armor was off, I began swimming back toward the surface, the Bloodletter slowing me considerably.*

I finally breached the surface and gasped for fresh air.

Then I took a head count: only three others bobbed on the lake's surface: Froggy, Eagan, and my dad. Two more appeared, one was Glam, still holding on to an unconscious Lake.

"Where's Ari?" Eagan shouted.

I took a deep breath and then dove back under. The water was dark, the city lights only reflecting above me on the surface.

---

* All things considered, given what eventually happened, I should have just cut it loose then and there and let it sink to the bottom of the lake. But that's a story for another time, perhaps.

But the Bloodletter began glowing blue on my back. I saw a large fish dart away to my right, and then I saw her faintly in the hazy light ahead of me, the armor dragging her down as she struggled.

I kicked toward her and grabbed the dagger from her belt. I cut at the armor straps. By the time Ari was freed, she was no longer struggling, but completely lifeless. Desperate energy surged through me as I kicked, towing her to the surface. We finally got there and I immediately swam toward shore.

"Is she okay?" Glam gulped behind me, swallowing lake water in the process.

I didn't answer, but just kept swimming, Ari's shirt clenched in one hand. Eagan grabbed her feet and kicked behind me, propelling us even faster. We reached the concrete pier that ran the length of the lake between the public beaches. I pulled myself up first and then hoisted Ari onto the landing.

Eagan followed. The rest of our party, Froggy, Glam, Lake, and my dad were still ten feet from shore, working together to tow in Lake. I was convinced that either Eagan or myself would have to attempt CPR on Ari—something I had no idea how to do properly.

But she rolled over and coughed up a bunch of lake water on her own.

I breathed out a sigh of relief.

We helped the others climb onto the concrete pier. A jogger ran past, giving us a strange look. Lake showed a few signs of life as he rolled to the side and groaned.

My dad stood next to me. Panting and bleeding, but alive and freed.

We had done it! We had rescued my dad and made it out

alive—all of us. I looked up at the Hancock building, just a few blocks away. The small shattered window we had leaped from was barely visible high up in the night sky.

I smiled, but our victory was short-lived.

My dad gave me a final weak grin and then collapsed onto the ground in a heap.

CHAPTER 45

The Bloodletter Never Shuts Up

I 'm afraid there's nothing more I can do without an antidote."

I stared at Foggy Bloodbrew, the Underground's head physician, Council Elder, and my dad's good friend. She stroked her chin hairs and shook her head sadly. Then she lowered her gaze and left the room.

After everything, I possibly hadn't saved my dad in the end. He'd sustained a wound from a poisoned Elven blade. Foggy Bloodbrew explained to me earlier that morning that it would eventually prove fatal unless they could somehow figure out which poison had been used. It clearly had been an ancient Elven poison from Separate Earth—not detectable or curable with modern medicine (Dwarven or otherwise).

I stood next to the bed. My dad opened his bloodshot eyes.

"Dad, I'm so sorry," I said.

"No, you did well," he said, his voice strained. "Getting to see you one last time was more than enough."

"But . . . but I'll never get to beat you in chess," I said.

It was a lame thing to say. But my mind reeled with anguish, and it truly had been a moment I'd looked forward to my whole life. Something even he'd been looking forward to.

My dad smiled.

"Greg," he said. "You already have done so much more than that. You're going to be a great Dwarf. You already are. But you have to promise me something . . ."

I nodded.

"Do not let this lead to more violence," he said. "Do not let the Dwarves go to war. That's never what I wanted all those years searching for Galdervatn. It was meant to foster a lasting peace, not destroy it. Promise me."

"I promise," I said, hoping it wasn't a lie.

He smiled and nodded, looking exhausted, before closing his eyes and passing out.

We can still save him.

The Bloodletter had been calling to me ever since we'd gotten back. I closed my eyes, trying to ignore it. But why would I? Perhaps it was right? There was, after all, still one way I might be able to get the antidote.

I grabbed my dad's limp hand and squeezed. I knew there was nothing more I needed to say. So I left.

Ari was out in the hallway.

She hugged me.

"I'm sorry I put you all in danger," I said.

"Don't say that," she said. "We would all do it again in an instant. And I know you'd do the same for us."

I nodded.

Come to me, Greg, we are not done yet.

"Plus, because of us," Ari continued, "the Council knows that the Elves have magic again. And the battle may have killed or seriously injured the Elf Lord. Your dad might pay the ultimate price, but it wasn't for *nothing*."

I nodded, knowing she was right. For me the cause had always been my dad. But now they were one and the same. Especially since it was the Elves who were responsible for his likely death. The other Dwarves were right, and had been all along: Elves could not and should not ever be trusted.

"So the Council is going to finally take action?" I asked.

"They're in discussions right now," Ari said. "The Council's spirits are renewed in light of what six mostly untrained Dwarven kids were able to do with just the element of surprise and some Galdervatn. If the Elf Lord really is dead, then the Elves are without a leader. They will be in disorganized anarchy for days, perhaps weeks, or longer. The Council will almost certainly formulate some sort of aggressive plan of action by tomorrow."

I nodded.

Greg, you must hurry if you still want to save your father.

"I need to go," I said, finally heeding the Bloodletter's calls.

"Are you sure you're okay?" Ari asked.

"Yeah, I just . . . need some time alone to process this."

Ari nodded and gave me another hug.

Greg . . .

"I know," I said softly as I stalked down the hallway toward our apartment. "I'm on my way."

CHAPTER 46

I Search for Fiery Vengeance
at the Public Library

The Bloodletter's normally black blade was glowing blue and hot with retribution when I arrived.

Let me help you get revenge.

"Revenge?" I said. "I thought you said we could save him."

We may be able to, but both revenge and possible salvation reside within the same person. And you know who that is, Greg. Don't you?

I nodded, grabbing the ax and stuffing it into a large duffel bag. I slung it over my shoulder and headed out to the library. Not the usual sort of place one goes to rain down furious vengeance on their mortal enemy. But it was where my path to either justice or possibly saving my dad would start.

There was an email already waiting for me when I signed in to one of the public computers. It was from Edwin and had been sent that morning at 5:23 a.m., just over an hour ago:

Greg, you really are a savage gwint just as bad as the rest of them. My parents were right all along: Dwarves are disgusting creatures barely above animals. Both of my parents have likely died in YOUR brutal attack on their sanctuary. Do you know what you have taken from me?

I typed a reply:

Yes, it's the same thing you've taken from me. Let's settle this ourselves: just you and me. No lackeys. No friends. No armies. You and me: Navy Pier at 7:30 a.m.

I only had to wait three minutes (the longest of my life) for his reply:

You're on, gwint.

———✠———

In my haste to leave the Underground, I'd forgotten to find more Galdervatn. I was going to head back to get some, but the Bloodletter stopped me.

You don't need it. I alone can help you make everything right.

I'd learned in the past few days that when a magical ax speaks to you, it's best to trust it. Especially since I'd never have gotten those last moments with my dad without it.

I headed directly to Navy Pier. People on the bus were chattering about the rolling power and Internet blackouts that had been hitting most major cities across the globe the past twenty-four hours. Scientists were still baffled as to what was causing such anomalies. I suspected I knew precisely what was behind them, but the prospects were more than I wanted to consider right then. All I could think about was Edwin. And how he might still know where to find the antidote for the ancient Elven poison.

I'd chosen Navy Pier because it was somewhere public enough to ensure the double-crosser (aka my *best friend*) wouldn't bring a whole army of Elven soldiers to help him defeat me. But it was early enough that it wouldn't be totally swarming with tourists and onlookers.

We met near the massive Ferris wheel.

I stood ten feet from him, the Bloodletter still in my duffel bag. He wore a billowing, long coat that I knew concealed an Elven sword. A few tourists walked past, entirely unaware of our intentions.

Rage burned in Edwin's eyes. They almost looked like they were on fire. Once the kindest person I knew, the Edwin in front of me was barely recognizable, his face distorted with pain and anger.

"I told you not to attack the Hancock building," Edwin said with his teeth clenched. "I could have helped you get your dad free without violence. But instead, you ignored my instructions. Like a bunch of gwinty Dwarves you barreled in, destroying everything in your path, only later asking what it was you had obliterated. Well, Greg, it was my parents you destroyed. Dwarves are not meant for this world anymore, you're like raging bulls in a fine china shop. My parents were right all along. I tirelessly defended you and your dad . . . and for what? Only to have you prove them right in the end."

"Your parents are . . . dead?" I asked, my stomach burning with guilt.

"Missing," Edwin said, his voice choked. "But presumed dead."

The few dozen tourists nearby ignored us completely. They

were distracted by a commotion at the end of the pier. But neither of us bothered to take notice.

"But *you* betrayed me first!" I yelled. "You knew I was a Dwarf and never told me. Your parents attacked our store! You sent Trolls to follow me to the Underground after our last meeting, where they then killed men, women, and children."

Edwin shook his head.

"You're lying," he said.

"No," I said. "I wish I was. Because then it would mean you hadn't tricked me—used me like you've been doing all along."

"I did no such thing, but I wouldn't expect a gwint like you to understand the nuances of my life," Edwin said. "How could you think I'd do that? *You came to me* yesterday, remember? How could I have possibly been ready with some Troll trap? My parents probably had Elves following me, and then *they* followed you after you showed up at the PEE again! Your own impulsiveness caused that, not me."

I hesitated. I didn't want to believe him. I couldn't.

"So I suppose you'll also claim to have no idea what my dad has been poisoned with?" I said. "Or how to save him? Tell me, tell me where to find the antidote to save my dad and I will show you some mercy."

Edwin actually laughed. But it wasn't triumphant or gloating. It was bitter and frustrated. He was close to tears.

"You still don't get it, do you?" he said. "I've *never* been in on *any* of this, Greg. I never knew. I've only been trying to *help* you! My parents *lied to me* the whole time. So I have no idea what they did to your dad, or about any Elven poisons. But you know what? My folks are probably dead—so they won't be home anytime soon. Why don't you just go break into our house and look for the antidote yourself? I don't care. You're good at breaking into places uninvited."

The Bloodletter glowed brilliantly right through my canvas duffel bag.

He's lying. You must force him to tell you.

I wasn't sure what to believe anymore. But Edwin wasn't going to give me a choice either way. Because he apparently had his own score to settle.

"But I can't let you just leave," Edwin said. "Not now. Not anymore." He drew a sword. It was four feet long with a curving, symmetrical blade that shone like it was made from diamonds. It almost seemed to hum with energy. "If you survive this, feel free to ransack my parents' homes. In fact, I'll even tell you to check behind the Chuck Close painting in their bedroom—it's where they stashed a lot of their secret Elven stuff. Consider it my last gift as your friend. Because I truly did always like you and your dad, Greg. Which is why it will be so bittersweet to end you today."

I pulled the glowing Bloodletter free from the bag.

"Edwin, don't," I said. "We don't have to do this."

"Yeah, we do," he said. "I guess we just can't escape our destiny after all."

"But we make our own destiny," I pleaded. "That's what you always told me. This will be too *ax*crutiating. Please *ax* yourself if we really need to do this. This is *sword* of silly. If you win, I'll be a real *sword* loser! Um, uh, I have more, just hang on . . ."

For a brief moment Edwin's scowl faded. A hint of that old grin flashed across his face, but then he closed his eyes and breathed. When he looked up again all the wrath was back, more intense than ever.

Then he charged.

CHAPTER 47

——◆→≫◆≪←◆——

I Do Declare Another Forthcoming Pun: My (Former) Best Friend Gets a Bit Carried Away

S parks erupted as our blades clanged together.

Edwin was fast and agile, and I struggled to defend his quick attacks. He clearly had had way more hand-to-hand-combat training. But the Bloodletter nearly acted on its own—helping me anticipate his moves.

For all the speed on Edwin's side, the sheer force of the Bloodletter evened the score. Every time I managed to mount an attack of my own, Edwin went sprawling backward several steps, even after a successful block. The ax blows were hard and impacted Edwin like an iron fist.

But they were few and far between—I was too busy deflecting his quicker strikes to take many swings myself. We spun and lunged and parried across the mostly deserted pier. Everyone else was at the end in a massive crowd, staring at something in the water.

We did not care.

We were only concerned with destroying each other.

After deflecting three quick slashes, I managed to throw my shoulder into his undefended chest. Edwin stumbled back toward the nonexistent line for the Ferris wheel. His back rested against a sign that read: Closed for Maintenance.

I quickly lunged forward and swung the Bloodletter overhead like I was about to chop a block of wood in two. He rolled away from the blow at the last second. My ax's blade sliced right through several thick, steel-enforced cables behind him.

The Ferris wheel groaned as a sudden gust of wind from the lake hit it. Edwin and I both looked up as it teetered unsteadily. The Bloodletter had just severed three of its load-bearing support cables.

We glanced at each other and then ran as the huge Ferris wheel finally toppled.

It crashed onto the pier with a mighty roar of twisted steel and shattered fiberglass. I used the Bloodletter to swipe away a metal beam that would surely have crushed me as the Ferris wheel collapsed around us.

We both stood among the twisted wreckage unharmed. Lightning erupted behind Edwin out on the lake among rolling, dark storm clouds. Thunder boomed seconds later.

I lifted the Bloodletter.

Edwin readied his sword.

But instead of attacking me again, he grinned deviously. His blade glowed orange and then burst into flames.

Edwin could do magic! I took a stunned step backward. I wasn't sure how exactly the whole Ability thing worked for Elves, but clearly Edwin had it.

He pointed his flaming sword at me and fire unfurled from the end and leaped out like some kind of blazing tongue. I dove out of the way. The fiberglass Ferris wheel car behind me began melting.

Edwin swung the blazing sword at me again. More fire leaped from the end. This time, I had no chance to escape. I shrugged back as the flames engulfed me.

I felt the heat of the flames, but there was no pain.

Only then did I realize I was being showered in sizzling, steaming water. It did not come from the sky, but seemed to be coming directly from *me.*

It was Dwarven magic.

How was that possible? I hadn't consumed any Galdervatn in nearly twelve hours. But I could feel magic coursing through me. Each time I'd taken Galdervatn, the feeling had become more familiar. It was less subtle now. I knew, somehow, magic had found me on its own.

Edwin readied for another attack. I focused on him, lowering my ax. He charged at me, grinning at my apparent lack of defense. But then he stopped abruptly and flew backward as a gust of wind slammed into his chest like an anvil.

The sword flew from his hand and clattered to the ground. I focused on it and more wind lifted Edwin's sword up into the air. It soared out over the marina, plunging down to the bottom of the lake.

Edwin recovered and climbed to his feet. He thrust out his palms and two bolts of green lightning fired from his hands right at me. I held up the Bloodletter and it absorbed the lightning easily.

Frustrated, Edwin screamed and tried again.

The Bloodletter easily absorbed his second attack, and then shot the energy right back at him. Edwin yelled out in pain as he dropped to the ground, his arms hanging lifelessly at his sides.

"Stay down," I said, standing over him.

Finish him.

The Bloodletter vibrated with the anticipation of revenge. It was, after all, what the powerful weapon was best at.

"No matter what you do to me"—Edwin scowled—"you'll still never be anything more than a worthless gwint."

"I never wanted this to happen," I said. "I didn't even do anything to your parents. It was Kurzol, their own Rock Troll, that caused their deaths. I was there, I saw it."

"But it wouldn't have happened if you'd listened to me and stayed away," he said. "I never wanted this either, Greg. I was always on your side; I *wanted* to help you get your dad back. I told you where he was, after all. All I ever wanted was to be your friend."

I knew he was telling the truth, and it broke my heart.

"Your parents held my dad prisoner," I said. "*That's* what started this. But it doesn't have to ruin us."

"They did," Edwin agreed. "It was their fault. But it's too late now. They're likely dead because of your attack and I can't ever let that go. What's done is done now. We're done."

I lifted the ax almost against my will—as if some unseen force was guiding my actions.

Do it. If you don't, this won't ever be over. You can't let him walk away, he has vowed to avenge his parents and the violence will never end until he does. You made a promise to your dad. Now keep it!

The Bloodletter pushed me, practically required me to swing the ax down with all the power I could muster. I obliged. But it slammed into the wooden pier right next to Edwin's head, missing by less than a foot.

I let go of the ax as he stared wide-eyed at the black blade.

As my hand left the handle, it was all gone. The lust for

the kill, for revenge, evaporated into the wind. Edwin made no move for the ax, but looked at me, shocked. Fury still gleamed in his eyes, but it was also laced with sorrow.

I shook my head.

This violent, vengeful person wasn't me. I never would or could harm Edwin, whether we were best friends or worst enemies. All I was doing was wasting time—Edwin himself had said the key to my dad's survival might still be in one of his parents' houses.

"Remember this moment," I said to Edwin. "The mercy I showed my best friend. If we ever meet again."

He scoffed and was about to say something but I didn't let him. Instead I summoned more wind. It lifted him off the ground and carried him a hundred yards out into the lake, plunging him into the water. His long swim back would provide me a head start to get to his house. There was still a chance I could save my dad.

I was about to walk away, leaving behind the Bloodletter.

But it called out to me.

You know you will need me again. This is far from over.

It was right. I sighed and pulled the ax from the pier. As soon as it was in my hand again, I felt some regret over letting Edwin go unharmed. I knew they weren't my real feelings, that the Bloodletter was trying to bend me, use me for its own selfish purposes, but I ignored it regardless. I had let Edwin go, and I'd do it all over again if I could.

I spun around and faced the city. Then stopped. The Bloodletter fell from my hand and clattered to the ground.

I stared in shock at what had distracted all the tourists on the pier during our fight.

CHAPTER 48

The Dawn of Magic

The city was completely still.

The buildings were dark, the entire skyline blacked out in the morning light. Every car on Lake Shore Drive was stalled and dead. The drivers walked around, collectively scratching their heads, dumbfounded.

No car horns blared. Nothing moved but the people. Cell phones rested lifelessly in hands, pockets, and purses, rendered completely useless.

The storm behind me shattered the silence with more thunder. A colorful, swirling haze rose up from the sewers. It hovered above the lake's surface like fog. The rainbow mist swirled between buildings, seeped from the cracks in the sidewalks.

It was Galdervatn.

The New Magical Age was beginning.

Nothing in this world would ever be the same again . . .

ACKNOWLEDGMENTS

—✛—

Thanks:

- Pete Harris for all the inspiration and hard work on this story
- All the people at Temple Hill and Putnam who helped make this book what it is: Wyck Godfrey, Jennifer Besser, Kate Meltzer, Katherine Perkins, and all others who I did not get to work with directly
- The two verified real goblins, Ginny and Fernet, who have been living in my house
- BBB (you guys bring out the worst in me and I love it)
- Beards
- Meat (especially offal)
- Large portions
- All the fantasy stuff I lovingly borrowed from and/or lovingly made fun of
- Steve Malk, like always

Special Thanks:

- People who care a lot about big houses, fancy cars, and money (for inspiring the bad guys)
- Sewer dwellers everywhere
- Hamburgers with bacon on them

No Thanks:

- Seitan